WAR COLLEGE

A Novel

Thomas A. Barnico

Kay Verbatim Press
2021

"An Irish Airman Foresees His Death"

by William Butler Yeats

I know that I shall meet my fate
Somewhere among the clouds above;
Those that I fight I do not hate,
Those that I guard I do not love;
My country is Kiltartan Cross,
My countrymen Kiltartan's poor,
No likely end could bring them loss
Or leave them happier than before.
Nor law, nor duty bade me fight,
Nor public men, nor cheering crowds,
A lonely impulse of delight
Drove to this tumult in the clouds;
I balanced all, brought all to mind,
The years to come seemed waste of breath,
A waste of breath the years behind
In balance with this life, this death.

For Kate, who loves a good story.

Contents

Book I

Chapter 1

The Veterans Hospital sat on the crest of a Vermont hill. Jack Dunne turned his battered '62 Buick into the hospital entrance and started up the driveway. He was eager to get back to his college, but this visit couldn't wait.

Trees lined the long, curving driveway that wound its way up the hill. Jack saw the hospital at the top but stopped the car halfway. He got out, walked through the tree line, and onto an open lawn. A gravel pathway cut thirty yards across the lawn, leading to a stone marker beside another line of trees. The marker was six feet tall, granite with a bronze plaque. It stood alone.

Jack approached the marker slowly, eyes glancing from side to side, up and down the hill. After nine months in Vietnam, he was allergic to open fields.

Twenty Vermont winters had taken their toll on the stone and the plaque. The small string of stone laurel was filled with dust and granite chips. The tarnished inscription read:

LIKE VIKINGS LEAVING HOME AND HEARTH,
THEIR LIVES AND FORTUNES ALL TO GIVE,
BORN IN THE COLD WINDS OF THE NORTH,
TO DIE THAT THOSE THEY LOVE MIGHT LIVE.

1914-1918
1941-1945
1950-1953

Jack remembered the first time that he had seen the plaque, and the hospital. As a freshman at the College, he had visited the veterans on Saturday mornings. As his campus slept, he played cards and talked with them about girls and sports. That's when he met Colonel Tiemo Turck.

Back in his car, Jack drove up the hill to the parking lot. It was a clear, bright Vermont fall day, the kind of day that Jack had achingly remembered as he sweated out the previous year far from school.

He jogged up the front steps and headed for the wing with the veterans in long-term care. He entered the main lobby, which was filled with men sitting in well-worn easy chairs. Some looked up at Jack as he passed. He stopped at the desk and said he was headed to Room 411. The man behind the desk nodded.

Jack climbed the stairs and found the room. When he looked through the doorway he saw Colonel Turck, seated upright in his chair, as if at attention. As he entered the room, he thought that he saw on the Colonel's face as much relief as joy.

"Jack."

"Colonel."

"You're back."

"Yes, sir."

"Sit down."

"Yes, sir."

Tiemo moved his chair closer to Jack's. When Tiemo talked he surrounded his listener. His shoulders hunched and tilted forward. His full head of pepper-and-salt hair stood at attention, rising from his forehead for an inch, then riding like a wave to the back of his head. His voice dove down to a low baritone. He looked his listener in the eyes and spoke slowly. His worn, blue-gray eyes brightened as he looked at Jack.

"You look like your father, Jack."

Jack nodded. Now twenty years old, it was not the first time that he had heard those words.

"How long are you back in the States?"

"Ten days."

"Special orders?"

"Yes. And I want to thank you and President Onion for arranging it. I went back to Iowa first. My mother sends her best. She said that it's kind of you all to remember her."

Tiemo nodded and smiled. "Your father—he was one of us. Tell me everything, Jack. What's going on over there?"

One hour passed.

"You've got to help our recruiting at the College, Jack," Tiemo said. "President Onion is still involved, still solid. Same for Professor McUsic. They will be glad you are back, even for a few days."

"I should get over to campus. I've got a lot to do," Jack said.

"Give the president and professor my best," Tiemo said. "Are you still living with Rocco?"

"Yes."

"Good man, Rocco. Smart, too. The professor says he couldn't do without him at the engineering school. An allegro spirit, he calls him."

Tiemo patted Jack on the knee. "Keep me posted."

"I will."

Jack stood up and walked to the door. He turned and gave Tiemo a wave as he left the room.

Tiemo leaned back in his chair and closed his eyes. He soon heard another knock on the door. His new next-room neighbor in the long-term care wing opened the door and stepped in.

"Come in, sit down," Tiemo said. "You just missed my young friend."

Tiemo's neighbor took Jack's chair. He was a thin, frail man with wire-rim glasses and a kindly smile. He wheezed as he walked, the result of a life-long love affair with cigarettes. He was a Navy veteran. The staff at the VA hospital had told him many things about his new neighbor, Colonel Turck. "You pronounce his name 'Tee-mo,'" they said, "but you might want to call him 'Colonel,' everyone else does."

Tiemo did not speak at first. His eyes remained on the window and the hills beyond. He had lived at the hospital for many years now. He hurt every minute, but his mind was clear and alive. He enjoyed living close to the College, the scene of so many of his youthful triumphs. He often enjoyed the company of his old classmates and comrades in the fight, some now in high places at the College and in government. They were engaged in a new fight, now, "The New War" they all called it. But all the rules seem changed. And why did so few from the College go to fight?

The years had taken many of his friends at the hospital. Three had died on his floor that month. Tiemo knew well the hushed tones, the murmurs, the cries, the scurrying about, the smell of death, the inevitable news, the clichéd regrets, the new neighbors, the first meetings, and the long goodbyes. Even Tiemo, who had seen war, grieved each loss. He took time after each death to write the next-of-kin, carefully enclosing an elegy from Henry Scott Holland, once rector at St. Paul's in London: "Death is nothing at all . . . ." They all had their stories, Tiemo thought.

But his memories were often his enemies, now. In the late afternoons his mind drifted into the hills beyond his window. Their different shades of forest green, ever changing in color from the shadows of the drifting clouds, lifted his heavy eyes. His new neighbor sat quietly in these moments.

"Who was the young guy?" his neighbor asked, quietly.

"Just the best we got," said Tiemo. "Jack Dunne. Just back from Vietnam."

"I knew his father," Tiemo said. "He was at the College after me. He left for the war. He dropped into France in '44, pre-D-Day, like me. He was a sabotage machine. Fluent French, looks from Hollywood. And fearless.

"He played hockey the same way when he got back. National champs his senior year. He was the captain. After every game, he went to the opponent's locker room to shake hands. No matter how hard they had hit him—clean or dirty—he went into that other locker room. Every time.

"He signed up again with the Agency after the war. Jack was two years old when we lost his father. Prague in '52 was a very dangerous place. The 'Cold War' was very hot. We were organizing Czech resistance groups. This was before the CIA. We were still under the wing of the OSS. We used our German occupation zone starting in 1946. Frankfurt and Regensburg were the U.S. base camps. We were running couriers from Austria and

Germany into Prague, Czech exiles, mostly. They had a taste for action. Some were from the old anti-Nazi resistance. They knew the soft spots in the border. But the border was tightening. Signal flares, border entrenchments. There was a twenty-meter wide clearing through the forest on the border. They plowed the clearing so they could see footprints. The fence was a combination of wooden posts and barbed wire, one, two, or three walls deep. One of the walls used electrified wire—2,000 to 6,000 volts. I saw pictures—people people hanging upside down on the barbed wire like a side of beef in a butcher's cold storage room.

"We had placed people in the Czech Ministry of Foreign Affairs radio group. They transmitted from that station out to exiles through encrypted messages. For a while, we had good radio contact with them. Then radio contact inside Czechoslovakia just stopped. We didn't know why. Jack's father volunteered to go in for a look."

Tiemo looked down, without expression.

"They found him in the Vlatva River. Never solved."

Tiemo looked up.

"Jack reminds me so much of him."

Tiemo paused again, then looked into the old eyes of his neighbor.

"I don't understand much about Vietnam, but if we can't get more guys like Jack to go, we don't belong there at all."

Chapter 2

Thomas "Rocco" Marconi worked part-time at the College Garage. He was an engineering student with good grades and good hands for engine work. He came, he said, from "Nowhere, Pennsylvania." He had brown, wavy hair and eyes as black as the coal of his native State. His dark eyebrows curved down like the wings of a bird, highlighting his eyes. He had a thin, wiry frame, a quick mind and a quicker smile. The manager of the Garage grabbed him as soon as he walked in the door of the gas station at the start of his freshman fall.

"Ever worked in a garage?" he asked Rocco.

"Yup, high school."

"Pump gas?"

"Yes, sir."

"Anything else?"

"Rebuilt my transmission."

"You're hired."

George Buttrey, the manager, saw something else about Rocco that he liked, too. On big weekends, space in the parking garage was scarce. Cars were parked in an elaborate system that left mere inches between even the priciest cars. The parking system required employees with keen eyes and steady nerves, capable of slipping the chariots of successful alumni carefully into their narrow spaces. And, most importantly, the system required one thin, agile, young man who could exit the back of the garage through a small window high on the back wall. Sam saw in Rocco his next Spiderman.

Rocco's scholarships did not cover his expenses, so he worked part-time jobs. Everywhere. The job at the garage was only one of many, which included the college dining hall, the College Inn kitchen, a local restaurant, grading papers, and selling sports programs at games. You couldn't walk one-hundred yards in the town or on campus without stepping on or into one of Rocco's places of employ.

The job he liked best was his new job in the lab at the engineering school. In his freshman year, Rocco and Professor Duncan McUsic had a very typical teacher-student relationship. But all that changed in the summer of '68. Rocco had stayed on campus that summer, working his usual array of jobs, and swimming in the river in the cool of the early evening after his day's work was done. In the mornings, he vacuumed the library in the engineering school, content among the engineering tomes and the quiet of the early morning hours.

Rocco had aced physics and math at his public high school. These subjects came easily to him. His parents had not attended college and were proud of his success. But they were unable to offer him much guidance or financial support for his dreams. As he entered his senior year in high school, he was unsure of his plans. A teacher pointed the way to a scholarship funded by a local mill-owner, an alumnus of the College. Rocco received the four-year scholarship and was on his way.

In his first week as a freshman Rocco learned about Professor McUsic. A student course guide described McUsic as "somewhat mysterious" and "exacting." The student reviewers wrote: "Be prepared to measure yourself; the man has a high standard, and few meet it." Rocco took the warning as a challenge.

There was no posting for the job of lab assistant to Professor McUsic. Rocco learned about it from the engineering department secretary. When Rocco stopped by her desk to pick up a graded paper, she put her finger to her lips and motioned Rocco to stand next to her at her desk. She looked up and down the hall from her desk.

"The professor asked me to give you this, Rocco," she said.

Rocco took the sealed envelope from her hand and walked out of the building and sat on a bench in the courtyard.

"Dear Mr. Marconi," the letter began.

Typical start, Rocco thought—he calls everyone "Mister" or "Miss."

"I am impressed by your work to date. If you would like to be my laboratory assistant this year, I have a few projects that might interest you. Sincerely, Professor McUsic."

They met the next day in the professor's office. Rocco appeared at his door; the professor motioned for him to sit in the chair in front of his large, clean desk.

"Come in Mr. Marconi, please sit down."

"Yes, sir."

"You are student of great promise."

"Thank you, sir."

"I need your help on one of my projects."

He eyed Rocco carefully, head to toe.

Rocco did not hesitate: "When do I start?"

"Right away."

"Professor?"

"Yes?"

"Can I keep my job cleaning the library?"

"You bet. Work for Cliff? Good man."

Rocco's supervisor on the cleaning job in the library was the school's janitor, Cliff Badger, the father of Rocco's co-worker, Townsend "Towny" Badger, at the College Garage. Soon after Rocco started at the garage, George had introduced him to a new part-time worker, a local high school student. A few years younger than Rocco, Towny Badger had a slim, athletic build, sloping shoulders and narrow hips, with fair skin, blue eyes and blonde hair. He played football and hockey for the local high school team.

Towny's father Cliff rose early each day and drove into town. He appreciated the job at the College; there weren't many jobs like it in the valley. "I love this job," he often told Rocco.

"What did you do before you worked at the College?" Rocco asked him one day.

"I was the janitor at the elementary school on Elm Street. God, I loved those kids. They made me Valentine cards, you know, the home-made ones with glitter and paper lace? They called me 'The Badger' behind my back. I pretended not to know.

"I left the school for better pay at the College. It almost broke my heart. On the day I left one of the teachers dressed up his class in 'badger' headgear and black and white striped shirts. I nearly fell on the floor laughing when I saw all those little 'badgers'."

"You've been a good friend to Towny," Cliff said to Rocco at the end of a shift in the library that summer. "Where did you learn so much about cars?"

"Home," Rocco said. "I worked in a garage in high school."

"It's not just how you help Towny with the cars," Cliff said, looking down. His lips suddenly tightened. "You've helped him on other things, too. Thinking things through. He really isn't sure about next year after he graduates from high school. He has some offers from colleges to play sports, but that's not what's on his mind. Some of his friends say that they are going to enlist. He talks about the war constantly. His mother is scared."

"We've talked about it," Rocco said. "I told him that if he went to college he wouldn't be drafted, maybe until after he graduates. The war might be over by then. That's all I said. He is not sure what to do."

Cliff nodded. "I know. And I don't what to say to him. We talk around it most of the time. I don't want to push him one way or another, you know? "

"He's a good guy and a smart guy, Mr. Badger. He'll decide what's right for him."

Chapter 3

Rocco's Saturday shift at the garage was ending when he heard a car wheel into the garage parking lot and blast its horn. Rocco recognized the horn and knew its owner without looking. He ran out to the car, banged on the hood, and yanked open the door. He pulled Jack out of the car and pounded him on the head and back. He gave him a tight hug, then stepped back and looked at his friend.

"You made it!"

"You bet," Jack said. "Great to see you! I went to Iowa to see my mom first. This afternoon, I stopped to see Tiemo. He mentioned you. Said that Professor McUsic likes your work."

"We'll talk about that later," Rocco said.

Towny walked slowly out of the garage bays and across the lot. He had heard a lot about Jack Dunne.

"Jack, this is Towny Badger. He works with me here," Rocco said. "Good man."

"Good to meet you." Jack gave Towny a look of wonder. "But one question: How do you put up with Rocco?" Towny smiled and said: "He's okay. I am putting up with him. But how do you *live* with him?"

Rocco jumped into the Buick and Jack blasted off, spinning wheels and kicking dust. Towny stared a long time at the car as it sped away. He turned to walk down Main Street toward home. Though still in high school, he had heard a lot about Jack from Rocco. Rocco had told him about Jack and the few other students who had left school to go to war. "Very few," Rocco said.

"Why do they go?" Towny asked Rocco that day. "They came here to learn, not to fight in a war, right?"

"Good question," Rocco said. "You'd have to ask them."

Rocco and Jack lived across the river, in a small, Cape-style brick house by a rushing, rocky stream. The stream followed a curving path behind other nearby houses, through fields, and down the gradual plain that led to the river. There it joined more cold water from the north and headed toward the sea, through miles of small towns and big cities, farmland and rolling hills.

Professor McUsic owned the house and rented it to students, usually a couple of his favorites. He visited often and didn't mind their occasional target practice in his two-acre back yard. The house had additions to its side and rear, giving Jack and Rocco plenty of room for guests. Rocco loved the heated garage, a haven for his latest projects. A shed outside held wood for the stone fireplace in the main room.

Jack dropped Rocco in the driveway of their house.

"I have a meeting tonight," Jack said. "President Onion and Professor McUsic. I have to be at the president's office at 6. They want to talk about recruiting."

"The professor hasn't asked me my plans," Rocco said. "I think he wants me to stay and work for him."

"He should," Jack said. "He couldn't find another Rocco."

"Don't know about that," Rocco said, as he climbed out of the car. "We'll see."

Jack pulled out of the driveway and drove down the hill to the road along the river and over the bridge to town. His mind drifted back to his first ride over that bridge and up the hill to the College. He arrived at the College for the first time two years before, almost to the day, for fall football practice in '67. He was six-foot two-inches, 220 pounds, from Madison, Iowa, dark-Irish handsome and a mobile, hostile linebacker to behold. The team ran the table his first year, ten wins, no losses, only four touchdowns given up by the defense all year. And, as his fellow linebacker Wayne "Earl" Warren liked to say, "Four of those were against the 'B' squad."

As Jack's athletic legend grew, the campus police came to forgive his high spirits and venal sins and treated him more like a lovable rogue. They let Jack ride in their squad cars, in the backseat, drinking beer and telling stories. Some of the old-timers on the force remembered his father and passed the word quietly to the younger officers to keep an eye out for Jack, who reminded them of his father in so many ways.

Jack pulled his car into the large parking lot of the fraternity
house. The car at the top of the lot had a large Viking head sten-
ciled on the two front doors. The stencil was the artwork of senior Pierre Loch, the Sergeant-at-Arms of Asgard Hall, Jack and
Rocco's fraternity, named for the dwelling place of the Viking
gods. The Sergeant was the keeper of house traditions. Pierre
took pride in his role: he saw the house as a bulwark against the
early signs of change reaching the campus in the 1960s. The
members were, in Pierre's eyes, the tenders of ancient and honorable flames.

Jack walked up the stairs from the parking lot to the side
of the house. Built in the 1920s, the house was long past its
neo-Georgian glory, a three-story brick with a large slate porch
facing the street. The front door oddly faced the side yard, but
those steeped in the history of the house knew that the architect
had chose a façade toward the College to underline the timeless
link between the fraternity and the College. Others said the door
gave groggy brothers a head start toward an early-morning class.

The front door also faced the church next door, another odd-
ity, given the weekend debauchery that had usually ended early
Sunday morning, only a few hours before the churchgoers made
their way up their walkway. Yet the relations between the pastor
and the house had been friendly for decades—better than relations with the College, in fact. The brothers were greedy buyers
at the annual church rummage sale, with a particular interest
in long coats with deep pockets, perfect pouches for flasks, bottles, and cans to smuggle into the football stadium and hockey
rink. A few of the boys attended services, quietly; others joined
in some volunteer work. A few had returned to marry in the
church, though their fiancées drew a line against a reception
in the house. Through the years, the pastor and the house had
reached a tacit agreement, if not a path to redemption: the pastor could conduct his missionary activity, while the boys gained a
character witness for hearings before the dean.

The yard of the house was covered with leaves, but someone

had taken quiet care to sweep off the five flat granite grave markers set in a row across the front yard. Beneath the plain stones lay thirty years of house dogs, four black labs and one mongrel, resting in peace, dreaming of their campus diet of ice cream and beer. The local health officers had loudly objected to the burials—full-blown affairs complete with a New Orleans-style parade with horns—but the appointment of a new, dog-loving town inspector quietly put the issue to rest.

The house had a large side yard, ideal for winter sports, of a sort. Rocco and the other house engineers had built a slide, long pieces of lumber lashed together with thick bolts. The slide ran from the roof of the porch to the side yard, and fed a long, iced path between snow banks, creating a fine bobsled run, choice of bob-sled design entirely at the whim of the rider.

At the other end of the large yard was a small skating area, perfect for another winter sport: barrel-jumping. In an early effort at re-cycling, discarded beer kegs were arrayed in a row, one keg added at a time as the jumpers cleared the row, like the gradual raising of a bar in the high jump. Inevitably, the organizers went a keg too far, and the resulting demolition of both kegs and jumpers resembled more a bowling alley, the humans taking the place of bowling balls, with predictable results.

Jack walked past the house, then cut in front of the dining hall and some dorms. As he approached the steps of the administration building, he remembered the first and second times that he had met President Samuel Onion.

In the first week of his freshman fall he went to the library looking for work. He entered the library and looked around. He went upstairs, with the vague notion that he could find some help there. He walked along a long corridor, then stopped and knocked on an unmarked door. No one answered at first, and Jack began to reconsider his plan. Then the door opened. A large man—probably in his sixties, Jack thought—answered.

"Can I help you?" the man asked.

Jack told him that he was looking for a job in the library. The man said that he might be able to help, and invited Jack into his office.

"What's your name?"

"Jack Dunne."

The man's face went blank and his eyes drifted downward.

"Sir?" Jack asked.

The man regained his focus and resumed his questions.

"Major?"

"Not sure yet."

"Sports?"

"Football."

The man looked him up and down and nodded.

"Where are you from?" he asked.

"I was born in DC but my mom and I moved to Iowa when I was small. She has family there." The man smiled and said that he, too, was from a small town in the Midwest. They talked about their homes and Jack's plans for his time at the College.

"Now about that job," the man said. He got up from his chair and motioned for Jack to follow. They went out the door, down the corridor, and into another office. The man said hello to the secretary but did not stop. Instead, he walked directly to the door to the inner office marked "Librarian of the College." Jack gulped a bit when he saw the sign.

The large man knocked as he opened the door to the inner office. He said hello to the librarian, who was seated at his desk. Then he said: "My friend, here, Mr. Jack Dunne, is a freshman who would like a job at the library. Do you think that we could help him?"

"Why yes, President Onion. I am sure that we could," said the librarian.

"President?" Jack thought, puzzled.

The man turned to Jack. "Well, Mr. Dunne, I think that I will leave you here. He shook Jack's hand and said: "Let's get together some time, to talk about your future." Then he left the room.

"President?" Jack asked the librarian.

As Jack approached the granite stairs to the administration building this evening, he recalled his second, and more fateful,

meeting with President Onion, later in the fall of his sophomore year. The town police were nonplussed by several Asgard
pranks, and fingered, not without probable cause, Jack as a party
involved. They complained loudly to the administration, citing
a threat to public safety and morals and a bad example for town
youth.

Eventually Jack was summoned to the president's office, not
to the office of the dean, who handled more minor discipline.
This must be bad, Jack thought. He entered the waiting room
and sat on a long leather couch, making small talk with the president's secretary and awaiting his fate.

The phone rang and the secretary said, "I'll send him right
in." She rose and opened the two large, oaken doors, each bearing a raised carving of the college symbol. The doors guarded
the entrance to the office. These Vikings look more foreboding
than the ones painted on Pierre's car, Jack thought.

On the president's office wall there was a ten-foot long photograph of Teddy Roosevelt standing in a line of well-dressed
men, all veterans of TR's beloved Rough Riders in the Span-
ish-American War. The photograph was taken, the president
often told visitors, at a reunion of the Riders at a well-appoint-
ed Manhattan club. "Harvard Club, 1908," the president told
them. "TR as host, my father in the crowd. Private event."

The president was reading papers on his desk as Jack sat
down silently. Looking up, the president said, "Sit down, boy."
Jack sat. "I'm starting to think, Jack, that our little ol' college
can't hold you right now."

"I think I know what you mean, sir."

"It's a shame, because I know the football coach wants you
around next year." The president paused. His expression had
changed. He smiled. "I can get you off the hook, you know that.
But I have an idea for a sabbatical," he said. "A cooling-off period. A type of foreign study, one might say. Listen up."

He nodded toward the large photo of the Rough Riders. "It
was my father who got me interested in the intelligence field. My
group was set up in 1940," he said. "They were chasing Nazis

in South America. The FBI international group was involved—there was no CIA then. Tommy Blackpool, Class of '32, was running the thing out of the White House. The State Department didn't like it—they thought he was poaching on their turf. But Roosevelt wanted it that way—he wanted Tommy's work on South America to be independent of State.

"So Tommy got me involved. I had worked at State in the '30s, and he needed someone who was still liked there. I didn't know Tommy at the College—I only knew of him. I saw him a few times after college and knew him just well enough so that when he was having troubles with State he thought I could help. So I left Wall Street and went back to State in 1940.

"We were kicking Axis agents out of South America. We were trying to stifle the Axis propaganda there. We tried to get American businesses there to drop their business agents who were backing the Nazis. You would not believe the infighting with State over our mission down there. It was intense. State didn't trust the FBI. And they didn't trust Tommy.

"Tommy recruited other guys from the College, too. Guys he could trust. That's how I met Tiemo Turck. He spoke fluent German and French. He had been Class of '33. His parents were German immigrants. They worked in the silver factories in Connecticut. I met him on assignment in Rio. God, it was wild. Tiemo later dropped into France. That's how he met your father."

The president paused. He realized that he had drifted far back in time. Finally, he said, "We all worked well behind the scenes. Off the record, if you will. That's why we have set this thing up at the College the way we have. Quiet. Clean. No paperwork. No committees. We just want to help. We are trying to find the right young guys for a little project of mine. I'm looking for well-bred boys who like a whiff of danger. Vietnam is not for everyone. We need boys with some brains and some guts."

He looked at Jack. "Interested?"

Chapter 4

President Onion and Professor McUsic met every Wednesday evening for bourbon and branch water, no interruptions, and no exceptions. They had known each other at the College as students. Lately their meetings went far into the night, each growing more frustrated with the course of the Vietnam War and its collateral damage on campus.

Sam Onion was the larger man, with broad shoulders and a black mustache. His jet black hair was greased straight back from his forehead and sideburns, giving the appearance that he was in constant, forward motion.

Duncan McUsic taught at the engineering school. He was a graduate of the school, Class of 1938. He liked to say that the engineering school's motto was "The College, Without the Bullshit."

Though only five-foot eight inches tall, he had an aura of command well-known to legions of engineering students. When a student met with him for the first time in his office, and saw him seated at his desk, he seemed to be a very large man. He had a large, wide forehead—like a marble bust of an ancient Greek in the College museum. His head was topped by a large tuft of gray hair, still speckled with the reddish brown color of his youth. The students noticed the wide shoulders and long torso and believed, upon their first meeting in the office, that he must be well over six feet tall. But when he moved out of his chair to grab a book, or open or close the office door, they noticed short, almost dainty legs and feet, like a dancer, or a featherweight boxer, one who danced away from every punch, moving, moving, moving, tiring his opponent as he set up his knockout blow.

The president poured two drinks and took a seat in his favorite leather chair. His eyes drifted away from the professor, toward the tall, wide windows that looked over the campus center.

"We want our boys in the fight. Lord knows Uncle Sam needs

guys like ours. There is risk. We know that. But the alternative is to do nothing, to be on the sidelines. We've never been on the sidelines before. What kind of college sits out a war?"

"Jack will be here in few minutes," the professor said. "I hear that he's done great work over there."

"That's what he's supposed to be doing."

"You could say 'Nicely done.'"

"I don't need to compliment a guy like Jack on his work. If you pick the right people, they know how good they are."

The president looked at the clock. "Do we have time for a quick round-up? Here goes: the faculty is killing me on ROTC. I don't care. ROTC stays as long as I breathe. Training has deep roots here; our boys marched on the college green in '17 and in the '40s. Protests are coming, I'm sure about that. We'll deal with them. But I won't be bending over for a spanking like some of my fellow presidents around the country. No way. We have rules here. They can hang me in effigy if they want." He looked the professor in the eye. "What about recruits, Duncan? Anyone new?"

"Five started over there last month," the professor said, "after training in the States. We've heard very high praise for their work thus far."

"What about your little project at the engineering school? Funds flowing?"

"Plenty," the professor said. "You have the touch."

"Can we trust the help?"

"Yes, very well-vetted. And the pay is excellent."

Jack knocked on the heavy door guarding the president's office and he heard his name called inside. He entered. The president and the professor rose from their chairs and moved toward him, hands outstretched, closing in for a firm grip.

"Jack, welcome home."

"Great to be back," Jack smiled. "And thanks for making the arrangements for my trip, sir. Leave like this is hard to come by."

"Always happy to help our boys. See Colonel Turck yet?"

"I did. He sends his best."

The president smiled. "Give you any advice?"

"A lot."

"Not surprised," the president said. "Sit down, sit down. Drink?"

"No, thanks."

Jack took a seat at the long mahogany conference table.

"Jack, we have some new recruits that we'd like to run by you. Here is the list."

The president slid a single piece of heavy bond, cream-colored paper across the well-polished table. Jack looked at the six names and spoke as he read.

"Solid, solid, solid, solid, solid." Then he paused at the sixth. He said the name aloud. "Vietnam? Really?"

"You're not sure, Jack?"

"No, I'm not sure. Brains to spare. Rocco knows him from the engineering school—of course, Professor McUsic does, too." He nodded toward the professor, who remained silent. "Couldn't he be more help here with your research? I'm just not sure about the field part. We go out for 'assessments.' Things can go wrong in a hurry. Happened to me already. It's not for everyone. I'd give him a second thought for this assignment, if I were you."

Jack looked at the professor. "I think Rocco would agree," Jack said.

"Then we'll wait on the sixth. On the others, can you talk to them while you're back?"

"Yes, sir."

"We'll meet them all at Professor McUsic's house for dinner. Bring Rocco."

"If there's free food, he's there."

"These recruits—we've pounded them with the details—to see if they blink—but I want them to hear it from you, not some old goat. Tell them what you're doing and why it matters."

Jack said nothing. The president moved on.

"Is Stumpo Stewart still with your group in Saigon?"

"Yes."

"How is he?"

"Same."

"Good God," the professor laughed. "How is his commander is holding up? Better than our rugby coach?"

The president smiled, then laughed. Jack nodded and winced as he recalled, but did not relate, Stumpo's latest troubles with his captain.

"Are we all set?" the president asked.

"Yes, sir, I think we are. Oh, I just remembered, there is one more thing. This one is a bit awkward, sir."

"What is it? Anything, Jack."

"Well, could you tell the Alumni Office that I'm not an alum? They keeping sending me letters asking me for money."

"What? Sending you letters? Over there?"

"Very efficient fundraisers you have there, Sam," the professor smirked.

"I can't believe it," the president said, shaking his head. "I'll take care of it. Okay, are we all set now?" he asked, looking around.

"All set," the professor said. He and Jack rose from their chairs, shook hands with the president, and walked out of the office.

As the professor and Jack exited the administration building, the clock in the tower of the library began its hourly chimes. The tower, clock, and bells were a gift from a generous but controversial alumnus, Richard J. "Dickie" Crouchback. In the 1920s, College funds to build a new library fell short of need, leaving the College resigned to a long, flat, non-descript building, three stories of brick but without its planned, signature spire.

Enter Crouchback, a flamboyant businessmen whose family had "agricultural" interests in the South that dated to ante-bellum days. Dickie was a loyal supporter of his *alma mater* and jumped at the naming opportunity presented by the missing funds for the missing tower.

"Consider it done, Mr. President," he said when Dickie took the call from Sam Onion. Construction of the tower commenced quickly and pressed upward to a height of 300 feet, the climax

stone laid with great fanfare and applause from the people staring at the spire from below.

Meanwhile, close observers of the construction became anx-
ious to see the bells that would occupy the belfry. They said that
the donor had taken an unusually keen interest in the clock-bell,
and their suspicions were confirmed when they learned that the
inside of the bell was engraved with several scenes depicting ante-bellum life in the South and a series of initials ringing the ears
of the bells—R.E.L., T.J.J., and others—honoring its military
heroes.

The bells were made of melted tin and copper. The donor, it
was said, also took an unusually keen interest in the round balls
at the end of each bell clapper, choosing the shape and large di-
ameter—"the biggest around," said the admiring president—in
keeping with, the president noted to close friends, the rumored
source of the donor's valor in the Great War and rapid success
in business.

For years afterward, the bells in Crouchback Tower rang
without controversy, calling students to class and marking the
victories of the vaunted football team. In recent years, however,
the bells had come under the gaze of some students interested
in history and not at all pleased by the engravings on the bells.
They researched the relationship between the Crouchbacks
and the slave trade. They protested loudly and directly to the
president and the Board of Trustees. Black crepe mysteriously
appeared on the tower, covering the clock. The president took
calls from all sides, all irate. The president stood firm—donor's
wishes, tradition, and so forth, he said.

The protesters—not to be denied, and fueled by the unsleep-
ing humor and creativity of youth—informally renamed the
tower "The Dick." The president stewed with anger but was
powerless to blunt the student movement; his only option was to
call Mr. Crouchback to relay the news of the informal renaming
of the tower.

"I kind of like it," Dickie said. "And one more thing: tell
them I personally posed for the bell clappers."

The nine o'clock bells quieted as the president, one foot on the credenza, watched the professor and Jack walk away down the sidewalk. He looked out on the campus green.

"I am not taking sides," he said aloud. "And I am not talking to myself," he added. "I am just thinking out loud. I am counselor to our situation. Difficult times require difficult measures. Sometimes quiet measures. My predecessors had it easy. This thing could blow up any day."

Some days he felt like he was in the wilderness, like another of his predecessors, the founder, hacking and slashing and fording his way up the river, against the current. The founder was driven by a simple dream. The President saw his role today as similar, as a pathfinder through the chaos. The campuses—hell, the whole goddam country—had lost their way.

He looked more closely out the window and saw students and faculty crisscrossing the green. On the same green, his friends had marched in formation as Navy "V-12" units preparing for war with Germany and Japan. Row upon row, straight as a string, dress whites and no dissents. Where was that unity now?

"Gone forever," Sam Onion said out loud.

Chapter 5

Jack and Professor McUsic left the president's office and walked back to the professor's house. Walking along the green, Jack noticed the darkening tower of the library, splitting the sunset in half. At the top of the Crouchback Tower sat a weathervane cast as a Viking in full battle regalia.

The sky was filled with brushstrokes—thin, charcoal and light-gray clouds—strands and wisps that darted across the remaining blue, orange, and yellow backdrop. The Vermont hills ran the width of the scene to the west, rising and falling in a line across the bottom of the tableau, the hills already dark, and the thin clouds dancing above the line of hills.

The clock read 9:15 p.m. Jack was tired from the long drive and the long day. He kept walking with the professor, though, and thinking: maybe he'll mention his daughter, Clare.

"Clare called last night," the Professor said suddenly. "She asked about you." He paused. "She said she's worried about you. I don't worry about you, but I do worry about her. She said she was at another protest against the war. There were some arrests—not her, thank God. South Tapley isn't a quiet little town anymore, I guess.

"She's stubborn as hell, just like her mother. But I guess you know that. I wish her mother had lived. She could talk to Clare. She is her mother's daughter, sure enough. She looks for trouble, and even when she doesn't look for it, trouble finds her. There is no bend with her, no compromise. She sees black and white. A problem? There must be a solution. A wrong? It must be righted. An underdog? It must be defended. Standing between Clare and her goal is not a safe place to be. I know, I have been there."

He glanced at Jack.

"God it's been a ride with her," the professor continued. "Not that I would have missed it for the world. But if you two have a future, you'll need vacations from each other. Her mother and I did."

"Well," Jack answered. "We're pretty far apart these days . . . ."

The professor looked at Jack but said nothing.

After a fifteen-minute walk they approached the professor's house. He lived in one of a row of houses on a long hill that faced a pond near the campus. The backs of the houses overlooked the river to the west.

Built in the 1920s, the Victorian held many surprises, including a large wine cellar and a concrete and steel vault in the basement. The first owner was a local bank president who—anticipating the stock market crash—stopped construction at the house to add the wine cellar and the vault to safeguard his liquid assets. The bank president later sold the house to the dean of the engineering school, who sold it to the professor.

The library was a large room on the first floor that extended the length of the house. Large cherry bookcases lined the walls and reached the ceiling. One far corner held a globe, the other a six-foot long jet engine. "A Junkers Jumo 004," the professor explained to curious guests. "I couldn't get it in here until my wife passed away. It's the world's first turbojet. Junkers produced it for the Germans in the '40s. They put it in their first jet plane. We were very lucky that we ended the war before these things took flight. We studied it closely at the engineering school in the '40s and '50s. It was easy to get the thing here: only took a dolly, a truck, a small forklift, four large boys from the engineering school, a ramp, and the removal of two large doors."

At the far end of the library a large bowed window overlooked the pond to the east. The window measured ten feet by six feet. On the window sill below there was a small brass plate inscribed: "Tim 'The Big K' Kowantowski Memorial Window." "A party for some of the boys from Asgard Hall gone awry," the professor often noted for guests, "and a hard window to replace, you can be sure," feigning a grimace but secretly enjoying the memory.

Clare had grown up in this house and spent hours skating

on the pond. As Jack looked out the window that night, he recalled an early date with Clare. A hard rain followed by a cold
snap left a sheet of black ice on the pond. Jack and Clare laced
their skates on the bank and glided out to the center of the ice.
They bowed toward each other and laughed, then took off in a
race, then stopped, then raced again. They cut thin white circles
into the black sheet. Then, suddenly, they were holding hands,
matching stride for stride, glancing at each other quickly then
looking ahead. A few other people skated at the far end but Jack
and Clare did not see them.

They returned to the bank and kicked off their skates. He
told her how much fun he had, how much the day meant to him.
But he did not tell her that day how much the pond meant to
him.

Back at the house, the professor interrupted Jack's daydream.

"Your father played out there."

"I know. My mother told me. She still has his stick and a few
old programs."

"Do you play hockey? I forget."

"A little bit in high school. My football coach discouraged it."

"The varsity practiced out there then, in the '40s," the professor said. "Twenty guys, equipment thrown everywhere on the
banks. 'Thump, thump, thump,' that's what you heard when the
pucks slammed against the wooden boards around the pond.
You could here it all the way down to the dorms in the cold air.
The coach drilled them until they dropped. But when the games
came, they flew. He was so very proud of them. 'Natural players
on natural ice,' the coach called them. And when the call came
for World War II, they were the fittest guys around. Some didn't
come back. I think of them every day.

"Your dad came back, though. And no one flew faster than
your father on that ice. He was always the last to leave the pond.
He and a buddy would bring their cars down, keep them running, and point the headlights onto the pond so that they could
skate into the night. You couldn't see much—these were old-
time headlights, remember. But you could hear him. 'Scrunch,

scrunch, scrunch,' that heavy sound that a great skater makes when he digs in and pushes off from natural ice. And when they dribbled the puck you could hear that 'tock, tock, tock,' of a wooden stick on the frozen puck, with a meter, Jack, that told you that the player had done it a thousand times."

The professor turned his gaze from the pond to Jack and said, "Well, Jack, it's late. I guess you better go."

He shook Jack's hand and said, "Careful over there, boy. Got it?"

Chapter 6

Clare McUsic's apartment at her women's college in South Tapley was in a large Victorian house purchased long ago by her college and converted for student use. Six students lived there, three seniors and two other sophomores, like Clare. The sophomores lived in the two apartments on the third floor, tucked into the garrets where Irish servants had lived in earlier times.

Clare sat in her dorm room studying, then not, then studying, then not. She turned the pages of her textbook slowly, then turned them back. She took a sip of her drink and looked at the small clock on the top of her nightstand. Jack would be there in half-an-hour.

She left her desk chair and walked up to the mirror above the wooden bureau. At five-foot-seven, she was almost too tall to see herself in it. She brushed out auburn curls that cascaded from her temples to her shoulders in twisting, tangled threads. She had reddish-brown eyebrows that jutted at an angle down toward her nose, almost forcing the world to stare into her gray-green eyes. Her eyes were wide and almond-shaped. She had full lips and a few freckles dotting her high cheekbones. She lingered at the mirror, looking past her image, as if to see the future past her own reflection. If she looked closely, she thought, her reflected self might reveal what was to come. But she saw nothing, nothing at all, and turned away.

She thought about the first time that she had met Jack Dunne. She and her friends—all recent graduates of the local high school—were swimming and canoeing in the river near town that summer. They were pulling their canoe out of the water when a young man approached them.

"Need a hand?" he asked.

She looked up at him and felt a physical pain, deep inside her chest. Her breathing slowed. Her mind emptied. She stood motionless

"I'm Jack Dunne," he said. She did not answer. Then he said, "Nice to meet you." Seconds passed like hours. In her mind she screamed, "I'm not speaking!" More time passed, but she made no sound.

"Nice hat," he said. And then he smiled and walked away.

When she returned home from that day at the river, she asked her father about the boy she had met.

"Everyone knows Jack," his father said. "And they want to be him, too."

"Where is he from?"

"Iowa."

"What's he doing out here?"

"His father went to the College. And the football coach did the rest."

"What do you think of him?"

The professor paused, not sure whether to answer truthfully.

"He's a boy every father would be proud to call 'son.'"

"Oh," Clare said. "So I guess you like him, Dad." She laughed.

"Does he have a girlfriend?"

"Not that I know of."

A phone call from Jack followed that summer, then another, then a visit to the McUsic house. Jack and Clare went on long walks. They walked around the pond and down to the river and hiked some of the nearby hills. They talked a lot about the women's college she was starting in the fall, two hours away.

"South Tapley's not that far," Jack said. She wasn't sure what he meant by that. She knew that she did not want their summer to end.

Clare looked from the mirror and toward Jack's picture on the bureau. He was confident and he was smart. He was not a bookworm but he was a lover of books and curious about all things. And, she thought from that first day at the river, he was strikingly handsome. But she thought his looks had less to do with his features—dark-Irish, widow's peak, and strong jaw and wide smile—than with his expressions. These didn't show in most photographs. Rather, he seemed most handsome at a glance, in a quick encounter, when he laughed, or in a photo taken on the run, when the camera caught him by surprise.

As she sat in her apartment that evening, she recalled his first visit to her at school. They walked to a nearby park. As they walked, they talked about the first time they had met by the river. Jack smiled.

"I don't remember much about the first time we met," he said. He rolled his eyes to their tops, as if searching his memory. "Oh, I guess I remember a bit. I remember the guy I was talking to. I remember one of the guys with you down by the river. He joked that you were his 'sister.' I remember what you wore. I remember your shirt. I remember your shorts. I remember your sandals."

He smiled. "But other than that, darlin', I don't remember a thing."

She laughed, but she wanted to cry. He could surprise her like that.

He always seemed ready for life, for the next adventure; he always seemed poised on the balls of his feet. And what a listener, she thought. When he looked at you he cocked his head at an angle—it was his way of staying with you, in the moment, locked in, not looking away to survey the room, like the other young men she knew. Yet, despite all his confidence, and his talent, she saw too a certain shyness, a "Yes, sir," "No, Sir," "Not sure," sometimes no more than a quiet smile. He shared very little, even about the war. Especially about the war. Older men liked these traits—she knew all about their respect for him from her father, who never seemed to tire of talking about Jack Dunne.

One day she asked her father about Jack and Colonel Turck.

"Dad, he often mentions Colonel Turck—Tiemo, he calls him. Who is he?"

"His name is Colonel Tiemo Turck. You pronounce his name 'Tee-mo.' He was born in Brandenberg, Germany. The family name is actually Turckhauser von Zweigenbury Freiherr zu Egkh und Hungarspach. It goes back at least as far as the 1100s. He came here as a child, 'steerage from Hamburg,' he often said. His father and uncles worked in the silver factories in Connecticut. The rivers drove the mills, but even after coal fired the plants, the mills stayed. Workers came from Germany in the 1800s and they stayed, too. They were tough Lutherans who were good with their hands. They made those factories go.

"When World War I came, they hit trouble. You don't hear about it in school much anymore, but there was a lot of bad feeling about German immigrants when we were fighting the Germans in Europe. So many of the immigrants changed their names to make them sound less German. Tiemo's family dropped the rest of their name and left it at "Turck."

"Tiemo came to school here in the early '30s. He was on a scholarship funded by one of the big Connecticut mill owners. He played hockey but his real love was history and foreign affairs, what was going on in the world. Europe. Russia. Japan. He spoke three languages. He was keeping a close eye on what was happening in Germany, of course. He still had family there."

"Nothing good happening at that point, I'm sure," Clare said.

" 'Nothing good' is mild. He and his family were very worried."

"How did he meet Jack?"

"After he left college here Tiemo went into the American intelligence corps. They always did a lot of recruiting here at the College. That's how Tiemo met Jack's father. And that's how he knows Jack. Every since we lost Jack's father in Prague . . . Tiemo kind of keeps an eye out for Jack."

"Clare!" Clare was jolted from her memories of her father's stories by a loud female voice calling from the foyer of her house. Clare heard a few of the doors of her housemates open as some heavy footsteps started up the stairs. She opened the door to her room just as Jack reached the top of the stairs on the third floor.

"Missed you," she said, as their eyes locked.

"Me, too."

Clare threw her arms around Jack and gave him a long, passionate kiss, as if it were the first, or the last, kiss between them.

"I missed you so much," she nearly shouted. "I can't tell you how much. Every day."

"Me, too," Jack said.

Clare grabbed his hand and said, "Come on in, soldier boy. You're all mine now."

Some time later, Jack and Clare descended the stairs and walked out the door of her house and onto the sidewalk. They walked slowly along the main street toward the campus. Old gaslight-style lamps flickered, then brightened as Jack and Clare walked in the dusk. The fall chill came later in South Tapley than in the north, at the College, but Jack felt any cool air as a welcome change from the tropics.

The women's college in South Tapley was a frequent destination for students from the College in the north, the terminus of trips down the two-lane that ran the length of the long, winding river that connected the campuses over the one-hundred mile route. In earlier days, South Tapley clubs were mobbed by students on the night before registration for classes to the north, and florists in South Tapley—keenly aware that the cross-border trade in emotion could spur trade in goods—advertised in the Viking campus newspaper for deliveries to the south.

Road trips south—often spontaneous—were raised by some of the students to an art form. "Cultural exchanges," Pierre Loch called them. And Pierre relished the lore of the trips, passing on to the younger brothers the tales of late night caravans, flat tires, empty gas tanks, and a thousand laughs. He had business cards printed for the journeys south: "Viking Traveling Party and Associated Zoo. Free Home Deliveries. Authorized Representative." One story—known by a generation at Asgard Hall simply as "The Arrest" was *primus inter pares*—first among equally hilarious tales. It arose from the highly volatile coincidence that, on the same winter night in '54 in South Tapley, there assembled both a group of marauding Vikings looking for fun and a glee club from a rival men's college performing in the ornate sitting room in one of the stately women's residence halls. The concert had already begun when the men of Asgard arrived late, per their usual schedule. They surveyed the scene. Their leader had been tipped to the concert by his girlfriend in another residence. He was carrying a large plastic garbage bag. He left his friends for a moment and disappeared around a corner of the building. When he returned he was wearing the full uniform of a campus police officer.

"Officer Smith, reporting for duty," he said. "Shall we go in, gentlemen?"

The "officer" stepped in first. The others slipped inside the door and found a spot in the hallway where they could watch the fun undetected. "Officer Smith" strode to the front of the room, head up, chest out, arms swinging. The glee club stopped their song in mid-chorus. The house mother rushed from her chair to the "officer" and said,

"Officer, is there something wrong?"

"Sorry ma'am, but I am afraid there is. I am arresting this man."

He pointed to the leader of the glee club.

"For, for, for . . . what?" the young man stammered.

"Yes, for what?" the house mother asked, her mouth and eyes wide open in disbelief.

"For crimes against the laws of man, nature, and this State," he said gravely to the house mother. "Committed in this very house last night, ma'am."

"What kind of crimes?"

"I'd rather not say in front of these young women, ma'am." "You," he said pointing to the glee club leader, whose mouth still hung open. "Come with me." He grabbed the young man and led him to the door.

"And that," Jack said to Clare when he first recounted the lore, "is what we call simply 'The Arrest.' It has assumed its place as a revered entry in what we call 'The Journal of Stray Beasts,' the ancient log of road trips."

"You people are beyond hope," Clare said then, rolling her

eyes while suppressing a smile.

This night, groups of students passed by them on the sidewalk. Some waved and smiled at Clare. When they reached the campus they turned down a long, cobblestone path that led to the dining hall. They entered through the large, oaken door. A hundred or so students—ninety-five women, five or so male visitors—stood in the line or sat quietly at rectangular wooden tables set in rows.

The hall was built in 1902. It had a high ceiling with a large transom that cast bright, shining light into the interior on sunny days. The transom was joined and supported by a dozen wooden arches that rose from the bases of the sidewalls toward the apex. At the base of each arch was a flagpole bearing the flag of one of the dozen residence halls on campus. The college long ago had determined not to create dining spaces in the residence halls. Central dining, it was said, would foster unity among the students.

Jack and Clare took their food trays to one of the tables. Clare looked around for familiar faces but saw none right away.

"Well, I made it this far," Jack said. Clare knew that he was referring to an incident on his last visit.

"I don't think she's here this term."

"Oh," Jack said. "Study abroad? I know some guys doing that myself. Fully funded by Uncle Sam."

Clare did not laugh. "She's okay, I guess. A little intense."

"Yes," Jack said. "A little intense. Like a hurricane."

They sat down at a table. Jack became serious. "I can only stay one night. I have to leave tomorrow. I might be back in the summer, if your father and President Onion can arrange it. My tour is up at the end of December next year."

"Then what?" Clare asked.

"Good question."

"Not much of an answer, Jack."

Clare waited a few minutes to speak again. Her stomach had knotted and she looked down at the ground.

"I haven't told you *my* latest. You might not like it," she began.

"Try me."

"I am going to speak at the next draft board meeting in town."

"About what?"

"The war."

"What about it?"

"It's illegal."

"I heard."

"No, really. No declaration of war by Congress, so it's not a legal war. They have no right to draft guys. They have no right to deny the appeals that the draft board hears."

She looked into Jack's eyes. Her own green eyes were burning with the intensity that Jack knew and loved. "What do you think?"

"I think you've decided what to do already. But you're not alone on this one. A lot of people are saying the same thing."

Jack looked at her closely. She was sitting up straight, neck and head forward, as if she were rehearsing her posture for the board. She was deadly serious and Jack in that instant saw what had always so attracted him to Clare—her commitment, her passion, and, at times, her barely-controlled fury, her I-don't-care what-others-think abandon, her desire to right any wrong, at any cost.

"Why the draft board?" he asked.

"No one else around here has any authority. I'm tired of talking to professors who agree with me, or are afraid to disagree with the students. I want to do something. At least the people on the board have some power. I want to push them."

"There will be some older vets on the board, I'll bet."

"I know."

"Not a friendly audience. An away game, for sure."

"Right."

"One thing?"

"What?"

"Remember, they are just doing a job, too. Some of them

know that this thing is turning out badly. They just won't say it in public. Anyone going with you?"

"A friend might come."

"Plan on getting arrested?"

"No, no plans."

She stared at him, he at her. He smiled slightly. "You're the best," he said.

She was still in battle-ready posture, sitting at attention. His kind words had put her off-balance. "Why do you say that?"

"Because you know what you think and you're willing to act on it."

She nodded but did not smile. "You do, too, Jack. Doesn't everyone?"

"No."

They had almost finished their meal when a young woman approached their table. She had long, dark hair and piercing emerald eyes. She wore an embroidered cotton shirt and faded blue bell-bottomed jeans.

"Hello Sarah," Clare said without expression. She looked down at her tray and then nervously at Jack. "Remember Jack?"

"Sure do," Sarah said. "And I remember what he's up to these days. How are you, soldier boy?"

Here we go, Jack thought.

"How do you sleep?" Sarah said, raising her voice.

"Not well. It's hot as hell."

"You know what I mean."

"I know what you mean." He shrugged. "I sleep fine. I sleep where they sent me."

"You volunteered, I heard."

"True."

"You could have . . . ."

"Careful. Don't assume . . . ."

"You had options."

"Oh yeah . . . *those* 'options.' They weren't for me."

"Enough," Clare interrupted, holding up her hand.

"Not impressed," Sarah said. She suddenly moved her hand

toward the end of the table and knocked Jack's drink to the floor.

"I said enough!" Clare shouted. "Sarah!"

Sarah turned quickly and walked away. Jack and Clare stared at each other but said nothing. After a few minutes, they rose. They cleaned up the mess on the floor and walked out of the cafeteria. Other students stared and whispered as Jack and Clare left the room.

They reached the sidewalk and turned to walk back to Clare's house. It was dark and quiet and they both sighed deeply as they walked, as if under a burden that they were now carrying on a steeper grade. They stopped in front of Clare's house. Jack turned to her and said, "I guess I shouldn't have expected to get clear of the war, even down here. Anyone who knows me is going to want to rumble. It's like I'm bringing back a disease. Or maybe that's wrong—maybe I don't bring it with me, maybe it's everywhere already. Everyone has an opinion and they think I should hear it. Or they feel they need to change my opinion, or at least the opinion they think I have. And I'm not even sure I have an opinion that they could change.

"I'm like the lightening rod on the barn. All the high voltage floating around—even in your dining hall—finds me. It's not really fair, though. It's the rod's job to draw the lightening bolts. But I didn't sign up for that job. No, I'm more like the tree in the field. The bolt hits the tree. It burns. Poof. It's not really personal—the bolt doesn't even know the tree. In fact, the bolt is not even trying to hit the tree. But that doesn't help the tree much. It's still toast in the end."

Clare said nothing. She let Jack finish. She loved his visits, but she knew he was right. She knew she should try to change the subject for Jack's time with her. But she felt carried into the same vortex, the same issues, even when she knew she should stop.

"One of my friends worked this summer in Los Angeles," she said, looking down the sidewalk toward the hill and her house. "She was helping out at a veterans hospital. Know what she saw? Ten floors of pain. One-thousand patients. Amputees everywhere. The four-limbs got carried around in a thing that looked like a child's car seat. She said that there were doctors, nurses, therapists, and psychiatrists everywhere, no let-up, no mercy for anyone—soldiers, families, anyone. It drove her crazy."

She stopped and looked at Jack.

"Is it worth it? What does all your work there accomplish? What is the point?"

"I don't see it that way."

"Why not?"

"I don't understand your question."

"We're going to lose this war anyway, so why do you . . . ."

"I don't know about winning or losing. I don't even know what those words mean. He looked down. I have no idea."

"You really don't seem to feel anything about this."

"I feel plenty."

"Where does all this lead for you?"

"Some people are counting on me."

"Oh yeah, I heard. They think you are committed, like them. They think you love your country. And you know what price they want you to pay for your commitment, for your love of country? The price is you will die for the country that they say you represent so well. Well, I don't think you should buy it. Think about the others on your campus. You're a star, the big man up there. People respect you. You know all the stories. You know all the codes. The others take their cues from you." She looked him in the eye. "That's why you shouldn't do this."

He did not move, not even an eyelid. Then he said, "Don't you have it backwards? Isn't that *why* I should do this? Because people know me? Because they'll want to know why I am going? Because no one else we know is going over there?"

"Towny is going," Clare said suddenly.

"What?"

"He's going to enlist next spring."

"Oh, shit," Jack said. "No."

"Yeah, well, he is. He wrote and told me. Rocco knows, too." Clare eyed Jack carefully. "Rocco says that Towny talks about you a lot."

Jack frowned.

"What's the matter? Why are you so surprised? Maybe he sees you as someone to look up to. You can't have it both ways, Jack – you're either a role model or you're not."

Jack shook his head. They stood in silence under the streetlight in front of Clare's house.

"I just thought I should tell you about him," Clare said. "I didn't want to ruin our night—we we don't get many." She took his hand and smiled and put her other hand around his neck. "So let's make the most of the time we have."

Chapter 7

Back at the house, boiling some pasta, Rocco reflected on his work on the professor's new project. Secrecy was paramount, he was told on his first day.

"What you see here, what you do here, what I say here, stays here. Got it? Some people just wouldn't understand what we're doing, or why we're doing it."

"Got it, Professor."

Rocco relished the work, despite some early stumbles. He had appeared at the professor's office with his first twenty-page background research report on the project, still general in concept because at that point he knew so few of the details. He was proud of his work and expected some praise.

"Come in and sit down, Rocco."

The professor quietly read the report from beginning to end without making or taking any notes. He then reached toward a coffee mug filled with pencils and pens. He carefully removed a bright red, recently sharpened pencil. He examined the first page of the report. Then he drew a long, red line from the top left corner of the page to the bottom right corner. Then he turned to the second page and did exactly the same thing. Then he did the same for the third and fourth pages. He said nothing as he turned to the fifth page.

Rocco shifted in his seat. This is not going well, he thought.

The professor turned to the fifth page and, in the middle, made a large "X" at the beginning of a paragraph.

"I think that you will agree that you should begin here," he said, pointing the pencil at the 'X.'"

"Yes, sir."

"That's all for today."

"Thank you, sir."

Yet, despite sessions like these, Rocco thought that the professor was generally pleased with his work. He heard no praise, true. Not a word. And the professor never compared his work to that of others. But slowly, with each day in the lab and each day writing reports, Rocco began to see the truth: he *was* being measured each day, silently, against the professor's own high standards. To succeed was to meet the standards.

Rocco heard his back door open and looked up from the stove. It was Jack, back from his visit to Clare in South Tapley.

"How did it go at the lab today?" Jack asked.

"Same. Hard to work for a riddle wrapped in a mystery inside an enigma."

"Sounds hard."

"Fascinating, more like it."

"What's he like to work for? Tiemo told me that the government and industry offer him jobs all the time."

"I've heard that too," Rocco said.

"Why does he stay?"

"Hard to say. He likes it here, I guess. He likes the guys. He sees big things for them. Ever tell you the one about him at the faculty parties at the fraternities? He loves going to them. At ours he was standing next to me, drink in his hand, smiling away. He looked around the room, then, with a great gleam in his eye turned to me and said: 'I wish I could invest in these guys!' I guess that he stays because he knows what he wants. He doesn't want to be someone else, or somewhere else. He likes it here. Maybe it makes him feel young again."

Rocco pointed over to the coffee table. "You have some mail there."

Jack walked over to the table and saw a letter addressed to him in his mother's hand. He wrote to her often, from the College and Vietnam. I guess she wanted to have a letter waiting for me here, Jack thought.

Her early letters to Jack at the College made a few references to Jack's father's time on campus. Jack read each carefully, memorizing the details and never throwing one out. He wrote a reply each night when he received one, and ended every letter with the words: "Thanks for everything. I never walk across the campus without thinking that I am the luckiest guy on the planet. Love always, Jack."

Jack put down the letter and leaned back on the couch.

"How was your visit with Clare?" Rocco asked.

"Fine with her—with her classmates, not so fine."

"What happened?"

"Nothing too bad. At least I didn't get called a baby-killer this time."

"Enough. Let's eat."

After dinner Rocco sat on the couch reading a newspaper.

"Draft lottery in December, Jack."

"I know, Rocco."

"I think I'll get to stay here and graduate, whatever number I get," Rocco said. "After that, I don't know. Grad school deferment? I don't think they work anymore. People are already crazy around here about the whole thing. I've heard it all—and I mean all—while you've been gone. Burning their cards, going to jail, going to Canada, eating themselves into oblivion. Everything is on the table."

Rocco got up and walked around the living room as he talked. "I really don't see me doing any of those things. I really don't handle things that way, you know. But I'm not there yet. We'll see."

"Why do you think people are doing these things?" Jack asked.

"I don't know—they don't want to die? Or maybe a little guilt?" Rocco ventured. "They are smart enough to know that someone will be going in their places. My high school—three killed already. No college, no deferment, no chance. Here they say 'Hell, no, we won't go.' I get it. But someone will go. People like Clare know this. She's got that right, at least. She hates the war, like them, but at least she sees the unfairness of it all."

Jack said nothing.

"When is the lottery?"

"December 1."

"That should be some shit-show here. Then what?"

"Physicals, inductions for some. It'll be wild."

"Seems funny for me to be on the outside, looking in. Or maybe I'm inside, looking out. I don't know what I mean. It's like I live in two places."

"You won't be outside of this for long, not if you hang around here."

"What do you mean?"

Rocco raised his voice. "Because they'll drag you in. They'll hate you for going, then they'll hate you for coming home. They'll hate what they think you represent. They will drag in you and the others who went over there. They'll hate everyone of you who went, even the ones who are lucky enough to make it back. You'll be in the middle of it either way."

Jack stared at him quietly. "I've already heard some of that. Here. Even from some guys on the team. Even from professors I thought I knew pretty well. One won't even look at me. And you should have heard the rant I got from a so-called friend of Clare's down in South Tapley last week."

"So the lottery's in December," Jack said, putting Clare's friend out of his mind. "You feeling lucky, Rocco?"

"Not really," Rocco said.

"Why not? Is this a real lottery? Or a fake? How are they going to do it? How are you going to know it's real?"

"They say they will write down the date of each day of the year on a slip of paper and assign them numbers, 1 through 366. Then they put each slip in a blue—beats me why it's blue—capsule. They mix all of the capsules in a big shoebox. Then they put the capsules in a big glass jar for someone to reach in a pull out a capsule, one by one. On live television."

"You're kidding. Live TV? And who is the poor bastard who gets to do the dirty deed in front of everyone? Shouldn't he wear a hood?"

"Don't know. Doubt it will be Nixon."

"So, you're the engineer—what could go wrong?"

"Easy. They'll muck up the mixing. The shoebox is the weak link. It won't be big enough for 366 capsules. It won't mix them in a statistically random way. Here's why it won't. The ones that get put in last won't get mixed well—they'll stay on top. And they'll still be on top when they get put in the jar. And bango, those will get taken out first. And remember, the birthdays that get taken out first get the low numbers, the unlucky ones. So if the December birthdays go into the jar last, they will come out first. And they will get a low number. And if you get a low number . . . ."

"You join me in paradise."

"Or worse," Rocco nodded. "So that's why I figure that the same dumb bastards who are running the war will screw up the lottery, too. I'm December 7, so I'm toast. It'll be Pearl Harbor Day all over again, this time for me."

They were quiet for a while. Jack looked over at Rocco, who had started writing at his desk.

"What are you writing? More stuff to the *Daily Viking?* Clare gets the paper at school. She likes the anonymous letters, she said, but she doesn't know it's you. I didn't tell her."

"Here. Look at this. Melville didn't just write whales tales."

Jack took the page from Rocco. The anonymous letter to the editor included the poem "The March into Manassas":

"To every just or larger end,
Whence should come the trust and cheer?

You must its ignorance impulse lend –
Age finds place in the rear.
All wars are boyish, and are fought by boys."

Jack finished reading the letter. "Whale of a poem, Rocco."
Rocco smirked.

"Melville got it right, though. You wouldn't believe how young some of the guys look over there. But they're not boys for long."

Jack stood up. "I've got to get my stuff. I'm leaving early tomorrow. Probably won't see you. I'm stopping to see Tiemo before I go to the airport."

"How has he been?"

"Okay, I guess. He's hard to read sometimes."

"Does he ever talk about your father?"

"Sometimes."

"What's that like?"

"It's strange. He talks to me like I knew the man. But I didn't. He and the others did. But since he knows so much about him, it's a little like talking to my father, or at least someone like him."

"Does he give you advice?"

"Plenty."

"Maybe I should get some. I've got some decisions ahead," Rocco said with a grimace, as he stood up. "Let's make a deal, friend: I won't do anything crazy on lottery night if you don't do anything crazy over there."

"Deal," Jack said.

Chapter 8

Jack rose early and made some coffee. Rocco was already up and off to his first job of the day. Jack looked out the kitchen window and saw two deer in the meadow behind the house, along the fence where Jack and Rocco liked to place their empty bottles for target practice.

He loaded the trunk of his Buick and went back into the kitchen to write Rocco a note. "Remember our deal," Jack wrote.

Jack turned the car out of the driveway and down the street to the two-lane that led to the VA hospital. Tiemo was up and in his chair when Jack arrived at his room.

"Hi, Jack. Headed back?"

"Yes, sir."

"When is your enlistment up?"

"December, '69. I might get back next summer. President Onion said that he could arrange it."

"Send me a letter about your work. The good, the bad, and the ugly. All of it."

"I will."

Tiemo looked out his window toward the familiar hills. The fall burst of colors would come soon, but today only offered a pale green-gray tableau. He turned his head back. He knew that he needed to make the most of this time with Jack.

"Ever told you this one about the professor? The US set up a new agency in '42. Roosevelt was worried about the Germans in occupied Europe. They were using propaganda, threats, and sabotage to create even more fear among the people that they had conquered. The Germans' idea was to drain the faith and hope of their victims. And the US and the Brits had very few means to stop them.

"I was recruited by the new group here in the States. We studied contacts with underground movements, bribery, subsidies, blackmail, counterfeiting, ration cards, passports, personal papers of enemy prisoners or their dead, rumors, abduction, chain letters, poisoning, assassination, illness and epidemics—the works.

"We had a ten-week course covering code practice, cryptography, security and procedure. We learned radio theory. We learned enough to take care of our equipment and make repairs in the field if necessary.

"They were looking for people with some technical background—college engineering, Army Signal Corps—anything. I was approached by the big brass, head honchos from the OSS. They were developing one of the first light-weight, portable radio stations. They managed to get the transmitter, receiver, and power pack all into a unit the size of a suitcase. They called it the 'suitcase radio.'

"Other groups produced other gadgets. When you are going to be undercover, you need different things. They had a lab in Maryland, but they couldn't keep up with the work. So they had to get some universities and private labs into the act.

"That's how I met Professor McUsic. He was back on campus, teaching at the engineering school. The agency sent me up here because I was an alumnus. I met him at the Inn for drinks. I had a whiskey, neat; he had sparkling water. It was secret work, but he came highly recommended, and was an alumnus himself.

"I told him that the agency was working on what they called a submersible raft. They needed something powered by sail or an electric motor, which could be transported in a submarine. Their request specified that the raft should be capable of carrying 400 pounds of dead weight, including the entire radio apparatus needed by the agent. Obviously, the radio had to be carried in dry storage. After an agent had gone ashore from a submarine on this raft, he should be able to submerge the raft in twenty-five feet of sea water and leave it there until the agent was sure that he was secure at his landing spot. It was also required that the raft surface itself and re-submerge at least eight times from a depth of twenty-five feet in order that the agent might be able to use his radio or obtain new supplies, and between those times submerge it for concealment purposes. So, you see, the Agency was looking for what was essentially a midget submarine.

"Professor McUsic was intrigued. So he said he would quietly arrange for a group of engineering students—those still at the College during the war—to give it a try. Well, they ran with it. They worked nights in the sub-basement of the engineering school. I don't know how they kept up with their classes. They produced a prototype in six weeks. The OSS could not believe it. They thought he was a miracle worker. But he's not. He's just someone who gets things done. And you know what else? He knows where to find the talent. He still does."

Tiemo looked Jack in the eye.

"So we took all of our gadgets to England, then we parachuted into France. It was May '44. They dropped guns and food and radios with us. They gave us a message to be broadcast over the BBC at a certain time. The same message for the French groups we would try to contact.

"We met another team dropped into the same area. We started to make contact with the resistance. They had a few thousand men, scattered all around. About half of them were living in tents in the woods and the others in farmhouses. They were organized in groups of six or fifteen. These were common people: a blacksmith, his wife, and his mistress. An old seamstress good with her hands. A student and his brother. A farmhand who had a cousin living in Brooklyn. A cooper and a tailor. And on and on. They were ordinary people doing extraordinary things.

"They needed food and clothes. They had only a few arms— mostly revolvers and machine guns, and only a little ammunition. About three-quarters of them were trained in the use of arms. When we got there they were impatient. They were ready for action.

"We gave them targets to hit on D-Day in June but we had a hard time keeping them on a leash. We weren't supposed to be playing offense there. We were to train, organize, and arm them, then wait for the Allies to invade. We knew that after D-Day Brittany would get hot very quickly.

"We started taking German prisoners and interrogating them. They were young. One was seventeen. They all believed in Hitler. They said, without remorse, that they had burned farms and killed farmers, their wives, and their children all over the area. They had French jewelry and coins and identification cards on them. They did not blink an eye as they said these things.

"What did the French do with them? They gave them no quarter. There was no way would could stop the French from doing this. Too much had happened to them, to their country. Too many civilians massacred. We were coming in late—we could not speak to the French about these things. It was war."

His voice lowered. "Well, all of this was a long time ago, Jack. I'm glad you are going back. But I've got no idea where we're headed. We're in it—I know that. We're there. So the troops deserve our support.

"Guys like you are a big help. It's all about intelligence—every war is. I think I have something to teach you about that. I wouldn't bore you with these old stories if I didn't think it would help you. There were times over in France when I thought we were outsmarting the Germans. We knew what they would do before they knew it. Not always, of course. There were some big SNAFUs, real cock-ups.

"In the summer after D-Day we were still operating in France. We sent some of the French resistance to find the American forces and guide them in the area. The French brought the Americans to our camp—they had been separated from their outfit when it ran into some Germans. But the French were creating a larger problem after D-Day. The French in nearly every town that saw the Americans went crazy—raising flags, cheering the Americans, well into the next day. But the Germans weren't gone—far from it. They were still around. And they didn't appreciate the flags. They entered one of the towns and butchered dozens of people. They found an American column and wiped it out.

"It didn't have to happen. Bad intelligence. The guys in London knew exactly where we were. They should have told the

US units where we were. If the US commander of that column could have contacted us, we could have steered him around those Germans. But they didn't know we were there. I still think about that one.

"I'm not a big-picture guy, Jack. I'll leave that to the professor and others. In Vietnam? Out? Stay? Go? How do I know? We're there. It's The New War. The job is the job. Intel is intel. There is trial and error. You lose your friends. You bury your dead. You cry and curse. You write a letter to their families. You keep going. It's always been this way."

He paused.

"Why do we want you guys? Because West Point, Annapolis—they need some help. They can't do it all. Your classmates? Nowhere to be found. Not like the past. Look at the bronze plaques on the walls at our football field. They are filled with the names of our guys. Civil War? Students on both sides. World War One. World War Two. Korea. Whatever our flaws, we have always remembered our guys. And even with these memorials, we fall short of Princeton: they have a star on the wall outside the window of every dorm room of a Son of Nassau killed in action. A remarkable tribute, indeed.

"But now? Protests against ROTC. Our recruits drying up . . . ." He looked at Jack and frowned. "I'm sorry, there I go again, boring you with the gripes of an old soldier."

Tiemo struggled to get out of his chair, huffing and puffing. Jack moved forward to close the distance and grabbed him by the arm, steadying Tiemo as he fixed his eyes on Jack.

"Take care, my young friend. Do good."

Book II

Chapter 1

Jack walked across the yard of the compound in Saigon, all too familiar by now. He walked quickly to the main door of the large building in the center. He opened the door, entered the lobby, and took the metal stairs two at a time. He was trying to make a meeting for new recruits, their first day of orientation. He slipped in the back door of the room and into a chair next to his college friend and in-country colleague, Aidan "Stumpo" Stewart.

Stumpo had received his name from the senior rugby players at Asgard Hall. They took the small but fierce freshman under their large wings. He was short and bow-legged and hard to knock off his feet on a rugby pitch. He rocked from side to side as he walked, as if had just dismounted from a horse or had been hit by a truck. He had sandy hair and hazel eyes and big ears. His smile appeared more like a grimace and he spoke in a Western rasp, the sounds of his native Montana. He was smart and fearless on and off the pitch, and jumped at the chance offered by President Onion and Professor McUsic to leave the College behind for a while, for something more dangerous.

"Welcome back to paradise," Stumpo whispered.

"Thanks, Stumpo."

Jack had landed a few hours before, back from ten days in the States. As his plane taxied toward the tarmac he looked across the vast, busy airfield. Airfield workers unloaded cargo planes from the rear, the cargo bay opening like the yawning mouth of a great white whale. He saw row upon row of fighter jets. Fuel tanks filled another quarter of the sprawling complex. Behind the tanks, there was an unlikely flat patch of green: the Americans had brought their golf with them, Jack noticed.

Jack hailed a taxi and told the driver his destination. They passed through the shantytowns on the outskirts of the city. The towns were filled with thousands of refugees from the fighting in the countryside. Jack saw a few miles of tents and open, boiling pots and children playing in the muddy streets next to open streams of sewerage.

As they crossed the river—the "Big Muddy," the Americans called it—Jack could see scores of ships that had made their way up the river to the city. He saw a large white German hospital ship. Once across the river, the taxi drove down the long, wide boulevards lined with banyan trees, hundreds of years old.

The taxi slowly made its way through the center of the city at a crawl. Jack saw bicycles of every size and shape, their riders in hats, often large and round, so large as to tip the rider from side to side. Motorbikes dodged in and out of traffic, barely missing Jack's taxi. Sometimes a bike driver pulled alongside and waved and smiled. The taxi rolled through a large intersection dissected by a small booth with a policeman in a white uniform making futile gestures to slow and direct the manic drivers who careened past.

As they reached the center of the city, they passed several ornate buildings. The French influence had surprised Jack on his arrival, "the Paris of Southeast Asia," as the city was once known. The Americans had other names for it now.

The street sidewalks were filled on this bright, sunny day. Women used black umbrellas to block the sun. They walked in pairs wearing long dresses, sometimes holding hands. Two million people. More bars than New York and New Orleans combined. And more refugees were on the way, some carrying all they owned on their backs.

The captain was now talking, ending Jack's reverie. The captain stood six-foot two inches tall, two hundred pounds. His uniform was taught and pressed. The new men sat at attention in the front rows of the small room. They filled their tiny chairs and pushed up against the writing boards attached to the side of each chair. They had pencils and small notebooks.

"You college boys have some brains, I'm told. And now you're fit. You survived your training, to the surprise of many. That's why your country went looking for you. Through channels, I'm told that you're from some very fancy schools, some very pretty places. And now you're here. Volunteers. Well, I'll be damned. Bet your choice wasn't too popular on campus. But whatever way you got here, you're mine now. We need your help."

The young eyes followed the captain as he paced across the front of the room, then turned on his heel to march back the other way.

"For those of you who don't know me, I'm Captain Stokke. I've been in this hell-hole forever. I got here early, when were still cleaning the mess that the French made in '54. Goddam French—what a shit show. And it has been a long haul for Uncle Sam ever since.

"But just in case you were wondering, I have no doubt whatsoever—whatsoever—that we will defeat the Commies here. This is the determined, hard thinking of your government and your Army. What's needed is for us—that means you—to get done what needs to be done. So you need to know a few things about our mission here.

"We are in the security business. One of the best ways to measure how things are going in this war is the degree of security in the countryside. The Government of South Vietnam—the GVN—has made some gains against the Commies out there— we know that. But it's hard to make these gains stick. Security conditions fluctuate. There's a lot of low-level terrorism, political agitation, and propaganda efforts by the Viet Cong. A lot of the countryside is still contested, that is, controlled by . . . nobody. It's hard to measure the allegiance of the people and the security of individual villages and hamlets. In other words, it's hard for us to measure progress, gentlemen. But someone has to do it, and that someone is you. You will help us gather information in the field by traveling to the hamlets and you will help us analyze it back here.

"The procedure we are using is called the Hamlet Evaluation System, the 'HES'. We set this up a few years ago. We make monthly reports on the state of Saigon's control over each of the 12,650 hamlets in South Vietnam. Only 8,650 hamlets are actually evaluated, since 4,000 are considered under permanent Viet Cong control. We get our reports from officers in the field. Saigon has a word for how you take the sixty percent of the South Vietnamese people who are peasant rice farmers and get them under your control—you 'pacify' them. We feed the people, give them medical treatment, and establish a local government. But above all we provide security, we 'pacify'.

"We need to gather the intel and put it in one place—a big computer, gentlemen. The police have some of the information. Our military intelligence has some. Everyone working in the villages and hamlets has some. You will go out there and get more.

"We try to measure the security of each of the thousands of hamlets once a month. In its raw form, most of the information is useless. When we try to make sense of this stuff, we find ourselves walking in the dark. So here is the system we run."

Some of the new recruits glanced at each other.

"So what is a hamlet? It is part of a larger village, but not a naturally distinct social unit—only a separate area for people who were once an integral part of a village. Over the years of the war, the social cohesion of these villages has declined, so they are no longer an effective unit. So instead of trying to rebuild the village, we have tried to prop up the hamlet, for better or worse.

"Here is the worksheet we use in the field to assess the hamlets. There are six major categories:

"The first category is Viet Cong military activities, including hamlet guerilla units, if any, external forces, and any military incidents affecting the hamlet.

"The second category is Viet Cong politically subversive activities.

"The third category is security, including the hamlet defense plan and friendly government support.

"The fourth category is administrative and political activity. These include management by the government.

"The fifth category is health, education, and welfare. This includes census information, medical services, and sanitation.

"The sixth category is economic development and self-help

activities, including public works."

The captain continued:

"In order to standardize the evaluation process, each village is rated according to a five-point scale, 'A' to 'E'.

"'A' means adequate security forces, Viet Cong infrastructure eliminated, public projects are underway, and the economic picture is improving.

"'B' means not immune to Viet Cong threat but security is organized and partially effective, infrastructure partially neutralized, self-help programs underway and economic progress started.

"'C' means subject to infrequent Viet Cong harassment, some infrastructure identified, some participation in self-help programs.

"'D' means Viet Cong activities reduced but still an internal threat, some VC terrorism and taxation, some local participation in hamlet government and economic programs. So, 'D' means contested but leaning toward government.

"'E' means Viet Cong are effective although some government control is evident, the Viet Cong infrastructure is intact, and government programs are nonexistent or just beginning.

"As I said, we supplement this information from our combat officers with our own field observations."

He paused and looked around the room. The new men glanced to the side at each other.

"That's when the fun starts. Sometimes we need to get in close. We have to get inside that human web that makes the Viet Cong incursions possible. We need to know which village chiefs are VC sympathizers, who supplies them and their villages, who are the spies, and who is stealing tax money from the government. And lie? Boy do they lie. And gentlemen, they are sometimes armed and dangerous.

"Lights, please." The room became dark. A projector cast a series of charts on a large screen hanging from the ceiling. The charts showed the hamlet security ratings—hundreds of them—with different colors for the different ratings.

"Project Haystack," Stumpo whispered, with a snort. "Pick your needle."

"These evaluations and—and the pacification program generally—are the most important thing we are doing right now. If we can take down the Viet Cong—hamlet by hamlet—the government of South Vietnam can raise its head up, the villages and hamlets can maintain themselves, and the government can take hold and do what a government should do—act like a government, not a goddam corrupt monarchy.

"I want to know what you are doing and how you could do it better. I will meet with each of you individually. I want complete freedom of speech in our group. I want your comments. I want criticism."

Jack felt another glance from Stumpo, a wave of sarcasm crashing against his right cheek. He fought the urge to look sideways and tried to stay at attention.

"That's it, dismissed."

The new men got up slowly, not sure how to proceed. They made no eye contact with the captain as they left the room.

Jack and Stumpo lingered behind, talking quietly. Stump nodded to Jack and then walked out of the room, leaving Jack as the only man in the room with the captain.

"Watch out for that guy," the captain said.

"Who, Stewart?"

"Yes. Trouble follows him like a cloud of flies around a steer, son."

"I know that, sir. I've met those flies."

The captain raised one eyebrow.

"You're right about the cloud," Jack said. "But he's a fine soldier, sir. Will that be all?"

Chapter 2

Jack met Stumpo that night at their usual place, Café Normandie. The owners, Jean David Pascal and his wife Chantal, had presided there since '52. The café attracted a mix of older French couples and young American diplomats and aid workers, all grateful that the French Government, when they bid *adieu* to Vietnam in '54, left behind their wine and food.

Business was in the air most evenings. There were buyers and sellers of all kinds, some trafficking in commodities, others in human beings. There were Asians and Europeans and an occasional man in a turban. Their tables were filled with whispers and furtive glances shrouded by puffs and swirls of smoke. The dining room and the courtyard were dimly lit, with small candles on the tables and metal fans that hung low and wobbled as they tried but failed to move the heavy air. Thick vegetation surrounded the courtyard, forever wet from the endless rain.

Jack and Stumpo were at their usual table near some aides from the American embassy when a man in a dinner jacket approached. It was the owner, Jean Pascal.

"*Bon soir*, Monsieur Jack, Monsieur Stumpo."

"*Bon soir*, Monsieur Pascal."

"Please tell us if we can be of any help to you this evening," he said pleasantly.

They nodded their thanks.

"And please do not fail to give my kind regards to Colonel Turck." He bowed at the waist and moved to another table.

"Tiemo knows him?" Stumpo asked, shaking his head.

"Tiemo knows everyone," Jack said. "His time in France in '44, I'd guess. He probably knows half the waiters in Hanoi, too."

Stumpo seemed distracted, Jack thought. Finally Stumpo took a napkin and some water and wiped the mist from his glasses. Jack sensed his mood. Stumpo never took the lectures from his commanders well. So Jack was ready for what followed.

"It all sounds so precise—down to one or two decimal plac-es," Stumpo began. "This many people are living in 'secure' ar-eas—areas "controlled" by the government.

Stumpo held up his fingers to make quotation marks. "'Se-cure.' Yeah, right. 'Controlled,' yeah, right. The government doesn't like the word 'contested', you know. They only want two categories: 'areas or hamlets controlled by the government' and 'areas or hamlets *not* controlled by the government.'

"And who thought up these questions? Some of them make no sense. What would you call these ratings? Are they facts? Do the data really exist? Do the guys in the field believe in this stuff? Do they even have time for this? The officer is out there, trying to keep his men alive. He's got a thousand things to do. And now they give him this checklist. What bullshit. And these guys are there in the daylight. How are they supposed to know what goes on at night? And most of them need interpreters. So what do you think the people in the hamlet will do if they don't un-derstand our questions or they feel that they have to lie to avoid getting whacked by the Viet Cong?

"I don't see that we are measuring loyalty. And without loyal-ty, there is no real security against the VC. What makes us think government control is the same thing as loyalty to the govern-ment? What makes us think that the people out there are behind us? Wouldn't we know that? Couldn't we tell? Actually, I think it's worse than that. You think that there is civil disobedience at home? They ain't seen nothing like the civil disobedience here. The guys don't want to enlist in the army. The ones in the ham-lets don't want to fight. They don't want to pay more taxes to the government. They don't want to help us with the intel because they're still playing both sides. They're not sure who'll win, so they're hedging their bets."

Jack said nothing for a while. "We'll be out there again soon enough," Jack said, finally.

"Lovely," Stumpo said. He slumped his shoulders and looked down at his boots. He said nothing for a while. The bar was filling with people.

"Heard from Clare?" Stumpo asked, finally.

"Saw her when I was home, one night."

"She's sweet."

"Sure is," Jack said. He changed the subject. "Speaking of sweet, whatever became of Candy?"

"Who?"

"Candy, from Vassar."

"Oh, yes, the lovely Candy. Not so sweet. Not like candy at all. More like the candy wrapper, come to think of it . . . clingy, transparent, made to be easily stripped. No, I would not say sweet. No."

"Sorry I asked," Jack said, with a grimace.

"No offense taken," Stumpo shrugged. "Love will find a way. Maybe tonight. My luck may change at any time."

They looked at each other across the table.

"I guess I shouldn't have said that," Stumpo said.

They finished their drinks, left money on the table, and walked out of the café. They stood together at the curb outside. People choked the sidewalk, talking quickly and loudly. "Like stepping from one world into another," Jack said. Behind him he smelled something inviting. He turned and saw a pushcart groaning with baguettes and croissants, two more survivors of the French defeat in '54. Behind the cart was another, this one carrying jewelry. He glanced at the pieces to check for something for Clare. People on bicycles and cyclos flowed by them in a stream on the street, inches from the curb, dodging taxis and swearing at the drivers. Police cars whizzed by, blaring their sirens.

Jack was silent for a moment as he looked at the jewelry. An old feeling crept in. I'm a long way from home, he thought. Lost for a moment, he stepped absent-mindedly off the curb. Stumpo suddenly and violently pulled him back by one arm as two speeding bicycles whizzed past.

"You trying to get killed?" Stumpo held Jack's arm in a death-grip.

Jack blinked, as if waking.

"Sorry, sorry, I wasn't paying attention," he said, sheepishly.

"I know you weren't. You gotta stop that. What would I tell Rocco? 'Oh, Jack got killed in Vietnam—he got run over by a bicycle outside a café.' How would that look in the *Alumni Magazine?*"

Chapter 3

The nights were long and often sleepless. Jack spent many late hours writing. He sat at a small, metal desk with a gray lamp and wrote letters back home—letters to his mother, to Clare, to Rocco. His letters to Tiemo were different; they were more like reports.

The window was open and the sounds of the city rolled in. There was fun to be had and Stumpo could find it, some relief, Jack thought, from a life that seemed to swing between boredom and terror. But the local nightlife had lost its allure for Jack.

He owed Tiemo a letter. "Tell me everything," Tiemo liked to say. Jack tore out a few pages from a notebook and started writing.

"Dear Colonel Turck,

"It has been a while since I've written and even longer since I promised you a 'report' from here, sir. I think I waited because I have had a hard time understanding what I am seeing and hearing. So maybe I'll just try to stick to some facts and tell you what I worry about. I guess like all my letters to you, this one will get 'overlooked' by the censors, too. Thank you and President Onion for that arrangement, sir.

"This whole effort started I guess because the Americans just didn't think that they had enough intel on what was going on in the countryside. So they created a new system that they would run and they hoped it would eventually improve their control over the rural areas. Maybe it has, maybe it hasn't, but one thing I noticed is that a system designed to measure the government control is slowly becoming a system to measure our success in the war. I don't think that's good.

"I also wonder a lot about how we get our info. We have 8,650 hamlets to evaluate. But we only have 232 officers who are the advisers on local security to the Vietnamese chiefs of the 232 districts. These Vietnamese chiefs are usually South Vietnamese

officers. They run the districts. So our 232 advisers have an average of 37 villages to evaluate each month. Our officer—the
district adviser or one of his two or three assistants—is supposed
to visit each hamlet in his district at least once each month. And
remember that that is not their main job—they are supposed
to be running everything to do with 'pacification.' Sometimes
we go out to assist the visits, but I saw pretty early that it is im-
possible for the advisers to hit every district every month. I was
told by some officers who are district advisers that some hamlets
are not visited for as long as twelve months—even though the
same hamlets get graded each month. So, for as long as twelve
months, the evaluation for that hamlet may be totally unreliable,
but it will still be used in country-wide assessments of the Saigon
government and its pacification program.

"And there are even more problems than that. The normal
tour of duty for an officer is twelve months, so almost no district
adviser develops even close to a deep knowledge of the hamlets
in their district. They are fortunate if they have been able to visit
each hamlet at least once in their tours.

"And there is very little training for all these evaluations. I
know that there is no specific training for it—I didn't have any.
And the language is a big problem. Some officers are nearly fluent in the language, others know some, and the rest know only a
few phrases. This means we use a lot of interpreters. This does
not help our accuracy at all.

"Let me tell you more about what happens when we go out
to the hamlets. It is in daylight. We have uniforms and our inter-
preter is with us. We start questioning people. We know we only
have about an hour. We sometimes pick the people at random,
but our advisers say that they get most of the useful information from the district, village, or hamlet chiefs. We know that
the chiefs are worried about what the Viet Cong does to persons
who inform on them and later fall into their control. They know
that the Viet Cong may be there long after we're gone. We ask
one whether the VC are in his hamlet at night, whether they
have been identified, whether their organization is still function-

ing. But how can we expect a Vietnamese peasant to risk his life to tell this stuff to a uniformed American who does not even speak his own language and who will not be in the hamlet that night when the Viet Cong comes back around?

"And there is another problem with these Vietnamese district chiefs. They know where the money is coming from—us. They want the money to keep flowing. They know what we want to hear. So they have an incentive to say there is 'high' security in order to qualify for more funds and supplies. Why should he tell us the hamlet is contested if that means his funds will dry up?

"Sorry to sound so down. I don't know what I would do without Stumpo here. We talk about home and the College and complain to each other when things get tough.

"Wish us luck—the captain says we'll be going back out to Badville soon.

"Kinsmen to kinsmen should be true,

Jack."

Book III

Chapter 1

Sturgis "Spike" Smith enjoyed being governor of his small state. He liked the marble halls of the state house, the long row of portraits of his predecessors hanging on the walls. He liked the long line of people camped outside his door. The line was very long on Mondays, and this Monday was no exception. But today he had bigger things than favor-seekers on his mind.

He had been mayor of his hometown in the Valley. He liked the executive chair—he was no legislative man. He detested their endless talk, their vanities, their constant preening for the press. He liked action, preferably the out-of-sight kind. Open government had gotten out of hand.

The College charter made the governor a member of the College Board of Trustees, *ex officio*. This pleased him, though the campus politics did not. He knew a lot about the College— he was Class of '41. He left that year for the intelligence service, "rural France" was all he ever said about it. He came back and took his degree in '46. Success in politics in his home State followed. Spike was a tall, imposing figure on the campaign trail and in office, with his wavy blonde hair, intense blue eyes, wide shoulders, and a vice-like handshake. The years had not dimmed his looks, his strength, or his legendary energy. A force of nature, his admirers said. A freight train to be avoided, said his detractors.

Today it was the College on the agenda, President Onion scheduled for a telephone call. Maybe the governor would get some good news for a change—on his project. It was about time.

As he waited for Sam Onion's call, the governor looked through the large window behind the desk onto the square. A statute of Senator Nathaniel Fletcher—graduate of the College, Class of 1810—commanded the capitol park. It was said that Fletcher's hat was the "biggest in the Senate, and contained its greatest brain." It was a bright sunny day in the capital, and the governor noticed that the sunlight reflected brightly off Fletcher's massive dome.

The governor's secretary routed the president's call when it came. "How are things up there, Sam?" Spike asked.

"Been better."

"New recruits?"

"Only a few. The rest are too soft, too suburban, no skills. Too much pot. The faculty is on the warpath about ROTC again. God this is getting hard."

"Where's the Board on the protest stuff?"

"Starting to wobble."

"What can I do?"

"Nothing, right now. You've got your own trouble down there in the House, I hear—do they really want to get into the foreign policy business? They're not going to be too happy if you keep saying nice things about Nixon."

"I can handle them," Spike said. "And Washington. I am tired of dealing with them, too. It's not just our little effort. It's everything. They've got their mitts on every little thing now."

"Agreed," said Sam.

"It started with Roosevelt. Ike didn't fight it. With Johnson and now the war, it's all Washington, all the time. A new agency every day. More laws, more rules, more power out of our hands. And you know what? They'll screw up the draft this year. Just like they've screwed up Vietnam."

Chapter 2

The day after his call with the governor, President Onion took a break from his letter-writing—mostly pleas for money from wealthy alumni—and stood up at his large, carved mahogany desk. He stretched his arms and walked across his office to the large windows that surveyed the campus green.

It was Friday afternoon, often a quiet time on campus, as the students finished classes and made plans for the weekend. There was a football game on campus that Saturday, an event that in the past had served as a unifying event—a "gathering of the tribe," he thought—but even that force seemed to be waning.

The large rectangular green was the focal point of the campus, green in color and name, crisscrossed by walkways of fine gravel. The walkways joined at the center, forging a crossroads for chance meetings of friends. The center of the green also served as a common site for other unifying events, such as the building of a giant snow sculpture—often a tribute to a Norse god—in winter and a bonfire to spur a pep rally on the eve of a big game.

Today, however, the president looked over a crowd that had a different purpose. Dozens, then hundreds of students were streaming from each corner to the center. The crowd pushed forward, then swelled back, like water pushing against a dam then recoiling back into a widening pool.

The president looked over toward his conference table. On the glossy surface lay the daily student newspaper with a headline that blared: "Rally for Peace Today on Green."

The president sighed and rubbed his forehead with his two large hands. "Here we go," he said aloud.

Many in the crowd carried signs. The president noted each without expression.

"Bring The Troops Home Now," one read.

Two students had climbed on a wooden table of the center

of the green. They led the crowd in chants.

"Hell no, we won't go!"

"Ho, Ho, Ho Chi Minh, Ho Chi Minh is gonna win!"

One of the students standing on the table reached down for a bullhorn passed from below.

Before he put the horn to his lips, he glanced all around him. The crowd had now spilled all the way back to the four streets surrounding the green. The chants grew louder.

The speaker began:

"We condemn the United States military action in Vietnam!"

"We demand the immediate withdrawal of all US troops!"

"We demand an end to recruiting on campus! NO military, NO CIA, NO Dow Chemical! No merchants of death! Not one! Go home and stay home!"

"We demand that the college immediately end the ROTC program!"

The speaker paused. He raised his fist as the crowd cheered. He did this four times, turning to each side of the green. As he reached the fourth side, he noticed a figure on the roof of one of the administration buildings that faced the green. The red, white, and blue flag of the United States flew over the building, snapping taught in the afternoon breeze.

"Tear it down!" he shouted in his bullhorn. "Tear it down!"

At that moment, the figure on the roof moved, cat-like, up the slope of the old slate roof of the building. The thin figure stopped and waved. The crowd roared with cheers.

"Tear it down!"

The figure hunched lower and balanced himself every step or two by placing one hand on the roof. He carried a tool of some kind in his other hand. When he reached the flagpole, he cut the lanyard of the flag. The flag fell quickly in the wind, turning upside down as it tumbled down the length of the roof and came to rest in the rain gutter. The crowd cheered again as the figure scrambled down to the fire escape, his deed done.

The president watched these events in silence. He did not move from his place at the window. Then he noticed movement in the far corner of the green closest to the town. Another group of students had formed, led by a student with a competing bullhorn. The second group gathered in two rows. Several were large, with athletic builds. Some carried United States flags. Their leader stepped forward, turned to his followers, and shouted through the bullhorn:

"It's YOUR flag they've torn! It's YOUR country they hate! It's YOUR high school friends that they mock! Now it's YOUR turn to give it right back!"

The groups advanced toward each other and collided. Wild punches tore into faces. Bodies fell like falling timber. As the warring groups battled, those on the ground were trampled. At one corner of the green, the president saw smoke. A flame appeared in the same corner, reaching six feet high, then higher. Through the smoke and flame, the President saw a North Vietnamese flag ablaze. As the fight ended, the counter-bullhorn blared: "Pay no attention to the commotion, folks—we're just working on some undecided voters."

A half-dozen bodies lay on the ground. Some called for help. Town and campus police tried to split the factions and remove the injured. The initial speaker, now screaming louder than before, shouted: "Fascist Pigs!" "Today pigs, tomorrow bacon!" The speaker continued but the president turned away. He walked back to his desk and sat in his large leather chair. His face was blank and his broad shoulders sagged. He stared across the room at the row of portraits of his predecessors. He thought for several minutes, drumming his fingers on his desk. Then he called his secretary at her desk outside his office and said:

"The governor, please."

Chapter 3

On the Monday after the protests that fall Professor John S. Randolph was bringing his 20th Century American Military History class to a close as the clock nudged noon. "Jack S.," as he liked to be called, ran his class like an engineer runs a freight train: on time, with no unscheduled stops.

Jack S. had a thick gray beard and mustache, and salt-and-pepper hair combed in a long sweep from one side of his head to the other, rising to a peak at the top of his head and then descending over his left ear. He had piercing, pale blue eyes that surveyed the entire class, from front row to back, often startling those in the front row and unsettling the sleepy inhabitants of the back row, who were not accustomed to such close surveillance. They never could tell if he was looking precisely at them, or not, as they moved uneasily in their hard-back wooden seats.

He stood at the podium with a military bearing, back arched. He stepped to the side from time to time to light one of the six Lucky Strike cigarettes he would smoke through the class, lighting each with the matchbook and cigarette in a single hand, the other hand still holding the podium or gesticulating on the point he was making. He dressed in a jacket and tie, sometimes in a blue pinstriped suit, always with a regimental striped tie and a small lapel pin of the American flag.

Each day he brought in large color prints of murals depicting the battles he would cover in class: the gleaming bayonet as it plunged into patriot Dr. Joseph Warren in the battle of Bunker Hill; Burgoyne's vivid redcoats in abject surrender at Saratoga; Washington, Greene, and Hamilton in their Continental blue on the decisive day at Yorktown, the day "The World Turned Upside-Down," and Lee and Grant, in their faded blue and gray, at Appomattox, former comrades, then foes. Students with a taste for drama swore that they could smell blood and gun smoke drifting from the murals.

Jack S. spoke with a slow, gravelly drawl of his native Virginia and his forbearers in the planter aristocracy. A graduate of Virginia Military Institute, he learned military history in classrooms that overlooked General Stonewall Jackson's grave in the campus cemetery. He and other cadets were required by VMI regulations to salute the statue of Jackson in the campus center each time they passed. A Ph.D. in history at Harvard had left him pining for somewhere, anywhere, beyond the swampy fevers of Cambridge politics, and he left as soon as he took his degree.

He found refuge at the College in the north, but now, it seemed, the same fevers had consumed his refuge in the hills. As a teacher of military history, he was now in harm's way—a target for the growing anti-military sentiments at the school. Students and faculty now called him "Stonewall."

He tried to avoid the issue. But in a class about war, this was hard. In the fall of 1969, a student challenged him, citing the looming student strike and the march to Washington D.C. to protest the war. "Don't you think this is the wrong time to be glorifying war?" the student asked.

"I do not glorify war," he said. "I recount it. How you judge it, and apply its lessons, it up to you. I do have some comments for those who may be skipping class in the near future."

"Some of you will go to Washington to march, no doubt. More of you will cut out and go to Florida for some fun. Others might stay here and go to class. I will be here. Our topic will be *The Prince*. In my opinion, that book will teach you more about politics and power than an afternoon on the Mall in D.C. But that's your choice.

"I am not the enemy, whatever you—and some of my colleagues—might think. I respect your views. I was your age, once, in another time of war. You didn't start this war, and you didn't ask for the draft. Your government decided these things. But now you—as citizens—are part of 'it.' It is therefore important to define what 'it' is, and what 'it' is not. It is, in my view, a struggle, a struggle between tyranny and freedom—a struggle as old as humankind.

"War has always been part of this struggle. Cain slew Abel. So there's your gasoline—human nature. But what's the match? Why Vietnam? Totalitarianism gives you an answer, but not a complete one. Beware the fallacy of the perfect analogy. I would be the first to admit that Vietnam is not Munich in 1938.

"As you consider this struggle—and your place in it—it is important to study things more closely than ever. You should not let your emotions skew your study. Rigorous, detached, close study—critical thinking—is, after all, what you are here to learn. You must learn that human affairs can be tragic, that they involve a good deal of mystery, and that we often stumble and grope through the dark to find our way.

"In this place—a place that now some of you view with contempt, as part of the "regime," the "establishment"—is the one place and time in your life when you can reach a deeper understanding of man's problems and the great issues that he confronts. Later, when you hold the levers of power in your own hands—as some of you surely will—you may benefit from your studies here.

"But time is of the essence. You know that world out there? You will meet it some day soon. It may not know who you are right now, but it will learn about you. It will put you to the test. It will see what you are made of. And as the world comes to know you, it will reflect your image right back at you—like a mirror. A mirror that you will not be able to duck. Will you like the way you look? Maybe you can't say right now. Will you look smaller than you thought? Bigger? Braver? Will you see the man you hoped to be? Or will you see someone that you hope that others would *never* see?

"Only a few of you will go to war. You need to ponder that singular fact. Of those who go, some will come back. How will you treat them? Will you ignore them? Or resent them? Or worse? What will be in your mind? Respect? Disgust? Guilt? How will you act?"

He paused and looked down at his watch.

"I understand. You think you're like Thoreau in jail that

night in Concord. He didn't like the slavery in the South. He didn't like the war with Mexico. He refused to pay the poll tax. Someone had to bail him out of the Concord jail. You want action, like him. I get it.

"I know that the war and the draft are front and center in your minds. Take your stances on them as you like. But do not mistake emotion for reason. If you must go to jail—like Thoreau—remember that someone is taking your place in that long line leading to Saigon. And for God's sake don't go to Canada—that's worse than jail and twice as cold."

Chapter 4

Saturday arrived clear and crisp and blue and the smoke from the burning flags and fiery hearts of the day before had cleared from the campus. The green filled again, but this time with fans headed to the football game. The fine weather continued through the day and the Viking football team—and many of their fans—purged the events of the week with a severe thrashing of the visiting team, a win recounted by Rocco in his weekly letter to Jack and Stumpo.

After the game, at the back door of the basement of the fraternity, an older man was supervising the delivery of kegs of beer. He had black, thick glasses, a red face, a big, bulbous nose and a wide smile, and talked in an open-mouthed bray. His name was Everett Finch.

"How *arrrrre* you boys?" he asked the crowd as they walked through the door. "Great game! Got some good stuff for the celebration!" In his arms Everett carried new equipment for the tap system and other accessories—tap handles, wall clocks, cups, and T-shirts, all bearing the logo of the boys' favorite beer.

"We had a big meeting downstate last week," Everett said. "The distributor had all us sales reps in for a year-end meeting. You wouldn't believe the story the boss told us. Seems that last month they had a meeting at the main brewery in St. Louis with all the top distributors in the country. They were looking the sales charts. They had a big map of the United States up on the wall and put stars to mark the location of the big distributors. The more beer sold, the bigger the star. They were moving west to east, and the numbers for the western guys looked impressive until they put up a hu-mon-gous star in the middle of nowhere in our little state. Everyone looked at each other. What's the story there, one of the big city guys asked. Where is that? Is there a city there? Another said: I know. 'It's near that college on the river. The one that *Playboy* refused to rank in its Top 20 drinking schools because the ranking was for amateurs, not professionals.' Well, my boss came back practically busting his buttons about that big star stuck on our little company."

Everett shook his head and smiled a big smile. He turned from the bar and gave a big wave as he stepped toward the back door of the basement. "Keep up the great work, boys! Great game today! See you next month."

The crowd around the bar now stood two deep and curved over toward a basement wall bearing an unusual painting. Fraternity basements of this type were not known for their art. So visitors to the basement of Asgard Hall were often struck by the full-length portrait, oil on wood, attached to the wall next to the bar. The artist had painted the *bella figura* as payment for his delinquent house dues. The subject—portrayed so lovingly—had now watched faithfully over the basement circus for decades. She had large black eyes, the size of coals, and she gathered her long, dark hair above her head with endless arms. She surveyed the scene with a serene pout, part boredom, part disgust, part quiet confidence that no one present—male or female—was her equal in looks, or lust. The artist had rendered the entire picture in a blazing burnt orange wash, with dark streaks surrounding the dark, curving lines of the figure known by the members simply as "The Lady."

Opposite The Lady on the other wall there was a large bronze plaque. In raised lettering it read, simply: "Last Among Equals." It had been presented years ago when Asgard had displaced a rival house as the fraternity with the lowest grade point average. The brothers of the rival house, dressed in robes and carrying torches, proceeded to the front of Asgard for a ceremony in which they solemnly transmitted what they called an "emblem of academic futility"—the plaque—to Asgard with "all best wishes" for continued academic "success."

Now the post-game crowd filled the house from top to bottom, toasting the latest win. Upstairs, older alumni and their spouses gathered, some with children. Trays of beer were ferried upstairs by means of a 24-slot metal tray used for milk bottles by door-to-door milkmen.

Rocco took his usual place on a bench at the fringe of the basement, watching a game of beer pong. He nodded briefly toward the scene—or more to himself—with a quiet smile. He slowly sipped beer from a plastic cup, right pinky finger underneath the cup to protect its contents if jostled in a crowd, as he had been taught as a freshman.

He recognized several younger alumni and their wives with children in tow. The children held their parents' hands or sat on their father's shoulders. Wives glanced at their watches, measuring the agreed-upon time limit for their husband's trip back in time. The regulars had taken care to leave their good shoes in their cars; boots stood a better chance of resisting spilt beer and were less likely to stick to the tar-like linoleum floor.

Some of the football players came down stairs, in twos and threes, and into the crowd. They smiled broadly at shouts of "Way to go!" and "Go Vikes!"   When they raised their fists, Rocco noticed the usual scars on their fingers, hands, and forearms—cuts and bruises and a color that looked like raw hamburger headed for black and blue.

Not all the faces were familiar to Rocco. Post-game parties always brought a mix of parents, sisters, brothers, and girlfriends, and others. Today Rocco noticed three young people standing to the side of the bar, watching the scene. They did not seem to know others there. Two girls had long blonde hair, wool coats, and faded bell-bottom jeans. One had large glasses with square lenses that nearly reached to the corners of her mouth. The other girl had turned from the bar and was looking carefully at The Lady, not quite sure how to react to the beauty staring down at her in the midst of the beer and the bedlam.

The young man was tall and thin and had black curly hair and wire-rimmed glasses. Rocco noticed that his eyes shifted constantly from person to person, side to side, up and down, never settling on one object. He did not smile. Rocco did not recognize him or the two girls.

Songs started around the bar, as if on cue: the Alma Mater, the Viking Fight Song, and country favorites that made the boys from the South feel more at home. Rocco smiled again.

The next song was "God Bless America."   Voices rose, off-key. The beer pong players stopped playing.

" . . . my home, sweet, home . . ."

The three strangers standing near The Lady did not sing. The two girls looked at their feet. The boy with the wire-rim glasses glared at the brother leading the song. The muscles in his neck bulged as he gritted his teeth. As the last note sounded, he looked across the bar and shouted: "Fuck America! Stop the War!"

The room fell silent. Brothers glanced around the room, searching for the source of the shout. Rocco looked at the bar and the three visitors who had been standing near the Lady, but the crowd had swelled and he could not be sure who had shouted. Then he heard another shout: "Shut up, asshole! If you don't like the songs, get the hell out!"   Now more eyes fixed on the curly-haired man. Then, a third voice, familiar to Rocco as another brother's:

"YOU shut up—he has the right to speak. Let him speak."

"No, not here, not in our house."

"What do you mean, your house? Not everyone thinks the way you do. Some of us thinks the war sucks, too."

Now the curly-haired man had gathered some courage.

"What's the matter? Afraid to debate the war?"

"No, I'm not, asshole."

"Then what's the problem with a little protest? You like your song, I say America sucks. You say God Bless America, I say 'I doubt it.'   God ain't blessing this goddam war, I'll tell you that."

The two women nodded several times, jaws set and arms locked with those of their friend.

The litigants glared at each other across the bar. Murmurs ran through the crowd. Children, unaware of the standoff, began to speak.

"Why are they yelling, Mommy?"

"Shhh . . . ."

The awkward silence continued, then was broken. There was a loud creaking sound from the basement door. Heads turned as two tall students entered, one pushing an older man in a wheelchair.

Tiemo was well known in these halls. He nodded and smiled and accepted warm greetings as he wheeled himself through the basement. The debate ceased in his presence. He had rendered the abstract debate suddenly and uncomfortably real. He alone in the room had seen violent death in war.

Chapter 5

Clare saw the notice for the next meeting of the local draft board and marked it on the calendar on her refrigerator. Time for some action, she thought.

On the night of the meeting of the board she checked her notes as she sipped tea in her kitchen. Her classmate, Sook-young "Sookie" Park, would be there soon to meet her and walk with her to the town hall. She read her speech aloud and thought about the evening ahead. She envisioned a room full of old men, mostly veterans of earlier wars and local politicians. Even as her school erupted in anti-war protests, most of the townspeople—and especially their leaders—did not share the dovish views engulfing the campus. Town and gown often disagreed, there was nothing new about that. But the past tensions were mild when compared to the new fights about the war.

The town had rejected a permit for students to hold an anti-war parade and rally in front of the town hall in South Tapley. The application for the permit was returned with a simple "Denied" stamped in red on the top of the first page, no explanation, no appeal. A few days later the city council had rejected as "out of order" a resolution submitted by a professor denouncing the war.

Clare heard a knock on the door of her room. It was Sookie, arriving early for the short walk to city hall. She was a foreign exchange student from South Korea. She had long, straight black hair, dark brown eyes, and a round mouth. She spoke slowly and quietly and, in the classroom, not at all. She lived in a dorm room double with another student from Asia, but lately had been spending more time at Clare's house. One of Clare's housemates had made fun of Sookie's reserve and her English but Clare cut her short. "She knows more about the world than you know about your own country," Clare had snapped. "And, by the way, with two-hundred American boys dying in Asia every week, you might want to learn more about that part of the world."

Sookie and Clare shared a love of literature and quickly became friends. Sookie often brought her books to Clare's house, but their study sessions often turned to the war.

"My uncle died in the Korean War," she told Clare one night. "He was my mother's brother. His picture hangs in my home. My mother always looks so sad when she says his name. Sometimes she wipes a tear from her eye."

"How old was he?" Clare asked.

"Twenty-two."

Sookie listened as Clare told her of the latest plans for protests. Sookie yearned to be more like this strong, auburn-haired woman who never feared to speak in class or in public. "We are often attracted to what we are not," a professor at home had written to Sookie, after she had described Clare in a letter to him.

Sookie sat down on Clare's old couch as Clare gathered her papers.

"Ready?" Sookie asked.

"Not really, but now or never, right?" Clare smiled.

They walked together slowly to the center of town. Outside the town hall, a large granite stone stood in one side of the small park. It bore bronze tablets with lists of names. The names were those of the sons of the town killed in past wars. The names shone in the soft glare of the streetlights facing the hall. The name of a Marine from South Tapley killed in Vietnam earlier that year had not yet been added to a tablet, Clare noticed. She wondered how many names might be added to a new tablet before the end of the endless war. She passed the monument and walked toward the granite steps leading to the large, wooden front doors of the hall.

The hearing room was on the second floor. In the front of the room, faded United States and state flags stood at attention, like bookends, at ends of the long wooden dais. A brass eagle perched at the top of each flag. Dusty old law books peered out from rows of glass-enclosed cases behind three worn chairs.

Underused, those law books, Clare thought. Let's open them tonight, maybe the one with the Constitution, to start.

The floor of the hearing room was yellow linoleum with gray specks. The dim fluorescent lights gave the floor a depressing pallor. The faces of the members of the board seemed to Clare to be of the same drab color as the floor, a pale yellow broken by thin red lines across each forehead and set in waves by a lower row of deep jowls across the three faces, left to right. The members sat uncomfortably in their too-small chairs, shifting their papers and peering out at the swelling crowd.

The chairman was a short, round man with a red face, blue eyes and gray hair cut in a military buzz cut. He wore a white shirt and plain red tie and blue blazer that was a size or two too small. A small American flag pin was stuck in his left lapel. He was a veteran of the Korean War and owner of the largest car dealership in town. He had served as chairman of the local draft board since the late 1950s. He smiled little and showed no patience for speakers at the hearings. Democracy had gotten out of hand, he thought.

The vice-chairman was also a veteran, a local postman. He was tall and thin and, even when seated, towered over his two colleagues at the table. He was quiet during most hearings, and motionless except for the rolling of his eyes during the longer of the chairman's endless speeches. In recent hearings he seemed to be hinting at reservations about Vietnam, and the chairman had scowled at some of the postman's expressions of sympathy for recent applicants for exemptions from the draft.

The third member and clerk of the board was a local lawyer. His hair was black and straight and thin. He wore brown horn-rimmed glasses over small, tired eyes. He had served as a lawyer in the Army Judge Advocate General Corps in the 1950s in Korea and after the war before returning home to open a law practice in the town.

The clerk of the board stood up and cleared his throat. He asked those present to stand while he led the Pledge of Allegiance. Many of those present stood, but not all. Not a good start, Clare noted. Things could be pretty tense by the time I talk, she thought.

The clerk ended the Pledge and sat down. He picked up a piece of paper from the table and read the notice of the hearing and the agenda.

The chairman first read a letter from the Defense Department, Selective Service. The letter stated the need for more troops.

"We'll do our best to fill these slots," the chairman said.

The board heard six cases. The final case concerned a young man by the name of Pacella. "Petition of John Pacella," the chairman said, looking up slowly, and scanning the room. A young man and an old man rose as one. The young man was thin, and his baggy grey flannel pants were hanging on his hips only by the grace of a worn leather belt. His white shirt was open at the neck, and he was holding a blue jacket on his arm. His jaw jutted from his neck, and he pulled at his chin as he rose, looking up, then down, then up again. He had sandy hair, clean cut, now less common among young men. He said nothing and gave no smile or recognition of his name. He reached his full height and stood, as if at attention.

The older man stood with him. He also was silent. He was shorter than the young man and somewhat stooped at the waist. He was balding and graying, and the patches of hair on the sides of his head stuck uncontrollably in all directions, as if they had been shot out of the sides of his head. He had a mustache of the same gray color, not trimmed. He wore a worn tweed jacket, a stained tie, and a button of some kind on his lapel. He carried a manila folder filled with papers.

The young man and the older man approached the table in front of the Board.

"Good evening, Mr. Pacella," said the chairman. "This is a hearing on your request for an exemption from your induction into the armed services. You claim status as a conscientious objector. The hearing tonight is informal. It is not a trial. You may present witnesses, but you may not ask us questions. You may not photograph or tape or audio-record this hearing in any way. You may request that this hearing remain open to the public. But we will not tolerate any commotion and will direct the police to remove any person who disrupts your hearing. We also may determine to close your hearing at any time, if necessary.

"I see that you have an advisor with you. Would you please identify him?"

"Professor Ernest N. Palmetto."

"You many consult with him but he may not participate in the hearing. Do you understand?"

"Yes."

"You may present evidence that is not already in our file from the earlier review of your claim for an exemption. Be careful what you and your witnesses say. There are very serious penalties for false statements made to this board. You may be put in jail for five years or fined a lot of money. Do you understand what I have told you? Do you want your hearing to be open?"

A loud noise echoed from the back of the room.

"Stop the war! Stop the draft!"

A young man had jumped up in the back row and begun to scream. He was small and wiry, with long black hair that reached his shoulders, and a thin moustache. His eyes were wide and wild, and they pushed so far forward from his head they looked as if they were about to exit the front of his skull. He waved his arms, up and down, in a jumping-jack motion, then moved his right arm forward and pointed with one finger to the board members.

"You are sending young men to die! For no reason! To die in a stupid, immoral war! Stop what you're doing, now!"

The chairman made no expression. Most of the recent meetings of the board had included a cameo like this, he thought. He spoke firmly: "Officers, please escort this gentleman (to use the term loosely) out of the hall, with the usual due process and respect for his right to dissent, of course."

The police moved in quickly and efficiently. Three officers grabbed the man by his wool coat. They held him horizontally, as if they were carrying a log as a battering ram. They moved as one to the entrance of the hall. The speaker flayed with his arms and legs. He continued to scream as he was removed. His voice trailed off, muffled by the sound of heavy footsteps as the three officers carried him down the stairs to the first floor.

The room quieted, though dozens of heads remained turned toward the back door, waiting for the next explosion. The petitioner and the professor had remained standing.

"We have the report of your earlier claim for a CO exemption. The report says that you are mentally and physically fit to serve. The report denied your claim."

"I understand. I have appealed," the petitioner said simply.

The room had become quiet. Clare felt her stomach turn, then turn again. She felt light-headed and wondered if she had made the right choice to come to speak.

The petitioner made no motion and said nothing.

"Do you have an opening statement?" the chairman asked.

"I do."

"Then let's hear it."

"I request classification as a conscientious objector to the war. I hold religious beliefs that do not permit me to serve in the military. I have explained my beliefs in my written filings, which you have. I have held these beliefs for my entire life. They guide my life to this day. 'Thou shalt not kill,' the commandment states, and I live by that command. I have submitted statements of my family and friends. They all testify under oath that I have consistently held these non-violent beliefs and have made them part of my life. For these moral, ethical, and religious reasons, I do not wish to participate in war. These reasons are not based on politics, expediency, or self interest."

"Thank you," the chairman said. "I have a question. Do you oppose all war or only this war?"

"All wars."

"Would you be willing to use force in self-defense or in defense of your home or family?"

"Yes, I view such actions to be different from acts of war."

"Do you concede that your views may change in the future?"

"I do. No one can see the future. But I should not be excluded from the classification now simply because my views might change."

"Do you have anything further?" the chairman asked.

"No."

"Well, then, the board takes your appeal under advisement. The three members present here tonight will decide your appeal. It will be based on what we have heard tonight and your existing file. You will receive a notice that tells you whether your request for an exemption is granted or denied. If it is denied, we will provide you with a statement of reasons for our decision. The notice will also inform you of your rights of further appeal under the Selective Service System.

"If we classify you as qualified for service but not available for combat or non-combat military service, you will receive a notice that you will be required to perform 24 months of alternative service. If we classify you as qualified for service and available for non-combat military service, you will receive a notice with an induction time and place."

The young man and his adviser gathered their papers, stood up, and slid their chairs back under the table. They slowly walked away, heads down. The room was silent. The chairman looked up from his notes and around the room, front to back and side to side.

"Any new business?

Clare rose.

"Name, Miss?"

"Clare McUsic. I would like to address the board."

"What would you like to address us about?"

"The war."

"Which one?" The chairman grinned and looked from side to side at his fellow board members but drew no laughs. Each was looking straight ahead at Clare.

Clare did not acknowledge the joke. She squared her shoulders and said,

"The one you keep sending young men to lose."

The chairman grimaced and looked at the clock in the rear of the hall. Ten minutes before ten. He then turned and looked quickly at the clock above him, which said ten minutes past ten. In this crowd, he thought, we will probably not even agree on the time of day.

"I have a resolution for the board to vote on," Clare said.

"You may read it. But we will decide if it is out of order for this meeting." Clare read from her paper, slowly:

> "Resolved, that this Board will cease its participation in the Selective Service System until further order of this Board. As grounds, we state that in the absence of a declaration of war by Congress under Article I of the United States Constitution, we have no power to conscript citizens into the armed forces, notwithstanding any directive from the Executive Branch or any power purportedly conferred on us by Congress under the Selective Service Act."

Clare finished reading the resolution and looked up from her papers. She said, "We ask that you adopt this resolution and immediately stop drafting people. You have no right to do this. Congress has never declared this war. You have no right to draft people to fight an undeclared war."

The chairman smiled, the kind of smile that an older person gives a young person before he delivers her a lecture.

"We hold an important office, Miss. We are sworn to enforce the law. Our doubts about the wisdom of the war do not matter to us in the exercise of our duties."

Clare responded quickly. She had planned for this point.

"If you doubt the wisdom of the war—even for a minute—then you must resign. You cannot in good conscience continue to enforce draft laws for a war that you feel is unconstitutional or unjust."

The chairman looked to his left and right at the other members. They nodded but looked straight ahead.

"We will not resign," he said. "And your resolution is hereby ruled out of order and so it is denied. I'm sorry, Miss. Do you have anything else?"

Clare looked at her notes.

"No," she said.

"This meeting is adjourned," the chairman said.

The large crowd slowly filed out of the hall and down the stairs. Clare found Sookie and made her way to the back of the hall.

"You tried," Sookie said. "You were great."

"Thanks," Clare said.

"What's next?" Sookie asked.

"I don't know," Clare said.

They went down the stairs and out to the front of the building. The fresh cool air felt good on Clare's face. She had blushed several times upstairs and still felt a bit dizzy. The air was at least some escape from the heat in the hall.

Clare and Sookie walked down the front steps and along the path toward the street. A young man was sitting on the fender of a car parked on the street in front of the hall. Bumper stickers on the car read: "Stop the War" and "Draft Beer Not Men." Clare recognized him as the man thrown out of the hearing. He saw Clare and Sookie and looked up and smiled.

"They're worthless cowards," he said. "They reject every appeal and wear the petitioners down. Meanwhile they encourage the local high school suckers to go to war."

Clare and Sookie did not respond at first. Sookie turned to Clare. "He wouldn't call Jack a sucker if he knew him, Clare," Sookie whispered, too loudly.

The young man narrowed his eyes. "Jack who?"

Clare sighed. This will not go well, she thought. "My boyfriend."

"Your boyfriend is over there?" A smirk formed on his thin lips, widening his moustache.

Clare shifted her feet.

"How do you feel about him killing people?" he asked. He looked at her closely, with raised eyebrows and without blinking.

"What do you mean 'How do I feel?' He's the one in the war, not me."

"Do you write to him?"

"Yeah, sure."

"Do you sign your letters with love?"

"None of your business."

"So you support him by writing him letters. You make him feel better so he can kill more people. Maybe kill women and children. So you are supporting the war."

"I don't support the war. If you hadn't shot off your mouth and got tossed out tonight you would know what I was here for. And I think you need some logic lessons."

"Why are you so pissed off?"

"Because you're a loser and I want to go home," Clare said, her voice now rising as Sookie moved closer to her friend.

"Well, maybe you just haven't asked yourself the hard questions," the young man said slyly.

"What is that supposed to mean? You saw me in there. I'm not afraid of the draft board and I'm not afraid of any questions, especially yours."

"Maybe, maybe not," he said. "We'll see." His eyes narrowed again. Then his sly smile returned. "You want it both ways: you oppose the war but you love and admire the guys fighting it."

"Not all of them."

"Some of them."

"Maybe."

He looked her up and down. Clare raised her hand up in the air, palm facing him.

"Enough," she said.

He squinted in the dark of the street, looking closely at Clare's arm.

"Is that a missing-in-action bracelet?"

Clare looked at her wrist quickly.

"None of your business."

"Who is it for?"

"Someone braver than you."

"Bitch. What's your problem? Whose side are you on, anyway?"

"I'm not on any side," Clare said. She was surprised to hear herself say these words. Sookie looked at her sideways but said nothing.

"So who's it for?"

"The name doesn't matter. He got drafted, he went, and now they can't find him."

Clare paused. Sookie recognized Clare's look, tongue in the side of her mouth and eyes darting. She had seen that look in class. Sookie knew Clare's next question before it came out of her mouth.

"What about you? Were you drafted?" Clare asked.

"Medical deferment."

"What for?"

"Bone spurs in my feet."

"Really? You seem to walk fine. And you seemed to have no problem kicking those cops when they were dragging you out of the hall."

"None of your business."

"Someone took your place over there, you know," Clare said.

"Doesn't matter to me."

"Really? That doesn't matter to you? Then why are you breaking up meetings screaming 'Stop the Draft'? I think that the ones who go do matter to you, a lot. So, as I see it, I feel sorry for the guys who are there, and you feel guilty about them. Are we so different?"

"Suit yourself," he said, and turned away and walked toward the driver's side of his car. "But you'll have to choose a side some time. Sounds like your boyfriend already has." He slid into the driver's seat, started the engine, and drove away.

The crowd had long left city hall and the lights of the building had been turned off. The street was quiet.

"Jerk," Sookie said.

"Didn't think I'd be getting shot at from that side, or out here, tonight," Clare said, shaking her head.

"You did great. I never could stand up to these people, the ones inside or out. I admire you, Clare."

"You did help, Sookie. You are here, aren't you? That's more than I can say about my other friends, the no-shows. And your family stories from Korea mean a lot to me. I'm glad you are here."

They started walking along the deserted street back toward Clare's apartment. "Want to get something to eat?" Sookie asked. "You must be hungry."

"No, thanks," Clare said. "I think I'll just go home. It's been a long night. And there are a lot more of these nights ahead of me."

They kept walking along the main street back to Clare's house.

"Who is the person whose name is on the bracelet, Clare?" Sookie asked.

"I don't know him. They make them for us to remember the soldiers who are prisoners of war or missing in action—'POW' or 'MIA', they call them. I sent them my address and the group that makes the bracelets mailed it back. He's been missing since 1966.

"You are good to wear it, Clare. I hope that that soldier comes home."

Clare sighed and nodded.

"I hope that Jack's name is never on a bracelet," Sookie said.

Clare stopped walking and looked straight ahead. "Me, too," she said.

Chapter 6

The thermometer attached to the front wall of the College Inn read zero degrees on a January day six weeks after the draft lottery in December, 1969. A few minutes before nine o'clock, as he hurried to class, Rocco saw a group of students at the corner huddling together in the cold. Two long coach buses were parked near the same corner, the engine running and tall plumes of vapor blasting from the tail pipe into the frigid air.

Theses buses usually carried the Viking sports teams on road trips. But this would be a short road trip, Rocco knew. The mix of non-athletes in the crowd confirmed the story that Rocco had read in the *Daily Viking* about looming draft induction physicals. He put his head down, changed his course away from the hotel and the bus and cut toward the center of the campus green. He contemplated his mid-range draft number for the rest of his walk and through all of his upper-level physics class.

The group on the corner had prepared well for their morning trip to the Veterans Hospital. This day had followed long nights spent with local lawyers, clergy, counselors, and medical students. The students had studied the Military Code of Physical Regulations with an intensity seldom shown in their undergraduate courses. One by one, their advisers had examined the physical and mental conditions of the students present. They asked questions that probed each, head to toe, head to heart, matching each draftee with likely—if not decisive—grounds for rejection from military service.

The study sessions were held in the common areas of the dorms. After one long night one of the medical students broke the tension with a summary of their efforts, a "gospel" reading of sorts, for the faithful:

"If you heed our words, these things shall come to pass:

The chubby shall become obese;
The thin shall become emaciated;
The unstable shall become stark, raving lunatics;
The meek shall tremble until they fall;
The bed-wetters shall void torrents that would float
battleships;
The flat-footed shall later jump with joy.
And, after all these things come to pass, you shall be
called
'Unqualified to Serve.'"

On the same morning that Rocco took his detour to class, less
than one-mile away, in the parking lot of the local high school, a
long yellow school bus sat idling in the cold. The bus had large
black tires rimmed by rusting wheel wells, the price of many long
northern winter trips through snow, ice, salt, and sand.

A man in his late forties sat in the driver's seat. Bill Spiggott
wore an old, puffy parka, a wool hat, and large gloves, a hedge
against the fact that the bus heater hadn't worked for a few years.
He had risen earlier than usual that morning for this special run
to the VA hospital. His sleep and routine had been disrupted that
night—he could not lay to rest the memory of his own bus ride
to the same hospital in '43. He and his high school friends were
quickly examined and approved that day. The road that followed
led Bill to the Navy and a job as a radioman on a transport ship
dodging kamikaze planes off Okinawa in 1945. The memories
of the landing boats returning the wounded from the beaches
and jungles of the island had disrupted many nights of his sleep
for years. He often recalled the day he was sitting at his radio below decks when he heard the news of the atomic bomb at Hiro-
shima. So long to the kamikazes, he thought, we're going home.

In the driver's seat, Bill looked at the large mirror attached
to the side of the bus. He could see the reflection of a couple
dozen teenagers milled about the parking lot, hands in their
pockets and rocking nervously back and forth on their feet. He
knew many of them—recent graduates of the high school—and

had driven them to games, matches, and meets. He knew their parents. He now wished he had turned down this run.

Towny Badger stood off to the side of the group. Already eighteen years old, he had quietly enlisted for duty after high school graduation in the spring, but had told few people in town. He watched closely as the big coach buses passed the high school parking lot.

The driver looked at his watch and saw that he was a minute late in leaving. He let another minute pass, then hit the horn. He slowly pulled the lever and closed the door.

At the hospital, from his window, Tiemo saw the two buses enter the grounds and crawl slowly up the hill. He had risen early that day to finish a letter to Jack. His neighbor poked his head into Tiemo's room.

"Remember your induction?" the neighbor asked.

"I do, but it was nothing—we all knew that they would take anyone that could breathe. And, as it turned out, we needed every one of them."

The buses pulled up to the parking lot outside the building that housed the ambulatory clinics. The young men were herded into a long line leading to the front door of the clinic building. Once in the lobby, they stood along its four walls. The boys from the college stood separately from the boys from town. From the college side, Towny heard excited tones and many medical-sounding terms. He heard the term "unqualified" many times.

"What are they talking about?" Towny's friend leaned in and whispered to him.

"Not sure," Towny said. He *was* sure: Rocco had told him about the many nights that the college boys had spent with doctors, lawyers, and counselors of all types.

His friend spoke again, his eyes locked on Towny's and his jaw set tight. "I think I know what it means," he said. "It means that more guys like me are going to go."

A single uniformed soldier appeared. He gave them trash bags to hold their clothes when they undressed for their physicals. They wore only their underwear and socks. The first of the men from the college bus entered a small examination room and sat on the chair. A doctor entered. He had a bow-tie and reading glasses held by a small cord around his neck. He was reading his notes as he entered the room and took no notice of the young man. He read his name and the young man nodded.

"Good morning. My name is Doctor Puerifoy." He looked at the young man from head to toe and gestured toward the scale placed against the wall of the room.

"Son, this is called an eye-level physician's beam scale. It has die-cast beam construction. It measures height up to 78 inches— that's six-foot-six, in case you flunked math. Please step up on the scale so I can measure your height."

He looked over his reading glasses at the student. "You are five-feet-eight inches tall. Now please step off the scale for a moment."

"We calibrated the scale this morning," the doctor continued. "It is built to measure weights up to 400 pounds. Let me show you how it works. When the large counter weight and the smaller sliding weight both read zero, the rotating beam should stop where it is completely horizontal and the needle on the far right lines up dead-on in the center of the slot. See? We usually ask you to estimate your weight so we'll know where to start measuring with the larger weight, then we adjust. Got it? Estimated weight?"

"275 pounds."

The doctor raised his eyebrows. The student stepped back on the scale.

The doctor slid the large counter-weight to a number far less than 250—all the way back to 150. He then slid the small weight slowly on the scale, notch by notch, resting briefly on each notch. He watched the balance beam closely without saying a word.

The balance beam rocked slowly then stopped. The large weight read "150." The small weight added "25."

"175 pounds," the doctor said.

"What?"

"I said, you weigh 175 pounds."

"That can't be right." The boy started to fidget, rubbing his hands together and shifting his weight from foot to foot.

"That's what the scale says, son."

"Well that scale's wrong! It's got to be wrong!"

"Not likely, son."

The doctor looked at the student from head to toe, glancing again at his abnormally large mid-section.

"Just this one time, son, I'm willing to re-calibrate the scale. Wait here while I get a screwdriver."

The doctor returned. He frowned deeply. He placed the screwdriver on the screw on one side of the beam to move it closer to zero. He nodded and grimaced.

"Well, you're right. It was off. Step back up on the scale."

"275. So now we have two weights measured—175 and 275. And now we know that 275 is correct. But let's think about this for a moment, son." He paused and looked the student in the eye. "What is your draft lottery number?"

"50."

"What did you weigh last year at this time?"

The student looked down. "I don't remember."

"Maybe 175? 200? And now you weigh 275 pounds."

The student did not look up.

"Let's say you weighed 175 last year. That would mean that both weights we measured today—175 and 275—could be *you*, couldn't they?"

"I guess. I'm not sure what you mean. Is this a trick question?"

The doctor paused again.

"Look me in the eye, son. Do you want to fight in Vietnam?"

"No, sir."

"Why not?"

"I think I can do more good for my country in some other role."

"Like what?"

"I want to be a doctor."

The doctor raised an eyebrow. "An admirable goal. Soldiers, you know, need doctors more than most people. Those high school boys over there may need a doctor soon." He nodded toward the door. "And some of those boys may have their own plans, I'll bet. Maybe some of them want to be doctors, too." The student said nothing and averted his eyes. "You've put on some weight lately?"

"A bit."

"Do you like candy?"

"What?"

"Do you like candy? Do you like fried food?"

"Sure."

"Funny thing about that food. It's not good for you, unless you're hoping to get diabetes. Or heart trouble. Or a stroke. Or eye damage. Or nerve damage. Or foot damage. Get the picture?"

"Yes."

"So you weighed 175 a year ago and now you weigh 275. Last year, you were probably qualified to serve; now you're not. So I have no choice but to say that I find your physical condition to be not acceptable for service in the Armed Forces of the United States. You may go."

The young man stood.

"One more thing, son. I have a story for you to consider. I had a friend in college in 1942. Hitler and Tojo were on the march. The world was a very dangerous place. My friend wanted to join the airborne troops, the best of the best. He took his physical, just like you are doing today. He was blind in his right eye. You know what he did? He covered his right eye twice and read the eye chart twice with his left eye. He parachuted into Normandy on D-Day in 1944."

The young man said nothing.

"You may go."

In the next room, a different doctor was examining Towny. The doctor conducted height, weight, and eye exams, a hearing exam, a blood pressure test, a rectal exam, and tapped his legs and ankles with a rubber hammer.

"No problems at all, son. I'm curious: bench press?"

"Two-hundred."

"Sports?"

"Football and hockey."

"You are in fine physical condition, son."

"Thank you, sir."

"I find that you are well qualified to serve in the armed forces of the United States. You may go."

Towny stood down from the examination table.

"Oh, and son?"

"Yes, sir?"

"Take care of yourself."

"Yes, sir."

Towny walked slowly outside and into the lot near the bus. He saw a former football and hockey teammate from his school. Towny had heard that his friend might be enlisting, too. His friend was bent over slightly from the head and neck and staring at the ground when Towny approached him.

"It's real now," his friend said. "It wasn't before."

Towny patted him on the back.

"C'mon, let's go."

Towny and his friend started to walk to the bus. Bill Spiggot driver motioned them toward the door and opened it with the long handle. As Towny moved toward the steps of the bus, he heard the coach buses from the college pass by, headed for the exit gate of the hospital. For a moment, Towny thought he heard laughter coming from the college buses, but he wasn't sure. He patted his friend on the back again, harder this time, and followed him up the steps.

Chapter 7

Rocco arrived at the College Garage early for his evening shift. He had put in a few hours at Professor McUsic's lab that afternoon. A slow evening at the garage would give him some time to do his homework for classes early the next day. He had the garage office to himself. The office window gave him a good look at the gas pumps and the street.

Across the street from the station was Joe's Variety Store, a fixture in town for as least as long as the garage. Its owner, Joe Goodale, Junior, was the son of its first owner, Joe Goodale, Senior. The store sold everything a college town needs, its narrow rows filled from floor to ceiling with goods. Milk, bread, cigarettes, and pornographic magazines were strong sellers, not necessarily in that order. The store's main profit center, however, was located in the rear of the store, at the shipping deck that extended off the back door. This was the site of the virtual monopoly that Joe's enjoyed for the sale of kegs of beer to thirsty students. Beer had a history long intertwined with the College, but the 1960s cemented the bond once and for all. The advent of refrigerated tap systems in the basement of each fraternity house had spiked demand. Each refrigerator could hold two 15 and one-half gallon kegs. On red-letter weekends, ten or twenty kegs could be seen stacked liked cordwood behind the wooden bars in the basements. Joe's was well positioned for the score. "We were playing the tuba the day it rained gold," Joe Sr., often said.

Joe's had two pick-up trucks with license plates "TAPS 1" and "TAPS 2," gifts of the then-governor—an alumnus of the college—and his pliant registrar of motor vehicles, with an assist from Everett Finch. Everett knew how to take care of his big customers, and he had been dining out on Joe's Variety for a few decades.

Joe Jr. was fifty years old. He was tall and thin and had the same ruddy complexion as his friends, all of whom loved the hiking, fishing, and hunting in the nearby mountains, woods, and streams. Most students liked Joe. He had an easy smile and enjoyed his banter with the students. The 18-year old drinking age took a big burden off the check for IDs.

Rocco knew Joe and often stopped by for a soda before his shift at the garage. He also knew that Joe's son—Joe III—was a teammate and good friend of Towny Badger.

Earlier that week, Rocco had crossed the street to the store and noticed a small sign on the glass front door. The sign had a small American flag and the words "Support Our Troops." Rocco bought his soda and said nothing to Joe but as he moved toward the same door to exit he saw the back of the same sign with the same flag and words. Trouble ahead, Rocco said to himself.

Trouble came to Joe's Variety sooner than Rocco expected. As he took his seat in the garage office one evening, he noticed a small crowd of students gathering outside the store.

"Boycott Joe!" one sign read.

"No Money for War-Mongers."

"Say No to Joe."

"Support Ho, Not Joe."

They were back the next day, and the day after that. The crowd grew, reaching 20 or 30 each night. And not all were students. A few faculty and townspeople joined. The number of customers had started to dwindle, Rocco noticed, from his perch across the street at the garage. When customers tried to enter, the crowd raised their voices and screamed their chants.

Late one night, after the protestors were gone, Rocco walked across the street at closing time. He walked into the store and approached Joe at the counter.

"Boycott hurting?"

"Yeah, Rocco," Joe said simply. "Some people from town have joined in. I didn't think they would, but . . . they did. And not just the professor-types."

"Do they know you served?"

"I don't talk about that much."

Joe sighed. "I wanted to show support for the troops. We have a few boys from town over there. And one Army nurse. Their parents are customers. They're scared to death about their kids. I didn't do it to pick a fight or become a target. Just to wanted support them."

"Everyone's a target these days," Rocco shrugged. "Open season in class, in the dorms, in the houses. Even the basements of the houses. No holds are barred. It's like the plague."

Joe nodded.

Rocco looked outside, as if sizing up the crowd, though it was now gone.

"I'll see what I can do," he said. Joe looked at him, uncertain of Rocco's meaning. "Have a good night," Rocco said.

A week later, on Saturday evening, the protesters again assembled in force. But a second crowd had also formed outside Joe's. The new crowd stood in a long line, in single file. The line started at the door and snaked west, away from the protestors. One by one, people appeared from both ends of the street and walked to the end of the second line. No one in the line spoke. Nor did they seem to pay any attention to the protestors.

The line grew to fifty yards long. As the line lengthened, the chanting from the protestors slowed, then stopped for a while. The single line reached a gentle rise at the end of the street. From the rise one could view the entire line and the store below.

There must be two-hundred people, Rocco nodded to himself at the very back of the line, where he motioned each newly-arriving person to step in front of him. Mostly students, Rocco thought, but he also saw a few dozen older men, some with veteran's hats or jackets, symbols of service in an older war.

"Nice turnout, Rocco," said a student, stepping in front of him.

"Thanks."

"How did you do it?"

"Asgard magic. Trade secret."

"No, really, how?"

"Word of mouth, mostly. Or no word at all. As Professor McUsic says, 'Never write when you can speak, and never speak when you can nod.'"

Rocco heard the protestors start chanting again. Two hours later, Rocco approached the door, still the last in line. When he reached the counter, he looked Joe in the eye. Joe looked tired but happy about his first busy night in weeks.

"'I'll see what I can do,' that's what you told me, Rocco."

Rocco smiled and nodded.

Joe continued, "The boys in the line said that you were covering the tab. What's that all about?"

Rocco held up his right hand, palm facing Joe.

"We're not done with you or Joe's Variety yet. I need to order kegs. Have sixty left?"

"Sixty? I think we do. It is Saturday night, and we are still in business, last I looked."

"Good. We want 'em all. Delivery around eight, usual houses, usual amounts."

"You got it."

"But one change."

"What's that?"

"When Bronco loads the kegs onto the trucks, tell him to bring the kegs out through the front door of the store, not out through the back. And tell him to park his trucks in front for the loading."

Joe smiled. "A final show of force?"

"Call it alcoh-diplomacy."

"You got it. Front it is."

"Now about payment," Rocco said, reaching into his coat pocket. "Bank check okay?"

Joe raised an eyebrow. "Well, yeah, sure. We don't get many."

Rocco handed him an opened envelope. It was addressed to the Asgard Hall post office box in town. It bore the return address of the largest brewery in the world. The post-mark read "St. Louis, MO."

Joe opened the envelope, removed the check, and stared at

the amount. It was made out to "Joe's Variety." It was issued by a St. Louis bank. The envelope held a note as well. The note was handwritten but not signed. It said simply: "Dear Mr. Marconi: It would give us great pleasure if you would use the enclosed for purchases at Joe's Variety, a fine establishment run by a great American."

"Does that take care of it?" Rocco asked.

"And then some," Joe said.

"Gotta get to my next job," Rocco said. He reached across the counter and shook Joe's hand.

"You sure? They'll need help drinking all that beer," Joe laughed.

"No, they won't," Rocco said.

Chapter 8

Jack had often noticed at the Veterans Hospital that the stone marker on the front lawn referred to the years of the Korean War. But he could find no marker at the College for that war, often referred to as "The Forgotten War." Not forgotten by the families of friends of the casualties of that war, Jack thought. During his sophomore fall term, Jack asked around campus, but no one seemed to know of any plans for a Korean War marker. Not a particularly good time for a ceremony about a war, someone told Jack. "We'll decide the right time," Jack replied, politely.

Tiemo had told him about a brother of Asgard Hall lost in Korea—Kitchi Martin, a member of the Cree Indian tribe—a Navy pilot shot down during the Inchon Landing. He left behind a wife and an infant daughter—the "papoose," the guys called her. In the late 1940s, Kitchi and his family had lived in the Quonset huts built for married students after World War II—the "Viking Long Huts," as the dorms were known. "I'll never forget the night the guys heard about Kitchi," Tiemo said. "I went over to the house. It was desolation. I always wondered," Tiemo mused to Jack, grimacing at the memory, "whatever happened to that little girl?"

During Jack's first months away from school, in the spring of 1969, Rocco executed Jack's plan for a Korean War memorial at Asgard Hall. It was a chilly night in March as the brothers assembled in the living room of the old brick mansion.

Rocco arrived at the house early that night. He took a seat on a worn, sunken couch along one wall. The living room filled quickly with large bodies. For decades, Asgard had had an unusually high representation on teams in contact sports. They were big and loud and intimidating to visitors. Professor McUsic once explained it to Clare. "Their maleness is pervading. Their energy is electric, sometimes excessive. Their timing is often poor, their subtlety non-existent. They see themselves as the protectors of College traditions, keepers of the faith. Their critics see an ancient anachronism, a relic of a rapidly fading past."

Asgard Hall was its name, but the group that gathered that night was no Nordic tribe. Its students came from all over the country: a Mongolian-American from New York City; a Puerto-Rican with an Irish surname from San Juan; a half-dozen Eastern European names from hardscrabble Pennsylvania and Ohio, cradles of football talent for the College for decades. They had one thing in common: they had big brains and big bodies and they were willing to throw both into risky ventures.

At 7:30 sharp, the brothers saw walking down the hall from the library three older men: President Onion, Professor McUsic, and a Roman Catholic priest. The undergraduate officers of Asgard followed. Behind them walked a beautiful young woman with high, round cheekbones and long black hair. She wore a full-length, burnt orange dress with dark blue diagonal lines and small beads lacing its neck. Her orange slippers made no sound as she walked behind the large, heavy-set men, who shuffled noisily in their dark, leather-soled shoes. She seemed to glide into the living room like an apparition. She was the only woman present and the instant focus of all.

The brothers immediately stopped their banter. They had expected the old guard and knew the purpose of the meeting. But nothing had prepared them for the impact of the stunning young woman.

Rocco stood up from his seat on the couch and squinted at the group entering the room. Her hair's so black it's blue, he said to himself. Then he thought: Wait—I've seen her. That's Kanti. She is a friend of Towny's. She's stopped by the garage a few times to say hello to him.

The older men and the young woman moved to the front of the room to a row of folding chairs near the fireplace, where Rocco had placed a podium bearing the Viking symbol. Professor McUsic welcomed the crowd and introduced the Reverend Alio Calamare. The old priest wore a black suit and a Roman collar. He rose stiffly from his seat, leaned on his cane, and moved to the podium to give the invocation. He said somberly: " 'O Valient Hearts' is a hymn by Sir John Arkwright, composed to honor the British dead of World War I. It reads:

O valiant hearts, who to your glory came
Through dust of conflict and through battle flame;
Tranquil you lie, your knightly virtue proved,
Your memory hallowed in the land you loved.
Splendid you passed, the great surrender made,
Into the light that never more shall fade;
Deep your contentment in that blest abode,
Who wait the last clear trumpet-call of God.
Long years ago, as earth lay dark and still,
Rose a loud cry upon a lonely hill,
While in the frailty of our human clay
Christ, our Redeemer, passed the self-same way.
These were his servants, in his steps they trod,
Following through death the martyred Son of God:
Victor he rose; victorious too shall rise
They who have drunk his cup of sacrifice.
O risen Lord, O Shepherd of our dead,
Whose Cross has brought them and whose staff has led,
In glorious hope their proud and sorrowing land
Commits her children to thy gracious hand.

The old priest looked up at the dozens of young faces before him. He met several eye-to-eye. "Amen," he said.

Professor McUsic returned to the podium. He thanked the priest and pulled a page of hand-written notes from his wool tweed jacket. He adjusted his reading glasses and looked out at the crowd. Without expression, he spoke:

"Those of us who stay involved with Asgard are sometimes asked, 'What goes on in that place, anyway?' And sometimes— against the advice of counsel—we answer. We say: Think of our house as a small but highly efficient manufacturing firm. We take young men and bind them together in life-long friendships, with loyalty to one another, to their fraternity, and to the College we all love. We have done this for more than one-hundred years. We do this better than anyone. We have our faults, and God knows we have our detractors, but we always, always remember our guys.

"Tonight we are called upon to demonstrate the ultimate loyalty—the pledge never to forget a brother who gave the last full measure of devotion in military service to his country. Kitchi lived here. He laughed here. He enjoyed the same bonds of fellowship that we all share. He shared what Augustine said he shared with his own fellow students: 'conversations and laughter and mutual deferrings.' But Kitchi did not come home to this room, to this house, ever again."

No one broke the silence that followed. Rocco glanced at the row of Kitchi's classmates, present for the ceremony honoring their departed friend. They stood motionless. Tears welled in their eyes.

"But Kitchi's spirit lives here tonight," Professor McUsic continued. "His daughter Kanti carries his spirit, and she is with us. Tonight she also carries a letter, a family keepsake written by Kitchi to the boys a few weeks before he died, delivered to the same mailbox in the hallway you passed as you entered this room tonight. Kanti would like to read you some excerpts."

Kanti took the podium and began:

"Thank you for the honor of joining you for the dedication of this memorial. I have a letter from my father addressed to Asgard Hall while he was in Korea. I know that this is a somber moment, but I picked this letter because it shows my father's sense of humor and his love for his brothers here.

> 'Dear Boys, I hope that you are all well. I
> am freezing! If you think it's cold in that
> old hockey rink, try the Korean coast in
> the winter. I have met another Cree here.
> He was at Cornell before the war. He is
> a very funny guy, and we spend a lot of

time together. He says that it is okay to
bomb the North Koreans. They deserve
to be punished, he says, for not walking
over the land bridge to Alaska and on to
the Americas. Seems like a stretch to me,
but war scrambles things in your mind
that way. All I know is that I need to get
out of here. I don't have long to go, and
can't wait to get home and see you boys
again.

"Kinsmen to kinsmen should be true,

Kitchi"

Kanti carefully folded the letter and placed it back in its envelope. She turned to the professor, who nodded and pointed
to the wall behind her. Several bronze memorial plaques hung
on the wall, bearing the names of brothers killed in action in
the Civil War, World War I, and World War II. A small United
States flag covered one plaque. A short white string hung from
the flag. Kanti stepped to the wall and pulled the string, revealing
the newest plaque. The plaque read: "In Loving Memory of
Kitchi Martin, Class of 1949, a Brother Who Gave His Life that
Liberty Might Live." The crowd applauded as Kanti returned
to her seat. Professor McUsic returned to the podium and introduced President Onion for closing remarks.

"We come together at a time when military service is dis-
dained," the president began. "Debate on the war is all around
you. I know that each of you boys will fulfill your duty as you see
it. We can help you on your course. But tonight, our duty is to
remember.

"Churchill once said: 'And wherever men are fighting against
barbarism, tyranny, and massacre, for freedom, law and honor,
let them remember that the fame of their deeds, even though
themselves be exterminated, may perhaps be celebrated as long

as the world rolls round.'"

The president surveyed the crowd. He nodded as if to bestow approval. He left the podium and took his seat in the front row of the folding chairs. A uniformed Navy officer rose, strode to the front of the plaques, and sang the College *alma mater*. As he finished the song, a campus police officer opened the front door of the house and walked directly to the front row of seats. He bent at the waist and spoke into the president's ear: "Sir, you are needed immediately at your office."

Chapter 9

The president and Professor McUsic reached the administration building at 9 p.m. They jogged up the marble stairs from the lobby without touching the long brass handrails. The president stopped in his outer office and greeted his secretary, Mrs. Penelope "Penny" Pole. She had a long thin nose and pale blue-gray eyes. She had auburn hair with strands of gray. She wore a dark, pin-striped blue suit, a sky blue cotton shirt, and white pearls.

Penny Lancaster—her maiden name—was a descendant of Harold Lancaster, Master of Her Majesty's Royal Mint, responsible for the production of all British Sovereigns and all other coinage for the realm. She had immigrated to the United States with her husband, William Pole, an American airman she met in England during World War II and who later taught at the College. He died in the late 1950s. Penny had not remarried and lived alone in a small house near the center of town, a short walk from the job and the campus she loved.

Working late that evening, Penny had asked the campus police to find the president at the ceremony. "What's going on?" the president asked her, when he arrived with the professor.

"We have credible word, sir," Penny said slowly, and somberly, in her finest British accent, "that students protesting the war plan to seize this building and your office tomorrow. Yes, indeed, tomorrow at 10. It is true."

"Well, it was only a matter of time," the president said, nodding slowly. "I guess it's our turn." He nodded to Penny. "Get me Judge Scruton on the phone. Wake him up if you have to."

The president and professor walked into the office and took seats across from each other at the conference table. The president had not turned on any lights in the room; it was dark except for the light from the streetlights entering the large front windows of the office. The president lit a cigar.

"It won't be this quiet tomorrow," he said.

"No."

"But it's not going down the way they think."

"Meaning?"

"Meaning I'm not making this us against them. That's not the look I want. I don't care about them occupying the office. I mean, I do care, but I want this to be about more than trespassing. I don't want to call in the state police just because some students are sitting at my desk and smoking my cigars. If that's all it is, the press will say it's a fight between property and free speech. And that will just enflame things. No, I want another angle for this debate: I want it to be about the authority of the courts and respect for our judges. So I'm not having them arrested for trespassing. I'm having them arrested for violating a lawful order of the court."

"What court?" the professor asked. "What order?"

"The circuit court, Judge Scruton. What order? The order I'm about to arrange."

They heard the phone ring at Penny's desk in the outer lobby. She answered, and called into the office. "Judge Scruton on the line."

"Judge? Sam Onion here. Sorry to disturb you. We have some trouble brewing on the campus here. Some damn students are going to take over my building and my office tomorrow at 10. I'll be talking to the governor and the state police, but there's something we will be asking you to do, too." Sam did not pause for the judge to respond. "Our lawyers will be at your court tomorrow at 9 sharp. They'll ask you for an emergency order, signed by you and bearing the great seal of our beloved State. Your order will prohibit the occupation of all college buildings and state that those who violate the order may be charge with contempt of court, jailed, and fined. I want the order clear and I want it to have teeth."

The president listened for half a minute while the judge spoke. As he listened, he nodded toward the professor and smiled.

"Ok, Judge. My best to Mrs. Scruton. Good night."

The president called out, "Mrs. Pole? I'll need calls placed to the governor and the chief of the campus police in a half-hour or so? Could you place those? Oh, and Mrs. Pole, could you come in here for a moment?"

Penny rose from her chair in the outer office and stepped into doorway.

"I appreciate your help tonight, as always," the president said. "I have no idea what I would do without you." He nodded to the professor to underline his compliment. "I want you to know right now that you are excused from work tomorrow. There's no need for you to get caught up in the circus. People might get hurt. I would never forgive myself if you were injured in the scrum."

Penny smiled. "That's kind of you, President Onion. But I would never forgive myself if I missed the show. I'll be here at my usual time, with coffee for our troops."

The president smiled. "I thought so, but I wanted to make the offer."

Penny smiled again. "Offer politely received and declined, sir."

"Next call, Mrs. Pole, to Bob Ward."

"Who?"

"He's a student. They call him Bullhorn Bob. He's the leader of tomorrow's séance. Call him. Tell him I want to see him here, tonight. Alone. Ten o'clock. Man to man. Let's get the cards on the table, face up for a change."

The president turned to the professor. "I'll take it from here tonight, Duncan. See you sometime tomorrow night, I hope, when the smoke clears."

The professor started toward the door.

"Wait. There is one more thing you can do for me. Take care of the old ship's wheel in the lobby." The Navy had donated the wheel to the College in 1946. A graduate of the College had been killed when a kamikaze plane hit a destroyer in 1945. When the destroyer was decommissioned after the war, the Navy sent the wheel from the ship's bridge to the College for a memorial.

It stood to the side of the lobby of the building. The president said: "Get Rocco and some of the other boys. Hide that ship's wheel in a safe place. I don't want anyone touching that wheel tomorrow. We see a memorial, but they may see a target. Take good care of it, in memory of our old pal."

"Will do," the professor said. "See you tomorrow."

The president's office was still dark when Penny peered in at 10 p.m. sharp.

"President Onion? Mr. Ward is here to see you."

Penny ushered in a tall, lean, broad-shouldered young man with long arms that seemed to reach halfway across the room as the president extended his hand.

"Bob Ward."

"Sam Onion. Please, sit down."

Bob had large, sunken eyes with wide, white sclera surrounding his pupils and long, thick lashes. He had long, cascading black hair that fell over his ears and his forehead. As he sat and talked, he ran his fingers through his hair, pushing it back as he tossed his head. He had the looks and the confidence to lead a crowd, the president thought. I know talent when I see it . . . and he looks a lot like his father, too.

"Thank you for coming, Mr. Ward." He motioned toward the sideboard.

"Drink?"

"No thanks."

"Mind if I?"

"No. "

"It is a pleasure to meet you. Your reputation as a fine student and gifted spokesman precedes you."

"Thank you."

"Major?"

"Government."

"Ah. Career plans? Law?"

"Undecided."

"Secondary school?

"Public. Brattle Hill, Pennsylvania."

"Lovely country. Those rolling hills, simply beautiful. Lots of steel plants in those valleys, right? Some hard-working folks, there." He paused. "Bet they've sent some sons to Vietnam."

Bob nodded, somberly. "Some from my high school."

"Many?"

"Yes, many."

"Any killed in action?"

"Two."

"I'm very sorry to hear that." The president abruptly changed the subject. "I know your father. We are classmates. He must be very happy to see you on this campus. He loves this College."

"I know that," Bob said. "But he hates war. Every year, on the anniversary of the landing at Guadalcanal, he pours himself a drink and toasts his fallen buddies. Then he recites the 'band of brothers' speech from *Henry V*. He does this every year. He hates the war in Vietnam. He hates all war, in fact. He's been protesting at home. Each Saturday night he organizes a candle-light vigil on the steps of our church."

"That's his right," the president nodded. "He saw war. Many of us did. Guadalcanal . . . that was very dirty business. We're not so different, your father and I. We know war. We hate it. And, yet, here we are, in a new war. So many lives lost already." He paused. Then he changed the subject again.

"Now about tomorrow's event."

"How did you find out?"

"Doesn't matter."

"What are you going to do?

"That doesn't matter tonight, either. You'll know soon enough. You will play your part, I will play mine."

The president took a short pull from his drink and rolled the ice cubes around in a circle at the bottom of the glass. He placed the glass on the table, leaned forward, put both of his elbows on the table, and folded his hands. Bob could smell the bourbon. The room seemed to grow darker. He felt the president driving closer to his point as he inched toward Bob.

"What do you hope to gain tomorrow?"

"We want to end the war. We want to stop the killing."

"We share that goal."

"No, I mean stop it now."

"Most wars are long."

"One more life lost is too many. Our college has already lost five men."

"I am well aware of that. I think of them every day. Do you know what classes they are from?

"1963, 1964, 1965, and 1966, and 1967."

"And do you know how many graduates were in each class?"

"One thousand."

"So, a total of five-thousand men in five classes. And do you know how many have served in Vietnam?"

"I don't know. "

"I do. Eighty-two. Out of five thousand."

The president was looking out the front windows of his office, toward the green.

"Have you been drafted?"

"No."

"Have a number?"

"Not yet."

"Would your draft number change your mind about the war?"

"I don't know what you mean."

"Would you lead the charge tomorrow if your number were 300? If you faced no risk at all from the draft?"

"Of course I would." Bob looked insulted.

The president nodded.

"Wars involve killing. Lots of it. Your father's war did. You know that. What is it about this war that you think is different, that leads you to protest in this way?"

"The war is illegal, immoral, and stupid. It's illegal because the people never voted to have their sons sent to die. Three presidents have rammed the country down this road, and not one of them dared put the issue to a vote. It's immoral because it sanctions the killing of thousands in the name of our view of what Vietnam should be. How immoral is that? We dictate the result we want and thousands on all sides die for our choice. Who are we to make that choice for them? And the war is stupid, too. We are losing, not winning. More are dying. There is no end in sight. There will be no victory, so why continue a lost cause? Get out now, that's what we say, and we'll say it loudly tomorrow."

The president was silent. He rubbed his face with both hands.

"Well said, Bob. You make a strong case. You speak from your heart. You have a well-deserved reputation for eloquence. But let me ask you this: why target your own college? Your father's college?"

"Because you're complicit."

"Complicit? How are we complicit?"

"ROTC. And your contracts with Dow Chemical and the others. And we've heard you're doing other things for the military, maybe research, we just can't figure out what. If we stop you, we stop the machine. We need to stop it all over the country. And we're not alone."

"That I know. What do you want here? My desk? My cigars? Or are you just using this building as a platform?"

"We want a campus-wide meeting. We want you and all of the trustees there. We want to debate the college's role in all of this. Your dirty hands. "

"I'll give that some thought, Bob. This is a liberal arts college. We believe in free speech and debate, John Stuart Mill and so forth, the marketplace of ideas. Let the best ideas win. After all, we are educating young men like yourself to assume leadership in the future. Seems to me you're well on your way, in fact."

The president placed his hands on the table, fingers wide and arched, as he pushed himself up to his full height.

"Well, I think that should do it for tonight. It's getting late, and I need to prepare for tomorrow. I have a school to run." He paused and looked at Bob, with a twinkle in his eye. "And I still need to clean and load my .45."

Bob had stood and turned toward the door, but jerked his

head backward when he thought he heard the president refer to a gun.

"Just kidding, son," the president chuckled.

The president walked to the doorway, reached for the doorknob, and opened the door. He smiled with taught lips. He look directly into Bob's wide eyes.

"It's a bit of a chess game, isn't it Bob?"

Bob smiled, with the confidence of youth. "Your move, sir."

"No, Bob, I've already moved."

"Sir?"

"You'll see."

Chapter 10

President Onion arrived early at the administration building the next morning. The building and front courtyard dominated the center of the campus and surveyed the green and surrounding buildings. To the left, the Crouchback Tower loomed, commanding attention as it tolled the time each hour. Two large black iron lamps stood watch at the sides of the main entrance to the building, which was framed by two rounded stone columns.

The building had no name other than "Administration." Its 19th-century donor preferred to remain anonymous, beyond a small circle of grateful trustees. He had made his fortune in the Civil War—his Pennsylvania firm had manufactured every shovel used by the Union Army. Lincoln had a hand in it—the great man himself had ordered that the contract be awarded to the donor. Hundreds of workers, laboring day and night along the Monongahela River, made the shovels that slammed into the soil of Antietam, Gettysburg, and Petersburg—especially Petersburg—and every bloodied patch of earth in between. Gun and cannon manufacturers were busy, too; their wares maimed and killed for four years. But the shovels were in even greater demand because they were more versatile—they dug the trenches for the Union lines before the carnage began and dug the graves when it ceased.

The donor made a fortune but lost two sons in the war. His sons were graduates of the College, as was he. After the war, he was happy to provide the funds for the new administration building but on one condition—that the College in the entrance to its library mount a bronze plaque bearing the names of the students of the College who had died in the Civil War. The donor made two further requests—that the names be enshrined in alphabetical order, and that the plaque not identify whether the student honored was from the Union or Confederate army. "The side for which they fought is not relevant to our task," he told the trustees. "For our purpose, we do not judge the merits of their causes, North or South. Rather, our task is to honor the memory of these young men. They are all sons of the College—beloved sons of their grieving *alma mater*—and they should appear on the memorial plaque together, as brother stands by brother, for as long as the College stands."

The president entered the lobby of the building that morning and greeted the old janitor, Tommy Snow. "Storm on the way today, Tommy," he said. "Take care of yourself. Leave if you have to. They'll be making quite a mess." Tommy frowned. He and his colleagues—like Cliff at the engineering school— prided themselves on the spotless halls and offices of the College. The president looked at the broom in Tommy's hand and shook his head with regret. "I'm sorry to have to say that, Tommy. But we'll get you some help cleaning up, after we take out the trash, so to speak."

"Thank you, Mr. President." The president started up the steps. "Sir?" Tommy asked. "Can I hit them with the broom?"

The president's eyes twinkled. "Come now, Tommy, you don't have to ask me that question. You're an old baseball player, aren't you? What do you do when you're batting and you've got two strikes on you?"

"Swing away?"

The president smiled. "But you didn't hear it from me."

He reached the top of the stairs and turned into his office. He walked straight to the front windows to see if anyone had arrived outside. He saw people in the center of the green, but not the ones the president had expected. Twenty or so older people were setting up tables and easels—he had completely forgotten about the town art show scheduled for that day.

"Life goes on," he mused.

At 9 a.m., Penny arrived in her outer office. "Good morning, Mr. President," she called in. "Mrs. Penelope Pole here, formerly of the Home Guard, reporting for duty."

The president looked out the window and saw a crowd

of three hundred students gathered outside the building. The crowd grew larger each minute, as students streamed from all over the campus and across the green. Banners and signs filled the street, the sidewalk, and the front courtyard of the building. "No More War." "Abolish ROTC." "ROTC Keeps the People Down and the Trustees Rich." "We Support the Occupation." "Dump Dow Chemical." "Peace Now." One waived the flag of North Vietnam, the "*co do sao vang*," a single gold star on a field of bright red. Four students wheeled a makeshift coffin along the sidewalk on a gurney, stolen from the student infirmary the night before. The coffin bore a white bed-sheet with the painted words "Bury ROTC." A second coffin on wheels followed, this one proclaiming "Peace Is the Beginning of Love."

Several students mounted the outside windows of the building and pulled themselves up to a narrow ledge that ran across its façade. They sat on the ledge, waving to friends. Some had cameras and were taking pictures of the crowd below. Two held a large bed sheet with the words "Liberation Zone" scrawled in red, with two red fists painted at each end. On the sidewalk, a student lit a fire inside a trash can. A light breeze had come up and it carried the foul-smelling smoke through the courtyard. The smoke and smell wafted up over the roof of the building and swung back over the center of the green, wrapping itself around the tables and easels in the art show.

The large crowd along the street cheered as a pickup truck pulled up to the sidewalk and stopped. Peace signs were painted on the doors of the truck. A tall, dark-haired man stood in the bed of the truck. It was Bullhorn Bob Ward, in his element and warming to the task. His bullhorn blared:

"Under no circumstances will we fight in Vietnam or surrender our opposition to this war. We demand an end to this college's complicity in this immoral war. We demand an end to ROTC. We demand an end to recruiting on this campus by the Central Intelligence Agency and Dow Chemical Company. We demand the withdrawal by the College from all contracts with the Department of Defense and the war criminals who run it.

We will now occupy this building and stay there until our demands are met."

The crowd moved, amoeba-like, toward the large front doors of the building. As they reached the top of the stairs, one of the two doors opened. The chief of the campus police, in full dress uniform, stepped out of the doorway and held up his hand. It contained a piece of paper. With his other hand he raised a bullhorn to his lips.

"I have in my hand an order issued by the Superior Court this morning. It reads as follows:

'Oyez, oyez, oyez, the Honorable Justice William Scruton of the Circuit Court has entered the following order, April 1 in the year of our Lord 1970:

'All persons are hereby enjoined from entry into the building and on the grounds located at One College Street, known as the Administration Building, without the express written permission of Samuel Onion, President, or the board of trustees, until further order of this Court. Persons found by this Court to have violated this injunction will be subject to prosecution for contempt of a lawful order of this Court and, if found guilty of criminal contempt of court, will be subject to fine, imprisonment, or both.'"

"Nice speech, Chief," said a student on the top step. "Now step aside. We're going in."

The crowd burst through the doors and up the stairs. They turned the corner on the second floor and headed for the outer office, chanting "Hey, Hey, Ho, Ho, ROTC has got to go."

Penny gave no expression as the crowd closed in. She sat motionless in a bankers swivel chair at her carved, antique desk. The desk and chair had been built in 1920 by Bond Brothers of London. The chair was worn on the insides of its wooden arms and on the edge of its seat. It had a faded black leather backing, tacked to the chair with round brass buttons. Five brass caster holders were mounted on the five-legged base, like a large starfish.

The desk and chair radiated authority, the sense that its occupant spoke *ex cathedra*. Its British craftsmen built it for the long haul, for people who sat at attention and gave orders and no quarter. They were no-frills, no-nonsense people, whose motto was "Do your job." In London offices, the Bond Brothers chairs had survived the bombs of the Nazi Blitz. The chair could swivel from side to side to meet any approaching threat, as if to face the world and echo Churchill himself: "Keep calm and carry on." The chair had held pride of place in the outer lobby of the president's office for decades, the seat of the gatekeeper for the College's chief officer, the guard governing entry to the *sanctum sanctorum*. It was a seat of responsibility and power, and no small measure of nuance.

Penny remained at attention as throngs of students bore down on her at her post.

"You have to leave the building, ma'am—everybody out," the first one to reach her said, curtly.

"You must be joking," Penny said, sharply. "I will not leave my captain so long as he is on the bridge. I will go down with the ship, if necessary."

"We're not joking, ma'am."

"Nor am I joking, young man. If the Nazi buzz bombs did not phase me, you and your colleagues certainly shall not."

"Well, ma'am, we'll have to take you out, then. We don't have much time."

Two men moved around the desk, one on each side, and grabbed the chair. One of them, a rattled freshman, sweating from his forehead down to his neck, moved one hand under the seat of the chair to grab a moving piece between the seat base, in order to lift Penny and the chair up over the desk. An English major with no mechanical bone in his body, he neglected the moving joint between the hub and the base. As the chair rose, Penny shifted her weight, and the hub pinched down on the fingers of his right hand.

"Shit, that hurts! I caught my finger! Dammit!" He took one hand off the chair. It tilted severely to one side as the freshman lost his grip.

"You're weak," Penny said, looking down on him as if he were a servant. "Are you sure you're cut out for kidnapping? You seem to be unable even to steal *furniture*. My dear nephew in London would boot your bottom from here to the river and send you to bed without your supper!"

Two more students joined the effort to remove Penny from her station. They grabbed the sides of the chair and the base and finally lifted Penny over the desk, down to the floor in front of the desk, and wheeled her toward the stairs.

"We won't hurt you," one said. "We're just taking you downstairs." They carried Penny down the wide, marble steps and toward the front doors. They placed the chair down on its casters and pushed her forward.

At the side of the lobby, Clare stared at the scene. She had arrived early that morning from South Tapley to join the demonstration. She carried a knapsack with food and water in case of an overnight stay in the building.

As the men rolled Penny across the lobby, Clare lowered her eyes. Oh, no, not Penny, she thought. Her father and Penny were good friends, and Penny had been a favorite of Clare's late mother. Clare looked down at the floor.

"Why Clare McUsic, what a *delight* to see you," Penny said, in her fine, undulating voice, as she rolled by. "How *are* you? Please, dear, don't get hurt, and try not to get arrested. Lawyers are so *expensive* these days!"

Clare managed a wan smile and gave a quick wave from her spot on the wall of the lobby.

"And you don't need to look so embarrassed standing over there, Clare. Truth be told, dear, I kind of like the women stepping out in front for a change. Long overdue! Oh, and one more thing—don't worry about me and my captors. I *adore* talking to men!"

The students who carried Penny outside looked out on a different scene from the one they had left minutes before. Fifty state police cars and vans had quietly taken positions on the green and the streets near the occupied building. The vans had steel cages in their back compartments and the state seal on their doors. Under the seal was the motto of the state police: "Protect and Serve."

Two hundred troopers assembled in rows on the edge of the green across the street from the administration building. They wore light blue jodhpur pants and polished black jackboots. They had riot helmets with clear facemasks pulled down from the tops of the helmets. They carried long, round wooden clubs, four feet in length, made of fine Kentucky white ash. Clubs harder than Mickey Mantle's bats, they liked to say, our own Louisville Sluggers. Their dark blue shirts had chrome buttons with the seal of the State and brass collar pins with the initials "SP." Across the breast pockets was a bar pin bearing a thin American flag.

The crowd jeered at the new arrivals. "Fascists Go Home." "Today's Pigs, Tomorrow's Bacon."

Back upstairs, twenty-five students filled the president's office, chanting "Hell, no, we won't go." Some sat down on the floor. Others and milled about, inspecting the walls of the high-ceiling roomed, walls filled with portraits of past presidents. One student posed, mockingly, for pictures with his arm around a bust of Mordecai Hatfield, fifth president of the College and a veteran of General Ulysses S. Grant's Virginia campaigns. Another student picked up a decanter of hard candy and quietly ate, piece by piece, as he surveyed the scene.

President Onion sat quietly at his desk as his office filled with the chanting students. He greeted Bob Ward from across the room.

"You're late, Mr. Ward. I've been waiting for you. Delayed in traffic?"

Bob motioned the crowd to quiet and approached the desk.

The president said: "I assume you listened to the chief's reading of the court order."

"Yes."

"I believe you're in violation of the order."

"We're not going anywhere until we get something in writing from you and the trustees."

"Oh, you'll get something in writing, alright. Maybe a summons to appear in court on a complaint of criminal contempt." He sighed. "Suit yourself, Bob. I for one would not want to be seen as violating a lawful order of the court. It might throw a wrench into your law school application. But that's your choice, now. Hope you all enjoy the ride on the road north to the jail. There are some nice views along the river. That is, if you can see anything from the back of those vans."

The president walked to the front window and looked out toward the police cars. He lit his cigar, the predetermined signal to the captain of the state police.

He turned back to Bob. "Have your fun with your gang here, at least while the fun lasts. Try to leave me a cigar or two and a few fingers of bourbon." He then walked toward the door, but stopped abruptly when saw a familiar female face. It was Clare.

"Why Miss McUsic. Up from South Tapley for the fun? A little early to be up here looking for a date for the Spring Festival, isn't it?"

Clare scowled. "Why are you so against us? Don't you want to stop the killing? Hasn't this war gone on long enough? Why won't this college take a stand for peace?"

The president nodded slowly but said nothing. He pushed through the crowd and out the door.

The State Police climbed the stairs and moved into the office to arrest the students. It was over within minutes. Handcuffs clicked hard against the smalls of thin young backs. White-ash clubs met flesh and bone. Some blood spilled from a head, though one officer dismissed the injury: "Hockey cut," he said, "half an inch of forehead skin and a gallon of blood. He's fine."

The police led the students out in handcuffs toward the waiting vans. The crowd cheered at the first sight of the students on the street, then howled in protest as they were pushed through the crowd to the street into the waiting vans.

Bob Ward and Clare were the last students dragged out of the building. They were brought to the last van in line. An older officer pointed them toward the small step at the back of the van. They paused there as the officer used his club to push others forward to the front of the van to make room. The older officer looked at Bob and Clare without expression and said quietly, almost casually: "Know anyone over there?" Clare was surprised by the question, coming in the midst of the chaos that engulfed them. She immediately thought of Jack. But she said nothing.

"I do," Bob said. "A high school friend."

"Where?"

"Quang Tri Province."

"A hell hole," the older officer said. "Better tell your friend there to keep his head down." Bob and Clare climbed up the rear step into the back of the crowded van. As the officer closed the door, he said: "And tell your friend to keep an eye out for my son—he's been missing in action since March."

Chapter 11

The protestors removed by the police were held overnight in the county jail, a drab concrete building behind the courthouse, five miles north of campus. Most of them refused to post bail and spent the night on cots crammed into small cells designed for a few town drunks and the occasional, transient thieves. The protestors slept little, more from excitement than the conditions. They talked all night about the occupation. A professor conducted a mock "class" on political resistance, offering Thoreau and Gandhi as guides, as the students voiced their approval. A different view about power and protest awaited them in the courtroom the next day.

They were arraigned the next morning in the three-story brick courthouse that faced the town green. The courthouse dated to 1825. Legend had it that the God-like Daniel Webster had argued a murder trial there, his words, one observer said, "like blows of a hammer." Another said that the jury had viewed him with awe, with the fascination that a snake must have for a bird. According to the lore, the county lawyers present at court were so shaken by the force of his personality that they could do no legal work—or any other kind of work, for that matter—for a week.

The main courtroom had dark wood paneling, rails, chairs, and benches. The wooden floor was scuffed and dusty. The walls bore the portraits of long-forgotten judges of the court, solemn, bearded, expressionless figures from a distant past with Old Testament names, Jeremiah, Samuel, Solomon, and Eleazar. Each had presided in his time like an Old Testament king, but no one recognized the names now. Now they seemed less like the main actors in the drama and more like a chorus, silently approving, disapproving, or remaining indifferent to the human comedies and tragedies that unfolded daily before their unblinking eyes.

The judge's bench was flanked by two flags. The United

States flag stood to the judge's right, a shining gold eagle atop the red, white, and blue cloth. To the judge's left, the state flag stood, bearing the state seal: a lofty mountain, and above it, a gleaming sword, and below it, the state motto, "Freedom or Death."

Shortly after dusk, crowds began to form in front of the courthouse, spilling onto the town green. There were newspaper reporters and television camera crews, some who had covered the takeover of the college building and stayed the night at the few modest motels nearby.

Protesters with signs took places across the street and on the sidewalks leading to the courthouse. Their signs read "Free Them," "Fascism on Parade," "Protect our Rights," and "End the War Now." Court workers placed six gray horizontal metal barriers along the sidewalk to protect the entrance from the crowds across the street.

Four state police cars, lights flashing, rolled to a stop in front of the courthouse. A dozen uniformed officers stepped out of the cars. They ignored the crowds and the cameras and walked—eyes straight ahead—up the granite stairs and into the courthouse.

Behind the courthouse in the jail, a county deputy sheriff walked Clare out of the lock-up to the back of a long line.

"What's a pretty girl like you doing with this crowd?" he asked, with a leering smile that Clare ignored. She kept her eyes to the front and on the long line of fellow protestors ahead of her.

"I like this crowd," she said. "It's my crowd."

The line moved slowly along the walkway to the back door of the courthouse.

In the courtroom, the long-time clerk sat in front of the judge's bench, framed by two large stacks of legal papers to the left and right on her desk. In front of her, she carefully arranged a third stack of papers for the morning's hearing.

The bailiff nervously studied the courtroom as it filled. The front entrance had an old metal detector but it sometimes malfunctioned. Not today, I hope, the bailiff thought. A dozen criminal defense lawyers hovered in the hallways and the back of the courtroom, waiting for one of the busier days in the sleepy, rural courthouse in a while. The younger ones were nervous—as they always were in front of this judge—but the older hands, like Maurice LeBlanc, took it all in stride: Maurice kept a half-smoked cigar burning on the side of the water bubbler in the hallway when he was called to business in the courtroom by the clerk.

The bailiff jumped up and snapped to attention as the door to the judge's chambers opened and the judge strode into the courtroom.

"All rise!" the bailiff shouted, louder than usual, surprising the courtroom clerk and the other regulars, including the many local defense counsel who would be representing the protestors that day. "The Honorable Oliver Scruton, now presiding."

The judge wore a black robe over a starched white, button down shirt and a blue tie with small gold emblems—anchors, some thought. He had a firm jaw and a sharp nose that jutted out over his jaw, the two so parallel that they looked like prongs of a pincer or the open mouth of a crocodile. The judge's blond hair was freshly cut, razor smooth on both sides. The top had a one-half-inch row of hair from front to back, like a blonde Mohawk.

The judge took his seat and leaned forward. He surveyed the scene as a commander surveys a battlefield. Some in the crowd felt that if he had had a pair of field glasses slung around his neck, he would have used them to get an even closer look at the crowd filling his courtroom. He missed nothing.

The first protestor entered the courtroom from the rear door and met his lawyer at the table for defendants.

"Call the first case, Madame Clerk."

"*State v. John Brown*," the clerk said in her precise voice, reading the criminal complaint.

"You may proceed, Mr. District Attorney," said the judge.

"The charge is contempt of court. The defendant is charged with the violation of a lawful injunction of this Honorable Court.

The State Police is here to testify, if necessary. We are prepared to dismiss the charge upon payment of $500 for court costs."

The lawyer for the defendant rose and said: "The defendant agrees to the dismissal on those terms."

For two hours, two-dozen more protestors appeared and met the same fate. On the advice of counsel—counsel painfully familiar with the temperament of the judge—no protestor rejected the terms of the dismissal. Five hundred dollars was a lot of money, they thought, but their lawyers convinced them that a guilty finding on their record and a week in jail would not help their cause or their future.

"Madame Clerk, please call the next case."

"*State v. Clare McUsic.*"

The judge's head jerked up from his papers. His eyes focused on a tall, striking, auburn-haired woman who had stood up with her lawyer when her name was called. President Onion had not told the judge that a McUsic would be part of the morning's proceedings.

"The defendant is here," her lawyer said. He looked nervously around the courtroom, his head turning to one side, then the other, his eyes widening as he took in the scene. Clare threw her shoulders back and tossed her head so as to push back her long, curled hair on both sides.

"Here under protest," she said.

Her lawyer rolled his eyes and raised his hand toward her, as if to ask her not to speak further. She took her own hand and pushed his down. The lawyer's face tightened.

The judge met Clare's steady gaze. Her name and looks were familiar. The judge was well acquainted with the reputation of her father, his exemplary research in support of World War II, his searing intellect, and his standing in the valley and beyond.

"Your honor, I have conferred with my client and she asks that you dismiss all charges against her on the ground that the war that she was protesting is an illegal, undeclared war."

Judge Scruton smiled and nodded his head: "Interesting question, counsel, but not a defense to these charges. It is beyond my jurisdiction. Tell your client she should write her congress-man—they are the ones with the power to declare war. What have they been doing? Missing in action? The defendant's motion is denied. What else do you have, counsel?"

"My client pleads not guilty."

The judge nodded. "Suit yourself." He turned to the district attorney. "You may call your first witness."

The trial was over in fifteen minutes, the State Police officer testifying that Clare had violated the order of the court against occupation of the building. Clare offered no defense, but asked her lawyer to renew her motion to dismiss on the ground that the war was illegal.

"Motion denied," said the judge. "Didn't you hear me the first time? Ms. McUsic, I find you guilty of criminal contempt. I impose a $500 fine, and a sentence of one week in jail, but I suspend your sentence for one year. You will be on probation for that time, and if you successfully complete your probation, you will not be jailed."

Clare stared at the judge but said nothing. The judge looked out over the courtroom, still filled with the other students and their lawyers who had watched Clare take her stand.

"I have a final word for all of you," he began. "What would your parents think of your misconduct yesterday? Fathers want sons, and daughters"—he paused and looked directly at Clare—"who obey. Who bring honor to their family name, not drag that name through the mud. You disobeyed the law. I must punish you. If I don't, I will be handing out a license to every other one like you. You can't run a college or a country that way. I am looking for the fair result, the just result. But you have openly disobeyed the law. You have tried to bring the law down, below yourself. You've tried to make it bow to your wishes, to your personal view of justice. That is your right, to try to do this. But you must now accept the consequences. I don't have the same luxury. I was put here to apply the law, not make it, or disagree with it."

A voice, first timid, then louder, rose from the group. It was Clare, back for more.

"You can resign your office."

The judge looked up from his notes and focused his stare on the group. The students looked down, shifting on their feet, side to side. There were a few nervous snickers, but most thought: there will be hell to pay, now.

"I will not resign," the judge said. "I will not join you in your disobedience, whatever I feel about the war."

There was more murmuring, this time in the crowd in the back of the courtroom. It grew louder.

"Order! You see, where there is no order, there's chaos! Courthouses, colleges, towns, homes, all the same. Without order, chaos! Listen to me. Your peers are fighting for this country in a God-forsaken jungle far away. In their lives, if their lines break, people die. Do you see? Without order, chaos! I won't have it, and I can't have it, here, in this courtroom."

There was a pause, long and ominous. The courtroom was still. The court reporter looked up from his machine. The clerk froze at attention in her chair in front of the judge. The judge gave one final look at the crowd and, without a word, jumped up from his chair, and walked quickly out of the courtroom.

Clare and her lawyer walked out of the courthouse and down the steps to the sidewalk. "Sorry I couldn't do more for you," her lawyer said. "He shouldn't have found you guilty. You should have been treated like all the others, with a dismissal of the charges and a fine."

"No, *I'm* sorry," Clare said. "It's not your fault, it's mine. I asked for it. I didn't want to just skip out, like the others. I wanted the guilty finding. That's my badge of honor. What's the point of all this, if you can't take the heat? The judge was right. And he should have hit the others harder, too. The big tough guys— the guys with the bullhorns and a lot to say—they got off easy. Not me. I can take it. Maybe they can't. Maybe women should be leading the way."

Chapter 12

Rocco heard a knock on the kitchen door and glanced up from his books. Only one person usually knocked on that door; strangers knocked on the front door, and friends from Asgard Hall simply opened the back door and walked through the kitchen to the refrigerator, ignoring any occupants. It had to be Clare, Rocco thought, and it was.

Rocco walked across the kitchen and opened the door with a smile. Clare stepped in, returned the smile and gave him a warm hug. "Hi, Rocco."

Clare often thought of Rocco as a refuge, of sorts, from the troubles that seemed to engulf her. He listened, he paused before he spoke, he pondered. He asked more questions. He started to speak, then often stopped to ask another question. Even when he spoke he was not quick to judge. No wonder Jack liked Rocco, Clare often thought.

Rocco took her coat and put it on the back of one of the kitchen chairs.

"What are you doing up here?" Then he thought a moment of the date and news of the last few days. "Oh, you're up for the fun on campus and the court case. Why the road trip? Not enough protests in South Tapley for you?"

"Not enough for me," Clare kidded back. "And I'll get two lectures for the price of one trip—one rant from the judge yesterday, and one from my father, still to come. He was out of town last night, so I missed him at the house. But he'll catch up with me, I'm sure."

"Must have been quite a scene at court."

"It was. Reporters, television cameras. Nothing like a couple dozen so-called 'elite' students in the dock in to bring out the paparazzi. I think they were hoping we would be taken away in handcuffs and leg-irons. Or maybe put in stocks—hand and feet—out in the town square, Puritan style. That's it! Maybe with a scarlet "A" for 'Anarchy' embroidered on our jackets. They didn't get that kind of drama, but the judge gave them the price of admission—plenty of good quotes in his tongue-lashing. He came out on the bench and like it was hunting season and we were the deer. 'I'm gonna get me a ten-point buck today. Maybe two dozen of 'em.' At least that was the look in his eye."

"C'mon, you're kidding. How bad could he be?"

"Pretty bad. Basically accused us of treason. Oh, and being a disgrace to our parents. And our schools. And our country. Did I miss anything? My father won't be much better. He'll think that he's a complete failure as a father."

She paused over that thought for a while. Rocco said nothing.

"When I talked to him last he said you and he have some work together."

Rocco nodded.

"How is that going?"

"Fine."

"I know you're not going to say much. My father doesn't. You—like Jack, come to think of it—never say a word. I keep thinking about you, though. You and Dad. Your work, Rocco. Whatever it is. It's gotta be for the military. Don't fool me, Rocco. It's kind of a problem for you, isn't it? By doing that kind of work, aren't you taking sides?"

"Good question," Rocco said quietly. "I have thought about it. I don't have an answer yet. When I do, I'll let you know. I might be taking sides. Let's assume," Rocco ventured slowly, "that we are working on something related to the military. Let's say that the device would kill more enemy soldiers but it would end the war sooner. Would that be good or bad? Moral or immoral? Which 'side' would that support?"

Clare nodded. Then she said: "What about women and children? Would it be okay to make something that would indirectly kill *them* faster if it meant a quicker end to the war?"

"Harder question," Rocco nodded. Then he said: "Or let's say we're working on something—say, equipment—that would bring more guys like Jack and Towny home alive? Good or bad?

Which 'side' would we be on?"

Clare thought for a while. Rocco knew that her mind had leaped to Jack and Towny and, for that moment, she faced the worst of her fears.

"Please, it's bad enough to know they are there. I can't even think about them not coming home. I think about Jack all the time, Rocco."

"He thinks about you, too," Rocco said. Clare looked up, hopefully.

"What does he say?"

"Well, not too much. You know Jack."

"I thought I did, but now I'm not so sure. I know I want to be with him, I know that I have never felt about anyone like I feel about him. It's just . . . ."

"Just what?"

"Well, he never says anything, never gives me a sign, about us, about our future, about what he's thinking . . . ."

Rocco nodded. Clare looked for a response, but Rocco was silent.

"Now it's all mixed up with this war," she continued. "It seems like we're on opposite sides of a gulf, a gulf that's getting wider and deeper every day. He's over there—God, he might even re-enlist—and I almost go to jail protesting the same war. It's killing me." She paused. "I guess that's not the right word for it."

"It'll do," Rocco said. He shrugged. "I wish I could tell you more, Clare. But he doesn't say much. But I think I know him as well as anyone, and I think that you are the only one he's ever cared about—really cared. He just doesn't say it."

They looked at each other. "That's all I got," Rocco said. "Sorry."

"I know. Not your fault." She looked at her watch. "My ride back to school will be here soon. What about you? Why haven't the president and the others recruited you for their foreign study program?"

"I don't know why," Rocco said, looking away. "I think that

they might want me working with your father."

Clare stood up and pointed at Rocco. "But don't you see? You have made a decision. It's a decision about how you use your talents and time. Your talents, my father's talents. Why are you doing this when you could be using your talents to end this goddam war? You're so smart. You could do anything you wanted to and do it well. We need help on *our* side."

Clare sighed. Rocco was so maddeningly reasonable. If she was looking to start a fight, she had picked the wrong guy. She was sad to end their talk but glad that Rocco still lived in some quiet corner of her crazy life.

"I think that the best that we all can do right now is just go on," he said. "Do what you are doing. I'll do the same."

The kitchen phone rang but neither moved.

Finally, Rocco walked over and picked it up. He nodded several times.

"Yes, sir. I'll be there tomorrow, first thing. Yes, I have it. Finished the notes today."

He looked at Clare. He knew that she knew who was at the other end of the call. She was nodding slowly, with a rueful look that Rocco often saw when and she and Jack had reached some impasse.

Rocco hung up the phone.

"I know," Clare said.

"Small town," Rocco smirked, rolling his eyes.

"You ain't kidding," she said, shaking her head and looking down at the floor. A car horn blared from outside the house. Clare brightened and grabbed her knapsack. "Gotta go. That's my ride. I'm a free woman! The judge said I can cross state lines!" Clare laughed and looked at Rocco: "So where are we?"

"Still friends," Rocco said. "Right?"

"Right," Clare said. "Thank you."

Chapter 13

Clare arrived back in South Tapley at 9 p.m. Her ride dropped her in front of her house and she put her bag on the sidewalk for a minute and looked toward the campus. It was quiet that evening, and it was hard for her to believe that only a few hours before she had been in a courthouse far away in the center of a storm. She looked up at the star-filled sky, thought about the past few days, and recalled a line from her reading: "And above it all, the stars."

She looked down at her bag and up at her house and her shoulders slumped forward. She knew that her father should be home by now, and that she owed him a call before he went to bed.

"First, are you okay?" he asked, as soon as he answered. "No one hurt you, right?"

"No, Dad, no injuries. Maybe to the soul, but no broken bones. How much do you know?"

"Everything."

"Figures. Small town, small state. That judge—do you know him? Where do they get these people? I thought that they were supposed to be fair and impartial. Yeah, right. We're lucky we all didn't hang from trees on the green."

"Well," said Duncan, not answering her question. "You did break the law."

"What laws are you talking about, Dad? Some order that Sam Onion finagled from a friendly judge? Law? Hah! How about the draft laws? Do you mean that some of the students are breaking those? Laws passed by our great Congress? What a joke! How many congressmen's sons are over there? They all find some way out. They are in college like me. Or grad school. And how many have gone from *your* beloved college so far? Hardly any. Only Jack and some of your other recruits, and maybe a few others from the ROTC. I don't understand any of them, by the way—why do they go voluntarily? But at least it's their choice. So, why does it matter if the judge or Congress passed some laws? There are more important things than law. What about peace? You go to church every Sunday. You pray to the 'Prince of Peace.' How would He like your goddam war?"

"Watch your language."

"I won't. I can't. These are men's laws—not God's laws. God's law is Love—Love Your God, Love Your Neighbor. You Shall Not Kill. What makes you think that judges, congressmen, and the President of the United States have a better idea than God? Those silly fat men in their dark, baggy suits in Congress—who do they think they are, sending poor boys to die? You know who goes? Guys like Towny. Janitors' sons, that's who. There are few—very few—like Jack."

Both were silent for a while.

"Anyway, I don't have to go to jail. I thought you'd be pleased."

"I'm glad to hear that."

"But if I violate probation and go to jail, will you visit me? If you do, you know what I will ask you? 'Why aren't you in here with me, Dad? What are you doing out there?'"

"I hope that you don't go to jail."

"That's not the point."

"You can't flout the law."

"I know the price I paid . . . I accepted it. That's what I told the judge. But what law will I have broken? A law against order? This whole *war* is out of order. It's my duty to speak. It is my right to speak. I can't stand it anymore. This is not about politics. I don't care about politics. This is about life and death."

Duncan sighed. "So now you're saying I should come down from my ivory tower and stand up for what *you* think is right. I know you think you see a lot of commitment among your peers when you protest on campus or on the streets. But you know what comes with commitment, sometimes? Malice. And you know what disappears? Charity. Ask yourself: What is *really* the kindest possible outcome here? Who would benefit from my new stance on the war, the one you want me to take? The Vietnamese people that we are trying to help? They can't dine on your friends' righteousness. They can't use it to save themselves from the North Vietnamese or Viet Cong. They just want to survive."

"So are we at war on this, you and I?" Clare asked. "I love you. How can my love for you turn into war?"

"You have me wrong, Clare. I'm not at war with you, and I'm not angry with you. I'm listening. You pushed things all the way—again—and I admire you for it. But you knew that the power was waiting for you, didn't you? The police, the courts. You knew you were on borrowed time. Yet you went ahead, as I knew you would. You *are* my daughter . . . ." He chuckled. "Well, on this one, actually, you are more your mother's daughter. How could I not know how you would handle this? How could you think I am surprised, when I know you best? But that does not mean I'm not worried. I don't know what you'll do next at your school. Maybe you shouldn't tell me. Whatever you do, don't get hurt. And don't forget our guys over there."

"Really Dad? And how could I do that?"

Chapter 14

One week after the occupation of the administration building, the Board of Trustees gathered in the conference room next to the president's office. Thomas "Gunner" Winchester was there from Boston. Hans "The Great Dane" Anderson flew from New York by private jet. "Damn expensive," he said, "and who were the geniuses that put an airport on the top of a mountain, anyway? Pilot couldn't see a damn thing. Reminds me of our parachute drop into France in '44. Good thing I had a flask in my jacket this time."

Thaddeus "Tat" Hudson flew up from Washington, despite his fear that—as a former White House aide with his fingerprints all over the war—he would present a large target. "Maybe I should wear a bulls-eye on my back," he grimaced. "Y'all might want to borrow my gun," drawled Peyton "Catfish" Cooper, a prolific fundraiser for the College who hailed from Baton Rouge and was now CEO of a chemical company, after a long stint, *sub rosa*, with the CIA. "Do they know what we've done in our lives? I mean *really* know?"

"They don't know history," answered the Great Dane. "No one does their homework anymore. They think the past is last week. But they do want our hides."

Each said that he would back the president to the hilt—for now, they added to each other, privately. Tat Hudson whispered to the Great Dane: "Sorry to say this, but in his cocoon up here, he has no idea about what's going on in the country, and the alarm growing among alumni about how he is handling things. The alums I talk to think the patients are now running the asylum."

Penny Pole poked her head into the conference room and peered through the cigar smoke. "It's time," she said. "Should I call for cars to the rink?"

"What, no limousines?" laughed the Great Dane.

President Onion said curtly, "We'll walk."

They walked in a group across the green and past the library tower.

"We could use Dickie Crouchback tonight," one said.

"Sure could. His humor would help."

"He's too smart to sit on this board right now."

"Agreed."

The college bells rang out from Crouchback Tower to announce the hour. This night they seemed to sound an alarm as well. In the mornings, they called sleepy student stragglers to class, but now they seemed to be calling to a larger audience, across the campus and into the town and beyond.

The meeting was held in the old hockey rink, ice-less now after construction of a new, lifeless arena that the students largely avoided. Old-time fans and players referred to the old rink as The Old Barn. Vestiges of its glory days remained: the old wooden boards, tattooed by a thousand pucks and, resting on the boards, a circumference of metal wire screening, a few feet in height, short enough for a fan to reach over and grab the stick of an opposing player during warm-ups, if the player absent-mindedly rested it on his shoulder or waved it over his head. The old wire screening had holes wide enough for a fan to grab the jersey of an opposing player when he lingered too long in a corner of the rink during play.

Visiting players despised The Old Barn. Its cramped locker rooms required both teams to dress in the gymnasium next door, then walk across a frigid, icy sidewalk, past a long line of students waiting to buy a ticket to the game. The visitors' welcome from the home crowd outside never changed: it was hostile and unrelenting. The visitors then entered the same front doors as the spectators, turned left, and walked around the back of the last row of stands through another gauntlet of abuse, finally reaching their small, cramped locker room. "The Bataan Death March at Ten-Below Zero," a visiting goalie once called it.

The Old Barn fit 600 spectators along its sides, strictly for standing room on its wide, long, wooden planks. At the far end of the rink there were twenty rows of seats for college staff and fans from town who arrived early to watch the shows on and off the ice.

Lines formed early for the 600 spots. In sub-zero weather, the crowd admitted was self-selected in the extreme: those willing to brave the cold for an hour outside were the most passionate fans and the most primed by flasks of the cheapest anti-freeze available. The intensity of this committed crowd, the surviving few of the fittest, could astonish even the home team at times.

Tiemo had once reminisced to Jack about the scene: "I was a captain in '33. They called me 'Slats.' They flooded the rink with water and opened the doors to make ice. The coach said we were his 'natural players on natural ice.' Your father came later—the best of the best. You could barely see him, only as a flash of the school colors and ice shavings flying up in the air. Even in the seats you could hear the deep crunch of his blades in the ice, powering him forward. And, early in the period, on the fresh, smooth ice, you could hear the 'tock, tock, tock' of the puck against his stick as he planned his next move around the hapless defenders. They froze as if they were stuck in the ice like poles on a slalom ski course."

As Sam Onion approached the Old Barn, he sighed. Great memories, but now this, he thought. The title page of his freshman book bore the inscription: "May this class always have a genius for unity." That's what the crowds in that old rink showed, he thought: a genius for unity. Now this. Division. Here, at the Old Barn. Sacrilege, Sam muttered to himself, as he walked though the large front doors of the rink.

The meeting was limited to faculty and students, who had shown their IDs at the front door. Nearly 1000 of them crowded onto the floorboards and sat in metal folding chairs. At the head of the rink was a long, raised table for the trustees and officers of the College and the invited faculty and student speakers.

Bullhorn Bob Ward took a seat at the end of the raised table. He wore a loose-fitting corduroy jacket with a yellow armband bearing a peace sign. He alone at the table had no necktie. He had a plain blue shirt open at the first two buttons.

Arriving a minute before the program, Rocco entered the rink from a side entrance that he used on the nights that he sold programs at the games. He had spent a long afternoon at the professor's lab. He was tired and hungry and hated long speeches but he felt he could not miss the show. And Jack and Stumpo would want a full, from-the-scene report; only Rocco, with his sharp pen and studied detachment, could provide it. Rocco slipped into the last row of seats and quickly pulled out some engineering papers to grade. In a mob filled with firm convictions, he felt uneasy, and quite alone, like his feet were planted firmly in mid-air. He felt that his ambivalence may show on his face and he could be discovered at any time. He was relieved when two faculty members unknown to him sat on either side.

The officials of the College and invited student speakers took their seats at the dais. At 7 p.m. sharp, the Secretary of the College, Styles Bridgestone, rose from his seat and moved toward the podium at the center of the long table. He was tall and thin and had a closely trimmed white mustache. He dressed each day in a three-piece suit, fall, winter, and spring, with the summer reserved for a two-piece seersucker and straw hat. He had enormous blue eyes and very large ears, like jug-handles. "When they were passing out ears, he thought they said beers, so he asked for two large," his detractors on the faculty joked. Others joked that he was the "eyes and ears" of the President, but this was literally true: Sam Onion counted on Styles to reconnoiter the campus and tell him who was up, who was down, who was sleeping with whom, who needed stroking, and who needed a kick in the rear. And, most importantly, Styles flagged for the president those who could be bought, and at what price.

Styles took a long stride toward the podium. Before he reached it, however, a student in the front row jumped up, mounted the stairs two at a time, beat Styles to the podium, and grabbed the microphone.

"We don't want your meetings or your due process. We don't want your dialogue. We want you to get rid of ROTC! We want you to get rid of the Defense Department contracts! We want you to kick out the chemical companies when they come here to recruit! We are not here to listen! We're here to speak!"

The president sat motionless a few feet from the speaker. He stared straight ahead, then whispered to the College counsel to his left: "Let them have their fun, let them raise the volume. Let them talk, loud and clear as they will. I want it all out on the floor. Nothing held back. They'll go too far, they always do. When I turn my glass upside down on the dais, it means I want to call a vote. Tell Styles."

The student stopped shouting. He looked at the Secretary with disgust and walked off the stage. The Secretary moved to the podium and declared: "This meeting is now open for debate. Mr. President?"

President Onion gathered his papers and reading glasses and moved to the podium.

"Students and faculty of the College:

"I agreed to this meeting because I believe in education. I began my education here many years ago. I believe that our meeting tonight can continue our mutual educations on the important issues of the day.

"Many here object to the war in Vietnam. Many also object to what they see as the support of the College for the war. Recent protests have escalated; laws have been broken; court orders ignored. The divisions among us seem sharp and deep.

"I do not denigrate your right to petition your government and the officials of the College we all love. I applaud it. But we can learn from each other only if we listen to one another and engage in rational debate.

"My second point is about consequences.

"The right to have a voice in the development of public policy carries with it a responsibility for the results of that policy. Our proposals may not be adopted, but what we say and how we say it will help shape what happens at the negotiating table and on the battlefield.

"History will render the final verdict on the wisdom of our

government's decision to enter the Vietnam conflict. There are those here tonight who are frustrated. They want an immediate, unilateral withdrawal of our troops. There are others, equally frustrated, who suggest that we escalate the war again. Both should consider the following. We cannot go back in time. The question whether to enter this war is behind us. We are in Vietnam. We must now choose the best course of action among the unpleasant paths before us.

"Will your proposed path make it more or less likely that we can achieve a negotiated settlement of the war? Would it mean an endless continuation of the war? How much more blood will be shed by the people of South Vietnam, either way? Do you believe in free choice for the South Vietnamese people? If we leave now, will it sow chaos? More bloodshed? I believe President Nixon wants peace in Vietnam. I believe the Nation is ready to support him in meaningful moves toward peace. I urge you to do the same, and to vote against the resolution to follow."

Bullhorn Bob took the podium next. He removed several lined pages from an envelope and began to read.

"We demand the abolition of ROTC. We have made our views on this subject known for months. I will not repeat them tonight. But I will remind you that ROTC is not a sin that stands alone. It's complicit with other policies—the support of big corporations, the exploitation of poor countries, all of this Nation's sins.

"We demand the end to military recruiting on campus. The College says that military and corporate recruiters are here on campus exercising their own rights of free speech and association. They do speak to students. They associate with them. These things are true. But if they are true, than we should have more speech, not less. Recruiters should be required to state their policies and the reasons for their policies before they enter the campus. Their policies should be subject to debate in some type of forum. The forum should be open to the public. All sides should be heard.

"And we demand an end to corporate recruiting by military

suppliers like Dow Chemical. They make the napalm. The military drops it on children and burns their homes. And we demand that you divest Dow stock from the college endowment. And we demand an end to military research on campus."

Rocco looked up from his papers. He felt eyes turn toward him, but no one had turned, from his front or to his sides. This is hitting close to home, he thought.

"We know military research is conducted on this campus," Bob continued, "but we don't know how much or on what projects. We know that the College makes money on this. On other campuses, this is even bigger business."

"We demand that all of this end, NOW!" A loud roar went up from the rink. Many students raised signs that they had smuggled into the rink, despite the efforts of the security guards. Some left their seats and walked up and down the side aisles in an impromptu demonstration. Secretary Bridgestone had regained the podium after Bob left and pounded on it with his gavel. "Order, order, I will have order or I will instruct the security officers to clear the hall!" After order was restored, "Gunner" Winchester took the podium to defend ROTC.

"You are making a big mistake about ROTC," he began. "We need officers from this College now more than ever. ROTC represents a large majority of the new officers in the Army. Many of them will become career officers. We need college graduates in this group and this College should do its share.

"You all need to wake up. To whom would you leave this mission, the leadership of our forces under fire? The enlisted men are mostly drawn from poor backgrounds. I think you know why. And I think that you know that their educations are not equivalent to yours. Why would you deny to them leaders educated like your privileged selves?

"It is now clear that we are facing an implacable enemy, whose avowed objective is world dominion by whatever means and at whatever costs. There are no rules in such a game. Acceptable norms of human conduct do not apply. If the United States is to survive, we must learn to subvert, sabotage, and destroy our enemies by more clever, more sophisticated, and more effective methods than those used against us."

Boos and jeers rained down on Gunner. He did not flinch. In fact, he seemed to be enjoying himself.

"We have a contract with the military regarding the ROTC. Should we break that contract? What would that mean for your federal scholarships? Have you thought about that? Some of you are in a closer relationship with your Uncle Sam than you think. Don't you think that the composition of the military should reflect the country, including institutions such as this college? And what about freedom to choose? Individuals should be able to choose whether to join ROTC or not, shouldn't they? It's a free country. Why should they be denied that choice here?"

Boos and hisses filled the rink. Bullhorn Bob jumped from his chair, interrupting the speaker. His voiced boomed out over the seats, as if the bullhorn that he had used daily for months had somehow become part of his vocal chords.

"We don't care! We demand the complete abolition of ROTC! ROTC casts the college as an instrument of an immoral military and foreign policy. Period. If we are training military leaders and granting them college credits, we are complicit in an unjust war. The fact that the military needs these men makes our role all the more evil. You say that the college is playing a crucial and indispensable role. We say: It must stop!"

Ward looked at Secretary Bridgestone: "I move the adoption of the following resolution:

"Resolved, That the College should (1) abolish ROTC, (2) bar recruiting on campus by any company that contracts with the United States Department of Defense or any other company engaged in research that could aid the military of the United States, and (3) cease any of its own research under contract with the Department of Defense."

"I second the motion," shouted a faculty member from far back in the crowd.

President Onion turned his water glass upside down.

"Are you ready to vote the question?" Secretary Bridgestone

asked the crowd. "Seeing no one claim the floor for further debate, I rule debate to be closed, and I will put the question to a voice vote, *viva voce.*

"On the resolution now pending, all those in favor signify by saying 'Aye.'"

A large roar filled the rink: "Aye!" Impressive, the president thought, though well short of the bedlam that followed any goal by the Vikings against Cornell in the old days.

"All those opposed, signify by saying 'Nay.'"

A second large roar, roughly as loud as the "Ayes," filled the rink: "Nay!"

Bridgestone looked out over the crowd and said, "It appears to be a vote *against* the resolution."

A third roar followed, "No, no, no! Count the votes! Count the votes!" the crowd shouted.

Bridgestone paused, but finally nodded. "We will proceed to a standing vote. All those in favor of the resolution will rise and stand until counted. The tellers will count the votes." The tellers wore red armbands and stood along the sides of the aisles in the rink. Now they moved up and down the aisles, pointing with their pencils to each person standing, counting each, and recording the number for each row on pink tally sheets. "All those opposed to the resolution will rise and stand until counted." The tellers again did their thankless work, under the suspicious eyes of both sides of the debate.

Rocco sat motionless through the standing count. No one seemed to notice that he had abstained from the vote. He looked out of the corners of his eyes—right and left—to the faculty members next to him, one who voted "aye" and one who voted "nay"—but their eyes were fixed on Bridgestone and did not seem to notice Rocco or his abstention. He was relieved by their oversight but not very happy with himself. "A real 'Profile in Courage,'" he said to himself. "Jack and Stumpo will give me huge grief for this some day soon."

When the tellers had completed their tallies, they walked their sheets—pink for those in favor, light blue for those opposed—up to the podium where the Secretary stood. He nervously checked his notes and thumbed a worn copy of the College rules that governed such a proceeding. He silently thanked Divine Providence for the fact that these circuses came to the campus only once during each Secretary's tenure. The murmuring of the crowd grew louder as he checked the tallies.

"Order! Order!" he shouted, and looked down at his notes with his half-glasses. As he towered over the podium and looked into the crowd over his glasses, those in the front rows thought they saw a trace of a smile on his lips. He cleared his throat to speak.

"On the question on the pending resolution, the ayes are 451, and the nays are . . . 451. The resolution is defeated." Cries of "No, no, recount, recount!" boomed through the Old Barn. Secretary Bridgestone slammed his gavel on the podium. "This meeting is adjourned, adjourned!"

Chapter 15

On the June day before Towny boarded a Greyhound Bus for the Army, he and Cliff left their house together for a favorite hike. The trail followed an old Native American path, first along a plateau overlooking the river and then into the nearby hills, leading to a fine rock ledge and a fire tower. They had walked the trail many times as father and son, sometimes in the bliss of silent companionship, sometimes with worries to share.

There were many trails in the hills near town. They could have chosen a different one every time they hiked. But Towny liked this trail. As a young boy, he took comfort in the ritual, the sense of order that came from following the footsteps of those who had lived in the hills near the river long ago. While he loved the changes that nature brought with the seasons of the North country, he did not like change in hikes with his father.

They left the car on the shoulder of the river road near the head of the trail. They moved under the shade of the trees and walked easily up the one-half mile to the first clearing. There, in the middle of a large field, was a single large, black rock, eight feet tall and twenty feet wide. The top of the rock had a commanding view of the river below. Local legend told of the rock and the ground below it as an old Native American burial site. As they walked the path around the rock, Towny and Cliff had often talked about the long-gone native people and their life along the river.

"Then the colonists came," Cliff said. "And they colonized. Not much of the Native American story is left, but they were here. Right here." He pointed to the rock, as he had done so many times before. "But they didn't get to choose their fate. Their enemies—disease, the Iroquois, and the colonists—decided it for them."

They walked past the rock and across the level field. They

walked through some taller grass and entered a grove of trees. The trail turned back down to the river, and Cliff and Towny could soon see in front of them the ruins of a small, brick factory near a rushing stream that fed the river. Piles of stones marked the site of a dam for a millpond. Built in the early 1800s, the factory once employed two hundred people, who turned the timber into hardwood blanks for the bobbins for the vast textile looms to the south. The "lords of the loom" paid good money for the bobbins and the factory thrived for a while. All that remained now were crumbling brick walls covered with ivy and other greenery, and half of a tall, round chimney that bore half of the company name, now unrecognizable from one-hundred north country winters.

"The workers here had ties to history," Cliff said to Towny. "Their fathers fought with General Allen at Ticonderoga and with General Stark at Bennington against the British. And their grandsons fought in the Civil War. They fought and died side-by-side because their regiments were formed by state and by town. Their names are on the monument in the center of town. But that was when everyone went to war," Cliff said, his voice trailing off. He wished he hadn't said that, he thought.

"That's not true now," Towny said. He looked at this father. Cliff frowned as he nodded toward his son. He tightened his lips and said nothing.

They headed up the trail from the ruins of the factory, using the natural stepping stones lying across the steeper parts of the trail. There were trees of every kind, but birch was Towny's favorite, from the days when he tried to write messages for his friends on its white bark. He picked up a fallen limb of birch and carefully peeled off the bark. It came off clean and he smiled at the memory of his writings. He heard the cry of a very angry blue jay.

They walked a half-mile through a large grove of white pines that lined the next stretch of the hike. There was a strong smell of pine needles from the ground. The tall pines were early prizes for the colonial settlers, who cut down the tallest and floated them down the river for later service as masts for the ships of His Majesty's fleet.

They entered another high clearing, often mistaken for the top.

Towny smiled and said: "The hills on this part always throw me, Dad. I never know whether we are at the highest point or not. I think we are still climbing, but then all of a sudden it seems we are not climbing, that we are headed down again." But just then they spied the final peak, with the fire tower at its top. They climbed the tower and looked up and down the river valley, bathed in late-afternoon sunlight.

"I love this place. I'll miss it."

"I know you will."

"Long bus ride tomorrow."

"That physical was very unfair to the guys from town," Cliff said.

"I know."

"Some of the same college guys took over the administration building, too, I heard. They smoked Sam Onion's cigars, that's what I heard from Tommy Snow. Heard about Tommy? He broomed out a few of them himself, he told me. The State Police loved it. They might make him an honorary trooper. And Rocco told me about the campus meeting. Wild. A tie vote? Old Sam Onion outfoxed them all again, I'd say. The man's a master. But it's hard for me to understand how much things have changed," Cliff said. "Some of those college boys—their fathers went to war with me in the '40s. The ones who came back built this country back up again."

"I guess it's different now," Towny shrugged. "Different time. Different war. I know one thing . . . college just isn't for me, not if it's anything like the one we have here. If all of the schools are getting like this one, count me out, at least for now. I'm not saying 'never'. Maybe when I get back I'll feel differently. About college, about the war, maybe about everything. I don't know how guys like Jack Dunne do it."

"Do what?"

"Balance. Live in two worlds. What do his friends think of him at school?"

"Depends which friends, I guess. I'll bet it's not easy. Rocco says that he and Jack talk about this. Everyone wants you to pick a side, Rocco says. He said that he and Jack really don't have a side. He worries about Jack all the time, though. And about the other guys who are there."

Cliff stopped and looked at Towny. "I don't want you to feel pressure to do this, just because I went."

"I don't. That's not it."

"Your mother is scared. I am sorry to say that to you, but it's true. You need to know that. She's a mom. She still thinks of you as her little guy, not a soldier. Give her a big hug tomorrow, will you?"

Towny looked at him and nodded. "I will. I'll write, too. You know I will."

They climbed down from the tower and walked back along the trail, past the large rock and down to the car. Cliff walked to the driver's door and Towny to the other side.

"I'm glad we've had the time together on these walks, Towny. It's different with fathers and sons these days. We won't be working in the coal mines together, or work in the same factory, but we've always been able to share these hills."

As they reached for the door handles, Towny suddenly said: "There's just one more thing, Dad." He stared down at the car and covered his mouth for a second with his hand. "I had a dream last night. I woke up sweating at three in the morning . . . .

"I dreamed that Jack Dunne died."

Book IV

Chapter 1

In the humid days of summer, 1970, Tiemo often sat on the screened porch on the fourth floor of the nursing home section of the veterans' hospital. He wheeled himself out the door and to the far end of the porch, across the scuffed wooden boards, to his favorite spot in the corner. The corner had good views and cool summer breezes. There Tiemo could see the Vermont hills, and, with his military-issue field glasses, the peaks of the mountains beyond. His glasses hung around his neck and he carried a book—today, Acheson's *Present at the Creation*—and a shiny, stainless steel canteen filled with cool water, in his lap.

He put the book and canteen down on the small table nearby and gazed out at the hills. They were a blessing and a curse, he thought. They give me strength to meet the day but they lure me back to the old days, old times and friends, some lost forever. He thanked God each day for bringing him home from France, body intact.

He often thought about his days at the College in the '40s, after the war. Maureen Connolly, a nurse on his floor, had asked him about the College and the veterans who were back on campus in those days. He smiled and said, "Are you sure you want to hear all this?"

"Try me," she said.

"After the war, my wife and I were here for two years while I was an assistant to the president," he had told her. "The campus was ninety percent veteran in 1945 and 1946. These were no 'silly sophomores.' These men were older. They had seen war. Many bore scars. When you saw a combat infantrymen badge on a jacket, you noticed. You gave way. Even the football locker room looked different. Many of the players had scars from bullets or hand-to-hand combat. There were jagged lines of stiches and raised skin from wounds and burns. It was the same for the young assistant coaches. The war was over, and yet the war was everywhere you looked.

"Most of the guys were at school on the 'GI Bill of Rights.' It paid for tuition, room, board, books, and a stipend. Men came here who would have had no hope of paying for college otherwise.

"Many were married. The College had to build a lot of housing, quickly. They found surplus trailers and hauled them up here for the married students. They set them all out in a long dusty field south of campus. They cost $20 a month to rent. They had kerosene stoves and the beds folded down from the living room walls. They had no individual sewerage hookups so everyone used communal baths and showers. It was like a little town, with door-to-door stops by the baker, the milkman, and the postman.

"For the single guys, they built long wooden huts that looked like barracks. Some of the guys probably felt like they had never left the service. But they were damn glad to be here.

"They were very diligent students. They were 'on the beam,' as we used to say. There was an air of maturity that probably didn't exist before or since. They were here to learn. The college had special courses devoted to foreign affairs. Marshall, Acheson, and Kennan all spoke to the courses. The Cold War was beginning, and the guys who were too young for World War II wondered if they were next up at bat in Europe or Asia. When they studied military history and diplomacy, they knew something about combat, something about the world. The professors could sense it, too. These were adults they were teaching. The teachers raised up their own games to match the war experiences of the students. Through it all, there seemed to be an unspoken code of some kind in force.

"It wasn't all business. But these guys were different even at play. Ah, the dances. Grown-up affairs. I remember the young men in black-tie, the women in gowns, the three-piece in the corner playing the sounds of the season. So different now. Tell me, why do the young people today insist on dancing apart? I liked dancing close—doesn't everyone?" he asked, raising his eyelids to show a gleam.

"Winter Weekend was special. The guys cleared out of their fraternities and dorms to make room for their female guests and chaperones. Chaperones were the wives of professors and mothers of students. There was a full page in a special edition of the student newspaper for the weekend, listing the names and colleges of the guests: Miss Angela Millescau, Smith; Jane Stidham, Skidmore; Nicole Marryat, Vassar; Jean Serenity, Wellesley; Margaret DeLisle, Colby Junior College. And so on, hundreds of names—in the newspaper! With the dorms that they were staying in! And the names of their chaperones! 'It reminds me of the *Daily Racing Form*,' one guy from Kentucky said. The last name on the list in the newspaper in '47 was simply 'Lady Love, New York City.' I think that it might have been a plant," Tiemo smiled. "At least I didn't meet her that weekend. But you get the idea. The place was Mecca for college women for one weekend each year. And their effect on the single men on campus could only be measured by the scale used for earthquakes.

"Many alumni returned for the Winter Weekend, too, even the older guys. They filled the College Inn or took rooms in Vermont. At night, they patrolled the fringes of the dance floor, then moved in quickly to cut in on the younger guys' dates, leaving their wives at the bar. Truth be told, I think the wives rather enjoyed the company of the younger men. And some enjoyed more than their company. Some of those stories live on, twenty-five years later . . . .

"Nobody that I knew smoked dope then. But they drank their share, and then some. The highballs flowed like water and—like the wine at the Wedding Feast at Cana—they never seem to run out. Cigarettes were everywhere, and everyone smoked. Even the lighters were statements. Monogramed lighters were *de rigueur*; I saw some dandies with diamond inlays, same for the cigarette cases. In the mornings on that weekend there were Bloody Marys and Screwdrivers at the ski jump. It was quite a thrill for those who had never seen men flying through the air on those boards.

"But still the war pervaded all things, even the ice sculpture competition. Guys cut very detailed, life-size figures of Japanese soldiers in various states of capture or under assault. These were not kind portraits of the Japanese. The figures were small with bulging eyes, round glasses, and enormous teeth. In the scenes in front of dormitories and fraternities, the figures cowered in front of the sculptured figures of much larger U.S. GIs. One sculpture had a Jap pulling a rickshaw for a couple of GIs holding whips and laughing. These were not sculptures designed to endear the College to their few Asian-American visitors. No. But you see, in their dreams, no, I should say, in their nightmares, everyone was still reliving Pearl Harbor, and Okinawa, and every bloody atoll in between. The war was still with us. A brooding omnipresence, you might say."

Tiemo sighed. "And now their sons are back in Asia. On the mainland, this time. Where we swore we would never be."

Tiemo stopped himself and looked around, past the nurse and back along the porch to the door, as if he were waking from a long afternoon daydream. He rubbed his eyes and checked to see who else was there.

"I'm sorry. You asked a question and got a monologue." He wiped a tear from his eye. "Sorry, I can't help it. It's just that . . . it was a time never to be repeated. It truly was, as they say, 'Once upon a time . . . .'"

Chapter 2

Jack visited campus on leave in late summer, 1970. He had been away for ten months. His two-year enlistment was not up until the end of December, but President Onion had arranged another special leave for him. Onion's recruits said they flew "Onion Air" for these unusual breaks.

Early in the morning of his first day back on campus, Jack drove to the Veterans Hospital. As he made his way up the long driveway, he thought about his many visits there and what Tiemo meant to him. His visits to Tiemo seemed less a choice than the work of magnetism: he was drawn to this man, and to his physical presence and wisdom, like iron filings to a magnet. Tiemo was a link to a father Jack never knew. When Tiemo spoke to Jack, his words touched something very deep in the younger man's soul, words new, yet familiar, traveling across space and time.

Jack parked the car and opened the rear door. He picked up three bags of   coffee and donuts from a shop in town. He carried them through the front entrance and up the stairs to Tiemo's floor. He saw a familiar face, Maureen Connolly, the charge nurse on the floor.

"Jack! So nice to see you back!" She hugged him and smiled.

"Thanks. It was a long trip. I go back in a week or so. How is Tiemo?"

"He's okay. He has some days when he really seems to drift off, somewhere in the past, or at least somewhere far away. Then the next day he seems fine. Physically, he seems the same. But there always seems to be a lot on his mind. He really takes the death of anyone here very hard. I've heard he had quite a war record in World War II, but he never talks about it." She paused and looked quizzically at Jack. "You know, I don't think I've ever asked you or him: Does he have any family?"

"Not that I know of. His wife died many years ago. He doesn't talk about personal things very much."

"Well, the young guys from the College still visit him every Saturday. They almost seem to worship him. And they show up like clockwork, like it's Sunday Mass. He calls them the boys from Asgard, but I don't know why."

Jack laughed. "It's a fraternity at the College. He is a member. A much-loved, I should say revered, member. They are his family, in a way. When you see him leave for a visit to the campus, Asgard Hall is bound to be one of his stops."

"Well, he is very kind to everyone here, no matter their rank, so to speak. Doctors, nurses, secretaries . . . everyone. And now he treats me like a daughter."

"Why do you say, now?" Jack asked, curious.

"I mean, after I told him my brother is in Vietnam."

Jack nodded slowly. "That would be like Tiemo. You know, if there is a time when you need to talk about your brother, or how much you miss him, or how afraid you are, talk to Tiemo. He understands. It's hard to find someone to talk to about these things these days. Everyone would rather ignore the war or fight about it."

She nodded. "That's good to know. I will. Thank you."

Maureen gave Jack another hug. He picked up the coffees and doughnuts and left them at the front desk for the other residents. Then he walked down the hall to Tiemo's room.

Tiemo was seated in his chair by his beside, reading. He looked up.

"Jack, you're back."

"Yes, sir."

"Onion Air?"

Jack laughed. He walked over to Tiemo and shook his hand. Tiemo motioned him to the empty chair.

"How's the work?"

"A lot of problems, Colonel. Do you have some time?"

"For you, always, Jack," Tiemo said.

Jack spoke slowly and carefully about the hamlet evaluation project. Tiemo preferred facts to speeches. He nodded as Jack made each point, as if to record the details in his mind by tape recorder or by engraving them on his mind, like a stone cutter at work on a tombstone. You really couldn't call this listening, Jack thought. This was something more permanent.

"There is another problem with these Vietnamese district chiefs," Jack continued. "They know where the money is coming from—us. They want the money to keep flowing. They know what we want to hear. So they have an incentive to say there is 'high' security in order to qualify for more funds and supplies. Why should the chief tell us that the hamlet is contested by the Viet Cong if that means his funds will dry up?

"And there's one more thing that bothers me, Sir, then I'll wrap this up. I don't like how these reports make the officers evaluate themselves. It seems dumb to me. During his first three months, the new officer is just trying to orient himself. So he continues the old evaluation grades. Maybe then he discovers that the previous guy has painted too rosy a picture. Now the new guy has to downgrade a lot of hamlets on his own watch. So he downgrades. Then all hell breaks loose at HQ, and my bosses all want to know why the hell some hamlets are getting downgraded. The new officer then has to burn his time—in a ninety-hour week—to justify his downgrades. And that's on top of everything else he has to do. And you know what, Colonel? It will be a cold day in-country before that officer downgrades any other hamlet, even if it's crawling with Viet Cong."

Tiemo nodded, this time a long, slow nod, as if to sum up, not as a speaker but as a listener. His manner spoke understanding and reflection, the measurement of what he just heard against a lifetime of training, study, and the crucible of combat. Finally, he spoke.

"Your caution is well-placed, my young friend. When you arrive at these hamlets to assess them, you enter a hall of mirrors. You are not quite sure what you see. Is it a reflection, or the real thing? Do some of the mirrors change the shape of things? Larger, smaller, wider, taller? It is all very hard to comprehend, given the tensions of the moment. We faced the same problems when we moved among the French, behind German lines in '44. Who were the friendlies? Who were the unfriendlies? How could you know which from which?

"These chiefs you meet. How is their English? Do you even think they understand your questions? And do you understand their answers? I'm not talking about translators. Ever heard the phrase 'lost in translation'? You may find yourself lost sometimes, too. We did.

"And your day at the hamlet may be all a show," Tiemo continued, as if he were dictating a memo. "It will be like inspection day at a state prison. The warden invites the governor and top aides. The warden wants to keep the money flowing—like your district chiefs do. So for a week, the inmates get fed steak and the cells get buffed to a shine. The whole place is cleaned, top to bottom. It looks like a cadet's room at West Point. The guards look busy and happy. It all seems to be 'working' when the governor arrives for his walk-through. The governor pats the warden on the back and says it's a 'model' prison. Then the governor leaves. One week later, it's all different. It's worse than Alcatraz again, and the warden reverts to his old mantra: 'The beatings will continue until moral improves.'"

Jack smiled, his eyes locked with Tiemo's.

"I know, Colonel. I know the problems. We just take it day-by-day, meeting to meeting, chart to chart, hamlet to hamlet. We don't talk much about the past or the future, let alone some grand strategy."

"And yet strategy is being made without you, and affecting your work." Tiemo said.

"What do you mean?" Jack asked.

"You have learned something about military intelligence. I am sure that you handle your intelligence with care. That is good. But by now you have also surely learned that your intelligence and conclusions are not the only factors in the final estimates that will emerge. Context is everything. Your superiors and their superiors and their head honchos and their political overlords—all these will supply the context for the final estimates. Their wishes will impose a steady, almost geological pressure downward on your intel, deforming your work with their preconceptions and desired outcomes. They do not want to hear evidence that undermines their beliefs, and they certainly do not want to see the same in writing, which may create a paper trail of dissent in the ranks. They know what they want to hear and they will ignore what they do not want to hear. This is the world of military 'estimates.'"

Tiemo changed the subject. "Meanwhile, the fires are burning here at home, too. President Onion and the governor both think that they are under siege. Sam just escaped that vote at the rink; how he pulled off that tie is beyond me. But the circus at the rink and the takeover of the administration building are really scuttling alumni support. The trustees are wavering, though the governor is solid. He is a trustee, *ex officio*, remember. The president talks tough, but doubts are creeping in: 'How long can this go on?' he asks me. But neither side offers a deal that the other wants. They want ROTC and all the other stuff gone but the president is not willing to bend the College out of shape. As I see it, he has two choices: he can concede on ROTC and Dow Chemical recruiting and all the rest for now, with a pledge that the protests cease. Or he can raise the stakes, arresting people until the students start to run out of money for bail and go home. But no one knows if that will slide the College over a cliff.

"I wish we could get you some help over there, Jack. Recruiting is still a slog. So says President Onion." Tiemo paused. His eyes left Jack and drifted toward the window and the hills, as if he had heard a distant sound. He shook his head, as if to say, 'No, no, no answers out there, not for me.'

"It's not in my nature to second-guess the young guys, Jack. Even the conscientious objectors. Why shouldn't they take the paths open to them? The paths of least resistance. The paths to a safe harbor. I knew what I signed up for. Some of us are born to do these jobs, this dirty work, and some aren't. Some might ask, though, if they're off the hook, why are they turning the campuses upside down? I think I know why. Because they know that some of you are in harm's way. Even while they are spitting on the soldiers who return, that knowledge gnaws at them. They have made their choices, but those choices still bother them. They're safe at home, but others like you are not. Guys their age are dying violent deaths. No wonder they want to tear down the colleges and the government. They want to strike back at the system that has condemned some to death and vouchsafed others. Why wouldn't they work day and night to wreck it?" He paused, shaking his head from side to side, eyes bulging and wild, the black bushy eyebrows arched like bridges. "Who *could* sleep?"

Tiemo bowed his head onto his chest and breathed in slowly, then exhaled one long breath, and gave a sigh.

"I admire you guys who go. You know that. But I worry about your future. I can see the days ahead, long after I'm gone. Vietnam will be over and, God willing, all the Vikings will be home. You'll take your place among your generation and you'll do all of the things that make up a life, the successes, the heartbreaks, and all the rest. But here is what I also see: There will always be a river, a mile wide and a mile deep, dividing the guys who went to war from the guys who did not. And nothing you can do will ever change that fact, or narrow that gap. And you shouldn't even try."

Chapter 3

Rocco had stayed on campus that summer after the end of spring classes. He enjoyed the calm that had briefly returned to the campus and the town. He worked his jobs at the garage and at school during the day, then headed for the river for a swim. The river was quiet in the long, summer evenings. With most of the students gone, he saw only a few single sculls and some fishermen, hanging their lines from the nearby bridge. The river was lower than in the spring, creeping slowly on its long journey from the north country to the sea. Rocco dove in off the dock, swimming as deeply as he could go. He was a strong swimmer and could hold his breath longer than most. He touched bottom, then moved his legs forward to push off the riverbed and back to the surface. The water was dark and cool and Rocco felt blessedly alone. As he pulled himself up onto the boathouse dock, he sat and looked out across the river to the opposite bank and the setting sun, arms folded across his body, his legs still in the water. He felt refreshed, and, for a moment, away from struggles near and far.

When the work from Professor McUsic piled up, Rocco left the river and went back to the engineering school for a long night in the lab. The lab was in a long, rectangular space that ran fifty feet by thirty feet in the sub-basement of the engineering school. Only he and the professor had keys.

At the end of the room were two large tanks, each fifteen feet by twenty feet, raised up one foot from the basement floor. Each was filled with water, discolored by what looked like mud and plants and some type of dark dye. The water was warm to the touch. There was an electric pump on one end of each tank, which circulated the water slowly in the tank. There was drain in the bottom of the tank and an outflow pipe. On the shelves opposite the tank there were large plastic bottles, three feet tall, containing what looked like exotic plants. Five other racks lined the wall from floor to ceiling next to the bottles. These racks held pieces of some sort of communications equipment.

The tanks had been donated by Wesley Sawchuck, Class of 1938, an old friend of the professor and a native of Maine, who had returned to his home after graduation and built the largest lobster company in the state.

"Let me tell you about Wes Sawchuck," the professor said to Rocco one night. "We call him 'The Crazy Uke.' His family was from Ukraine. Their name was Savchuk. They fled the Communists after the Russian Revolution. They were farmers and landed in Central Maine and started growing potatoes.

"Young Wesley wanted no part of the farm. He had a gift. His teachers at the local public high school did not know what to make of him. He arrived at the college like an uncut diamond, different than all those oh-so-polished prep-school boys. Soon, though, the professors knew what they had on their hands. He was odd, but brilliant. His smarts grew out of God's black earth, like the Maine potatoes he left behind. He left here *summa cum laude, Phi Beta Kappa.*

"We've stayed in touch. He stops by from time to time. A while ago he dragged me to the Inn for a long, liquid lunch. If he does that again I plan to be accompanied by a medical professional. Anyway, Wesley heard about our little project from mutual friends. He called me up. "Heard you boys need some tanks. I'll ship them over tomorrow. Now, did I tell you about the 1000-pound sturgeon we caught in the bay last weekend?"

"So here they are," the professor said, pointing to the tanks. "Remember this though, if he stops by, don't pay any attention to that down-East Maine routine. Don't let him fool you. He was a decorated Navy man, in underwater demolition in World War II. He knows his way around dark water, and he knows what we're up to here."

The professor had said surprisingly little about what he and Rocco were "up to" as the weeks sped by. Rocco learned early that the professor preferred distance to intimacy. He gave no grand speeches about a mission, theirs or anybody else's. He explained no connection between their project and Vietnam, or any war, for that matter.

One day that changed. Rocco had stayed late that day in the lab, putting some of the materials on the shelves into the tanks and measuring their resistance to water.

The professor appeared unexpectedly.

"Got a minute, Rocco?"

"Yes, sir.

He motioned toward an old wooden desk and two chairs along a concrete basement wall. "Pull up a chair."

The professor sat down on a hard, old desk chair and motioned for Rocco to do the same. He slid the second chair over to him.

"How are you doing here?"

"Great."

"Pay okay?"

"Better than okay."

"'It's about time I told you what we we're doing in here, I think."

He pulled his chair closer.

"It's about radios. This basement, Rocco, is hallowed ground. Early in World War II, they did some work on radios down here. The OSS needed a lightweight radio that they could carry through Europe without discovery. They spent a lot of time on the so-called 'suitcase radio,' one that looked like a suitcase. Here in this basement they tested transmitters, receivers, aerial wires, headphones, portable tappers, basically all of the key components. The final product was assembled elsewhere, but the key tests were done here.

"Now we're working on radios again, this time the ones they use in Vietnam. There is a radio they use all the time over there in the field. Its Army number is AN/PRC-25. 'AN' is the prefix they use for military electronics. 'PRC' stands for 'portable radio.' The number 25 means it is the twenty-fifth radio that the military has created and widely used.

He walked over to a wooden case on the side of the room

and removed what looked like a large case with dials and knobs.

"Here it is. The PRC-25. You won't be surprised to learn that the soldiers call it the '25' or the 'Prick.' I'll bet you've handled a few cases of beer in your time. Well, the Prick is just about the same size and weighs about the same. A little more, maybe 23 pounds.

"These handles on each side are for transport. Notice that the thing has really two parts, not one. Both are metal. The soldiers call them 'cans.' One is the radio and one is the battery pack. Here are diagrams of the radio."

"What is this second box?" Rocco asked, pointing to the second diagram.

"When it is used in a vehicle or an aircraft, the Prick has a second box attached. That's for a speaker and equipment to convert the system to the one used in the electrical system for the vehicle or, say, the helicopter."

The professor grabbed the radio and placed it so the controls were on top.

"Let's take a look at the controls. On the left is the antenna mount. See the antenna? It looks like the type of tape measure you buy at the hardware store. At the end, though, it has a tube that they use to screw the antenna into the set."

"What's this bag?" Rocco asked, pointing to a canvas bag attached the side.

"Long-range antenna," the professor said. "It screws in the same way for long-distance use. Long-distance use gets you about 18 miles, short-distance maybe three or four. The Prick doesn't like hills, though.

"Look back on the top for the controls. You turn it on with the 'function' switch. 'Squelch' removes the static. You can relay to another radio with the 'retrans' switch. You can set the dials for any frequency, but before they go out they usually do 'presets' at the base, to set you for the main frequency and maybe one other."

"Got it," Rocco nodded. "So where do we come in?"

"We come in because of the damn handset. It works fine

when it's dry. You can hear fine in the earpiece and you can even whisper and be heard into the microphone. But when it gets wet all bets are off. No radio, no communication. Bad things can happen. They need a better one. That's where we come in."

"So that's why the tanks."

"Yes."

"And why all the tests on waterproofing materials that I've been doing."

"Yes."

"And the stuff we've been adding to the tanks?"

"Rivers, swamps, jungles . . . these things need to go everywhere. And it rains all the time. Like you would not believe. It's like trying to live your life in the shower. Nothing ever dries out. Those poor bastards—the RTOs."

"The what?"

"Sorry—it stands for 'Radio Telephone Operator.' He's the go-to radio guy for the unit in the field. He's picked for his technical smarts and his cool under fire. He has to be someone who can step in if the commanding officer gets hit. He is a key part of the team. At night he sleeps close to the officer, the sergeant, and the medic. He never lets the radio get too far away. The radio is monitored all night. And in the daylight he is in a special kind of danger—the antenna makes him a marked man in the field. These are very prized guys in the platoon. And their job is a lot tougher when the damn handsets get wet. But I think I know a way to fix the problem. And I will."

"Got it," Rocco said.

The professor slapped Rocco on the knee and stood up.

"Good man. Any questions as we go along, let me know." He walked to the door of the lab, then turned back to Rocco. "Oh, and Rocco? Welcome to the fight." He turned again, opened the door, and left the room.

Rocco shifted in his chair. He tugged at his watch as he surveyed the room, the tanks, tables, and equipment, familiar to him yet now bearing some new meaning. "Welcome to the fight," the professor had said. "Maybe Clare was right," Rocco said out loud. "Maybe I have decided."

Chapter 4

Jack left Tiemo and drove the short distance from the hospital to his house. As he pulled his Buick into the driveway, he saw Rocco's car. There was a second car parked there, a red Chevy that Jack did not recognize. Jack had been back at the College for a few days but had not seen his roommate. This did not surprise Jack, as Rocco was always on the move, from the garage to class to his engineering projects, moving like a fine racing car, always humming, tank always full, and taking the banked turns at top speed. The ordinary markers of student life—light, dark, morning, night, mealtimes, errands—had no meaning for Rocco's rounds. A marvel, Jack thought. You either want it, or you don't, that's what Tiemo always said about people.

Jack entered the back door to the kitchen, and the screen door slammed shut behind him. Jack saw another young man seated at the kitchen table with Rocco. He was tall, thin, and loose limbed, with long forearms that he had draped over the kitchen table. He had long, thick, black hair that he parted down the middle of his head and held back from his face with a thin red headband. He wore large black glasses that sat on two pointed ears. Jack knew most of Rocco's friends, but didn't recognize this one.

Rocco stood up from the table with a big smile and walked quickly across the kitchen and gave Jack a bear hug, which always placed Rocco's head at about the level of Jack's chest. "How are you, big guy? Welcome home."

Rocco turned toward the table and pointed and said, "Jack, this is Harold Hankey. He's at the engineering school with me. We're talking about a project we're working on for class. Harold, this is Jack Dunne."

Harold did not get up from his chair. He nodded and smiled a half, closed-mouthed smile. "Ah, the famous Jack Dunne," he said. "I've heard a lot about you. Everyone around here has heard of you, I'd say. Football star. Big man on campus. Heard you're a soldier boy, now."

Jack did not smile. Rocco's eyes shifted quickly from Harold to Jack. Oh, shit, Rocco thought. I should have seen this coming. I should have cleared this guy out of here before Jack came home.

"Oh, yeah?" Jack said. "Where you'd hear that?"

"Everybody knows. They know the names of the other guys, too. You're buddy Stewart. The others."

"Nice of you to think of us," Jack said.

Harold grunted. "Not what I meant. We know your names because we can't believe anyone would volunteer to fight in the goddam war."

"We have our reasons," Jack said. Maybe you have your reasons for staying up here in the woods." Harold glared at Jack. "What are you afraid of?" Jack continued. "Getting killed by the Viet Cong? Or are you more afraid of getting spit on by your friends? C'mon Harold, which is it? Does it take more balls to go, or more balls to stay?"

Harold raised his voice. "It's an immoral war. We have no business there. You have no business there. You're a fool. And a tool of the war machine."

"That's for me to decide, Harold. You can sit things out if you want. I'm sure you'll find a way. But the guy sitting next to me over there is taking your place. I'll be sure to tell him you think he's a fool, too."

"Tell him whatever you like. You're both fools."

Rocco stepped between Jack and Harold, who was still sitting at the table. "You know, Harold and I have just wrapped things up. Maybe you should get going, Harold."

Harold grunted again. "Okay. I really don't want to get into it with the soldier boy, anyway."

Rocco quickly picked up the papers on the table and gave them to Harold. "I'll see you at class tomorrow," Rocco said, and motioned Harold toward the door. Jack gave him a menacing glare but let Harold pass. Harold gave Jack a mock salute and stepped out the back door.

Jack looked at Rocco. "Sorry," Rocco said. "I should have known this would happen. Harold's obsessed with the war. I can barely get him to focus on the class, or our project."

"Like everyone," Jack said. "I've heard worse. Like every time I visit Clare."

Jack grabbed two cold drinks from the refrigerator and sat down at the table with Rocco. "So what's new around here?"

"Well, I got a letter from Towny. He's okay, for now. He said he's already seen some bad stuff. His company has already lost guys. He said he's not writing this stuff to his family because they will get too worried. But he's worried, I can tell."

"I think I know where he is. Bad neighborhood."

"I don't think Cliff knows that," Rocco said. "I know he's worried, but I don't think Towny is saying much so far. What a guy Cliff is, though. He subbed for me one morning last week doing the vacuuming at the library. I was up all night in the lab, and he found me stretched out sleeping on one of the long study tables. He tapped me on the shoulder and said 'I got it. I'll wake you when I'm done.' What a guy."

Rocco finished his drink and said, "Hey, got some time? How about some target practice? Good for the nerves."

The backyard of the house opened to a long, gentle hill filled with golden grass waving in the soft summer breeze. Across the hill, an old rail fence stood, a reminder of the farm that once operated on the same ground. Rocco and Jack—in fact, all of Professor McUsic's tenants—enjoyed this view, especially at sunset.

Rocco and Jack used the hill for sports, today some target practice. Rocco stepped out of the back door and bent down to a box of empty beer bottles. He picked up the cardboard box with both hands, recognizing the smell of stale beer. A whiff of the Asgard Hall basement, he thought. Makes me feel right at home, he smiled.

As Jack watched from the yard, Rocco carried the box up the hill and set it down next to the rail fence. He selected a bottle from the box and set it on the flat top rail of the fence. Then he picked up another bottle and set it on the same rail, a foot apart from the first. Then another, and another, until he had placed fifty bottles on the fence, carefully spaced out, as an engineer would. Rocco walked back down the hill with the empty box.

"Ready?" Rocco asked. Jack was standing in the yard holding a large pistol that he had retrieved from the house. "Now remember, one thing: if we run out of bottles, I can always get Harold to come back and stand out there."

Jack burst out laughing. "Don't worry—I've forgotten him already. He's your problem, not mine."

Jack started firing at the bottles, missing a few but hitting most of his allotted twenty-five. "Where did you learn to shoot like that? Are you a soldier boy?" Rocco mimicked Harold with those last words and Jack laughed again. Rocco held his ears as Jack finished his rounds. Blam! Blam! Blam! "We need to get some ear plugs," he said. "Hope the cops don't come again." Rocco took his turn, next, missing more than he hit. "I'm not sure I'm soldier material," he said. When he finished his rounds, Rocco put the pistol back in its case. Jack took a seat on the lawn chairs while Rocco grabbed a couple of drinks from the kitchen.

Rocco returned, handed Jack his drink, and sat down next to him. Jack became serious.

"Any plans yet?" Jack asked.

"Plans for what?"

Jack rolled his eyes. "Rocco . . . ."

"Oh, those plans. No, not yet."

"What's your draft number? Remind me? High, right?" Jack asked, without looking at Rocco.

"Very high. 310."

"Lucky guy."

"I don't think so."

"Why not?"

"It makes it harder for me, I think. Now it really is my choice. The choice is not being made for me. If I had a low number, off I'd go. No choice. But with my number, I have a choice. Go or stay. But I'm wondering about that, too. Is it a choice? Is there any real choice here, true free will? Professor McUsic sometimes talks about what he calls 'subtle coercions'. He says it's a rare individual who actually has and can exercise free choice."

Jack cut him off. "Yeah, tell me about choice. I thought I had one at the time. Did I really choose what I'm doing? If I did, how come I can't say why I'm doing what I'm doing?"

Rocco nodded. "Well, that doesn't seem to help me much."

"You could take my place," Jack said. "Or Stumpo's. Or one of the other guys. We won't be over there forever. The president and professor are begging for guys."

"Maybe. Something's holding me back, though. I'm not sure what."

"Something like the fear of getting killed?"

"For one thing."

"Nothing crazy about fear. We don't go out to Badville much, but when we do . . . well, let's just say it focuses your attention. Learning a few prayers might help. Maybe Father Calamare can give you a few." He paused, and became serious, "But it's the guys like Towny who are really in the shit."

They both thought about that for a moment and said nothing.

Rocco changed the subject. "How are you and Clare?"

"Good question," Jack said. "I'll see tomorrow. Sometimes I think the distance isn't the worst thing right now. Eight-thousand miles might be just the right distance to keep us happy these days. You know how she is. She's always on, always shining, always moving forward. Like you, in a way, but not as quiet. But that passion, up close, in the middle of this mess of a war, it gets wearing, even the little I see her. Even her letters are intense. It's very strange. You're reading this beautiful, flowing cursive handwriting yet you feel that someone is shouting at you. How many letters do you get that use triple exclamation points?"

Rocco laughed. He knew Clare well enough to know that Jack was not exaggerating.

"She's just so intense, especially about the war. It makes me nervous about getting too close. She's like a star . . ."

"Oh, here we go, cue the music . . . ," Rocco interjected, rolling his eyes and tilting his head back.

"No, really. Think of a star. When you're far away, it looks beautiful. If you get too close, it burns you to a crisp. Poof. Ashes. You're gone."

"Well, that's a bit much," Rocco said.

"Don't get me wrong. I care for her very much. I really do. I can't see ever being with anyone else. I've never met anyone like her. When I'm with her I feel something that I never, ever have felt. It's just . . . the war. I feel like there are always three of us . . . Clare, me, and the war."

Rocco said nothing for a while. He was looking away. "Maybe the war's hard for her because she's in love with you."

Jack looked at Rocco but said nothing for a long time. "I won't see you in the morning," Jack said, finally. "I'm out of here early. Maybe I can sneak into Clare's place without getting spit on."

He stood up and looked down at Rocco. "Rocco, my boy, this is getting hard. All of it."

"Agreed," Rocco nodded. "Want to shoot anything?"

Chapter 5

Clare rose early and cleaned her apartment. She was on campus for the summer session but taking only one course and working as an articles editor for the student newspaper, *The Collegian*. She had a class in political philosophy in the morning and an editorial board meeting in the afternoon. Jack would arrive early that evening. She was looking forward to the day and especially the night.

There was time for her to do an errand or two in town. She stopped in a few stores, absent-mindedly looking at clothes, with a vague notion that she could use a new blouse. She found nothing, but stopped in the drugstore and bought a card for Jack's birthday and a scented candle for her room. As she left the drugstore, she looked at her watch. Oh, oh, she thought. Time to go back. The new editor of the newspaper was not kind toward late arrivals at her meetings.

Clare started up the sidewalk back toward campus. She crossed the street at the light and noticed a young couple with two children, a girl by their side, and a boy in a carriage, leaving a playground. The playground was filled with new, brightly colored swings and slides. It was surrounded by rows of flowers. They added a sweet, summer smell to the humid air. The young woman was about thirty, petite with black hair, and round, welcoming brown eyes and a wide smile. The young man looked about the same age, tall and thin, with a dirty blond forelock of hair falling down over his brow. He pushed his hair back off his face as he pushed the carriage out of the playground and onto the sidewalk. They were laughing as they watched the three-year old girl skip along, singing to herself. She was wearing jean overalls with short pants to her knees, pink ankle socks, and white sneakers with rainbows drawn on their sides. Clare overtook them as she picked up her pace toward the school.

"Hello! Beautiful little girl!" Clare said with a smile. "What's her name?"

"Molly," the woman said proudly.

"And one getting a ride from dad?"

"Yes he is!" the woman laughed, and the man nodded. "I'm Laura, and this is Jim."

"Live near here?" Clare asked.

"Green Street, about a half-mile away. We love this playground. It was so nice of the college to build it. And we love the flowers. All the kids come here. Molly calls it the 'New Prayground,' that's how she pronounces it, anyway."

"Cute," Clare said. "Work around here?" She knew she was late but she felt drawn to this happy scene.

"Jim teaches science at the junior high school; I work at the Veterans Hospital. Go to college here?"

"Yes, I'll be a junior in the fall. I'm here for the summer session."

"Major?"

"Political Science."

"A lot to talk about in class, these days, I'll bet."

The father, who had been nodding and smiling, suddenly shifted uneasily on his feet, and tried to get the attention of the mother, as if to say: Careful what you say.

"That's true." Clare said. Clare noticed his unease, so she changed the subject.

"What's the baby's name?"

"Jack. Well, it's John, but we call him Jack. He's named after his grandfather. He was killed in action in World War II."

Clare froze. She stared at the child.

"Is everything all right, Miss?" The mother reached toward Clare.

"Yes, yes, it's just that . . . That's such a nice name."

"We should get home," the woman said, glancing nervously at the man. "Jack needs a nap. Have a nice day, Miss. Oh, I'm so sorry, I didn't ask your name."

"Clare. Clare McUsic."

"Clare. What a beautiful name. Did you know that Clare

means 'bridge' in Gaelic?"

"No, I didn't know that," Clare said quietly.

Clare watched as they crossed the street and reached the far sidewalk. They turned and waved once more.

Clare knew she was late for her meeting now, but she noticed she could not move right away. She stood and stared at the beautiful, happy family, as if she were in a trance. She felt time moving back and forth in her mind, as if all time—past, present and future—had all become visible at once, like three theater stages, each with the curtains up, each commanding her attention. Am I looking at something that I *will* live, she thought? Or just *may* live? What if I don't get to live this scene? She's not that much older than I am now, at least I don't think so. But that life seems so far away right now. Is the man Jack? Is the woman me? I would love a couple of kids like that, she sighed.

She thought about the near future—and Jack's visit that night. Where was it all going? Her mind raced as she thought of Jack, the war, and her plans for a career in Washington. She blinked her eyes, trying to regain the present—her life, at that moment—and shake these visions that had enveloped her mind and pinned her feet to the sidewalk.

Finally, as if moving through water, she turned away from the sight of the family and slowly stepped forward toward the campus, and, with a great effort, started into a trot, headed for the meeting.

The newspaper had offices in the college's Miller Hall, named for a 19th-century benefactor of the college, a newspaper publisher who sent three daughters to the school while he editorialized against granting women the vote. *The Collegian*'s editorial board used an old, wood-paneled conference room on the first floor for its meetings. One end of the room was lined with glass-enclosed cherry bookcases dating to the 19th century. The bookcases held leather bound copies of previous editions of the newspaper. Several busts sat atop the bookcases: Ainslie Eads, the first president of the college, watched warily by Susan B. Anthony, Harriet Tubman, and Eleanor Roosevelt. At the end of one row of bookcases, near the door, stood another work of art, a favorite of the "Style and Humor" section editors: a life-size plaster-of-Paris of Mae West, in all her glory. An editor long ago had hung a placard around the neck of the curved figure. The placard, protruding from West's renowned chest, read: "*The Collegian*: Come Up and See Us Sometime." Twenty racks at the far end of the room held newspapers and magazines from cities across the United States and the world. The best writers at the school competed for prized slots as reporters and editors of this, the oldest women's college newspaper in the country.

The editor, Sarah Brown, sat at the head of the long, polished table, ringed by a dozen crimson leather chairs. She was from outside New York City. She had long, raven-black hair and piercing emerald eyes that could bring any listener, male or female, to their knees. She was tall and rail-thin and had long, shapely legs, legs that, a visitor from Williams had once noted, "she will gladly use to kick you in the balls." Her mother, an alumna of the college, was a Unitarian active in the peace movement. She had already been arrested for disturbing the peace in front of the town hall in her comely suburb outside New York. "*Love* the charge against me," she wrote to Sarah. "*I'm* disturbing the peace? They must be joking. Make sure this gets in my obit. Love, Mother."

After Sarah's first two years on the paper, she was the graduating seniors' clear-cut choice for editor-in-chief, even as a rising junior. If she accepted their offer, she would be the first junior elected editor in the history of the paper. As she mulled the offer, she thought about a new paper that had appeared on campus that winter. Started by two of Sarah's friends, *The Unvanquished* took a much harsher, even revolutionary editorial line, mixing firm opposition to the war with attacks on racism, capitalism, the subjugation of women, and almost every aspect of American life. "*The Unhinged*," the more conservative students called it.

Sarah's friends pleaded with her to join *The Unvanquished* and become its editor as a junior. Sarah shared this news with Clare.

"It's nice to be wanted," Clare said generously, but cautiously. "A choice of two editor's jobs, and as a junior, no less. You know, this reminds me of Robert E. Lee."

"The slave-owning traitor?"

"The general, I meant." Clare pressed on. "At the start of the Civil War, Lincoln offered him the command of the Union Army. He turned it down out of loyalty to his native State, the Commonwealth of Virginia."

"So you're saying I should stay with *The Collegian*?"

"I'm saying that you can follow your heart, or your head. It's your choice."

Several weeks later, Clare heard that Sarah had followed her head. A long line of editors of *The Collegian* had landed plum jobs in journalism and the large publishing houses of New York. Bomb throwing has its place, Clare thought, but business is business. Sarah was a zealot, but she was no fool.

The Collegian's early editorials on the war were cautious, with a restraint reflecting both pacifism and sadness as the killing surged in Vietnam. But in the spring and early summer session of 1970, with Sarah at the throttle, the editorials changed tone, first to anguish, then anger, then open rebellion. The Kent State shootings set even the staid old, conservative campus in South Tapley on its head. "End the Killing," one new headline demanded. "Divest Dow." "Dump Nixon." At the college's spring commencement, most of the students openly protested the war, wearing black armbands and mortarboards bearing peace signs. Some bore the Vietcong flag.

Members of the college board of trustees—particularly the males—took note of the trend at *The Collegian* and complained to the president. But the tradition at the college was that the paper's editorial judgments were kept free of college control. That principle would be tested soon.

Clare arrived a minute late for the meeting. As she opened the heavy, creaking wooden door to the conference room, she breathed in the scent of smoke that filled the room. She drew a withering glance of disapproval from Sarah. The younger members held their breath, expecting a volcanic eruption. There was a collective sigh of relief when Sarah, with curled lip, said nothing and took a drag from her signature cigarillo.

Sarah picked up the agenda with one hand and, with the other hand, her pen, a black fountain pen with a gold-plated nib that was passed down from editor to editor at a yearly ceremony. It was said by generations of editors to be equally useful in signing formal letters and prodding the staff.

The agenda was typed on a single piece of paper, a crisp bond, with the logo of *The Collegian* on the top. It read: "Item 1. Photographs on First Pages of a Future Edition. Discussion."

"You all know of the *Life Magazine* issue last year," Sarah began. "The 217 faces of soldiers killed in action they published? The title of the article was 'One Week's Dead.' I want us to do the same on our front page and the next few pages of an edition in July. I want photos of all of the dead from Western Massachusetts. Just like *Life Magazine*."

"What will be in there other than the photos?" a senior reporter asked.

"Name, age, branch of service, rank, and hometown. Like in *Life*."

"Will their parents know we are doing this?"

"We will get the photos from them or their friends."

Several pursed their lips as if to say, Oh, no. Around the table, several instantly realized that they would be assigned to make the calls to the families. In that moment, the war seemed to creep closer to their lives.

"Does anyone object to my plan?" Not expecting dissent, Sarah stared confidently out the large, palladian windows to the campus quad beyond. The summer afternoon sun had suddenly given way to dark, ominous clouds.

Objections are not likely, Clare thought. Except for mine. She raised her hand and caught Sarah's eye.

"Clare? Do you have an objection?"

Clare blushed but gathered her composure and spoke slowly and firmly. "I am concerned about the families and friends of the soldiers still over there. There are some families and friends in this town, right here in South Tapley. Their sons are over there. How will they feel if we run these pictures? Shouldn't we take their feelings into account before we do this?"

Sarah nodded slowly, not revealing her reaction, not at first. "Know anyone like that, Clare?" Sarah asked slyly, as if she were moving a chess piece into a "checkmate" position.

"I do. The families will think that their boy's next. It will scare the hell out of them."

Sarah put down her paper and pen and took a drag from her cigarillo. "Well, that's the point, isn't it? Isn't that what *Life* was trying to do? Scare the living hell out of everyone? Get them off their asses and into the streets to stop this war? That's our job, isn't it? To shake things up? To afflict the comfortable?"

"You think they're comfortable?" Clare shot back, as the younger members of the group held their breaths. "Sitting home waiting for an officer in uniform and a priest, or a minister, or a rabbi, to knock on your door and tell you that you've lost your son and your world is gone?"

Sarah was taken aback, but only for a moment.

"You know what I mean, Clare. Their comfort is in the fact that they are not trying to end this war sooner. Their comfort is their tacit support for this government and this war, the war that may, yes, end in the killing their sons."

"But why this way? With the pictures? Why now? Why do you want to use these poor men in this way?"

"The people need to see the faces. There's no better way to do it."

"But at what cost? You're using them, Sarah, using their faces, their memories, for your own political goals, or the newspaper's goals. The war isn't their policy. They were drafted. Or they volunteered. Who knows why? But why drag them into your war on the war? Why not keep them out of it?"

"They're already in it, one way or another, dead or live, whether they like it or not," Sarah replied. "Like we're all in it. And I'm sorry to say, they will always be in it, as casualties of an unjust and immoral war. So if their pictures can change things, I say we go with the pictures."

She looked around the table, chin extended well over the side of the table. "Any further discussion?"

At the far end of the table, one freshman whispered to another: "Clare's boyfriend's in the Army. In Vietnam." "No!" whispered the other, but not quietly enough.

"Ladies!" Sarah exploded, and pounded her fist on the table. "Could you please shut your poor little mouths and save the pitiful trivia on your lips for your next pointless talk in the cafeteria?" She glared at them for what seemed like days. The two freshman sunk in their chairs, nearly sliding under the table, a place that that they dearly wished to be. They had already endured many of Sarah's outbursts and commands, causing them to doubt their choice of career.

The room was silent.

"Any other objections?" She glanced quickly at Clare. "Then it's settled. We are going to run the photos. Assignments will follow. Meeting adjourned." Without a smile, she re-lit her cigarillo and shook the match like she was cutting off someone's hand.

Clare made her way out of the room without looking at Sarah. She spoke to no one, and headed straight to the front door of the building. She nearly tripped as she descended the granite steps. For the second time that day, she felt dizzy, her head spinning. Low gray clouds had covered the campus and a light summer rain had bounced blankets of mists off the walkways leading from the building to the street. Her vision blurred with the rain and she lost sight of the walkway. Peels of thunder sounded overhead, crackling into Clare's ears and reaching deep into her mind. A flash of lightening in the sky in front of her caused her to gasp and stumble. She held out her hand for balance, as she inhaled drops of rain and began to choke and cough. Another loud clap of thunder boomed. Is this what artillery fire sounds like, she wondered, as she stumbled on? The sound that bombs make when they drop, pulverizing the earth and the people on it? Is this what war is like? Clare struggled again to keep her balance. Oh, God, where am I?

Chapter 6

Jack rose early and packed his duffle bag for the trip south to South Tapley. He left a note for Rocco: "Nice shooting, yesterday, pardner. But your new friend is a load. Watch your back with him. See you in '71. Kinsmen to kinsmen should be true, Jack. "

Jack pointed the Buick up the ramp and onto the interstate, headed for South Tapley, and who knows what, he thought. With only a couple days of leave left, am I headed south for fun, or more trouble?

Jack's mind wandered as he viewed the rural, almost pastoral scenes that lined both sides of the highway. He saw red barns and lush green fields. Several high peaks loomed to his right, some with the open spaces of dormant ski trails. Some peaks had their lifts running for summer tourists to enjoy the views.

These were not the large, wide-open farms he knew from his native Iowa. Here, the early settlers had faced rocky soil, jagged hills, and a harsh winter. They must have been tough people, Jack mused, to get up here in the first place. They must have hacked their way up the old dirt trails, inching up the riverbanks, or pushed up against the southbound current of the river on crude boats. What were their dreams? What words did the endless green trees on the shores of this great blue river speak to them in the deep silence of their journey north? Could they possibly see what two-hundred years would bring to this valley?

Jack was thirsty and pulled off the interstate onto the long, winding two-lane that hugged the river. When he reached a traffic light he turned left over an old stone bridge that spanned the river at a narrow point. As he crossed the bridge he saw to his right a six-story old brick factory building, planted firmly against the river, the primal source for the water that had powered the mill. Painted on the red brick of the side of the factory were ten-foot high, worn, letters spelling the name of its former occupant:

"Remington Arms Co." Someone had draped a bed sheet from the roof of the same building with a newer message: "Peace Now."

After he grabbed a drink, Jack headed out of town, deciding to stay on the back road for a while and rejoin the interstate later. As he climbed the hill out of town, he passed a dozen imposing brick homes, built by the early mill owners and town founders, placed to ensure oversight, literal and figurative, of the town, its officials, and the mills.

Reaching the crest of the hill and heading south, he saw that his gas gauge was low and pulled off the road in to a Gulf station. He rolled slowly up to a row of pumps. A young boy of about sixteen came out of the office and walked around the front of Jack's old Buick. He was a red-haired boy with freckles on his face and his arms.

"Fill it, sir?"

"Yes, sir," Jack smiled.

"Where'd you get the Iowa plates?"

"Iowa," Jack said, laughing.

"What are those funny-looking things on the plates?"

"Ears of corn, wise guy," Jack smiled.

As the boy filled the tank, Jack glanced at the station. On the outside wall next to the door, he saw a small American flag above a small white sign which read, in red, white and blue letters: "Support Our Troops." In the office, he saw a young, well-built man about thirty years old. Like the boy, he had red hair and freckles on his face and arms.

Jack took a guess. "That your older brother inside?"

"Yes, sir. It's his station," the boy said proudly. "He bought it after he came back from the war."

"The war?"

"Yes, sir."

"Vietnam?"

"Yes, sir. He was in the Marines."

Jack looked back at the red-haired man, who was seated at his desk, looking through some papers. He wore a blue mechanic's jump suit with a orange "Gulf" patch on his left sleeve.

Jack paid for the gas and gave the boy a good tip. "Well, I'm glad he's home."

"Me, too," the boy said.

Jack pulled back out onto the road and drove for a few miles. There were very few houses on this stretch, only endless woods. His windows down, Jack smelled the summer forest, full of the aroma of pine needles and the beginnings of an evening mist rising from the river. He heard a long whistle of a freight train from tracks that curved along the riverbank below the road. Jack cut the corner as the road took a sharp turn toward a bridge, which crossed over the railroad tracks and the river and eased back onto the Vermont side. He had another two hours to go.

It was dusk when Jack approached South Tapley. In the sky about the town he saw clouds in thin lines across a full, rising blood-red moon, like the lines of musical scales. Jack turned down the main street and came to a stop at College Street, which bordered the front of the campus. In front of him was the main entrance to the campus. The entrance was flanked by two thirty-foot-tall brownstone turrets. A Grecian urn capped each turret. High across the entrance, extending from the top of one turret to the other, was an intricate arch of wrought iron. In the middle of the arch, the name of the college was woven into the metal design and highlighted with gold leaf.

Jack turned left on College Street and right into the entrance for the student parking lot, a short walk to Clare's house on the outskirts of the campus. He put his car in the far corner of the lot, where the campus police would be less likely to look for a parking sticker. He grabbed his green duffle bag and a small backpack from the trunk and closed the door. He could see Clare's house in the distance as he started up the paved hill back to College Street. To his left he saw dormitories with white objects hanging from the room windows. As he got closer, he saw bed sheets and blankets with writing on them: "Stop the War." "Peace Now." "Stop the Draft. "Ho Will Win."

Jack knocked on the front door of the house. One of Clare's

housemates answered the door and let Jack in. Without a word to Jack, she turned and yelled upstairs for Clare.

Jack said nothing and started quickly up the stairs. He saw Clare at the landing, where the stairs turned to go to the second floor.

"Jack!" He ran up the rest of the stairs and grabbed and lifted her in the air, turning her round and round. He lowered her to the floor and gave her a long kiss.

"It's been so long, Jack. I've missed you so much."

"I've missed you too, Clare. A lot."

She took his arms and wrapped them around her tightly. "C'mon, time for us to catch up."

———

Later, Clare grabbed two cold drinks from her small refrigerator and handed one to Jack. They sat down on Clare's couch.

"So, how was jail?" Jack smiled.

"Lovely. And Judge Scruton, he was a real doll. Almost threw me back in the cooler when I started mouthing off."

Jack smiled again. "Ever seen the judge before?"

"No, and I hope I don't again."

"His son is a Marine. He was wounded, pretty bad, last year. He's in a Veteran's Hospital in Philly."

"I didn't know that," Clare said, stunned for a moment. She nodded slowly and narrowed her eyes. "Well, that explains a few things about the injunction, the arrests, and the kangaroo court, I'd say. I'm sorry about his son. But we had a point to make and I think we made it. He didn't like the point."

"I'm sure you made your point," Jack said. "You're Clare."

"I will take that as a compliment, Mr. Dunne," she smiled. "And you know what else?" She pulled her head back and stood up straight.

"What?"

"We matter."

"Who?"

"Women. In the protests, on the streets, in the newspapers, we matter. We matter at all the colleges. We have roles. We plan the protests. We write. People read our stuff. People—even men—even professors, listen to us. We're out front. Look at the photos lately: women are everywhere, in the lead. And we're not going back, after all this is over. We're going forward. You'll see. We will run things, big things."

"Why not? Jack said. "The guys have been screwing things up for a while, and pretty badly. Take a look at the war."

Clare was slightly surprised at his response. "My point exactly," Clare said, nodding her head up and down quickly.

"I saw the bedding hanging out the windows. I'll have to tell Stumpo," Jack deadpanned. "Without their blankets and sheets, some of his old girlfriends might be cold this winter. It's a shame we can't send you some heat from Hell. We have plenty."

"Funny," Clare said, without laughing.

"I had a pretty rough day yesterday. Remember Sarah from the cafeteria? My editor at the paper?"

"The one who doesn't like me drinking Coke?"

"Very funny. She tore my head off at our editorial board meeting."

"What about?"

"I'm not sure you want to hear. Well, you know the *Life Magazine* article with the pictures of all of the guys killed in action in a week?"

"Yes, I heard about it."

"She wants to do the same in the *Collegian*."

"Great."

"I raised some questions. She didn't like it."

"I'll bet she didn't. When she put it to a vote, did she say 'All those opposed signify by saying 'I resign'?'"

"Not quite, but almost. It's not a democracy on the newspaper, by the way. There are no votes. Far from it."

An hour passed. Clare continued to talk about the meeting but did not mention her harrowing exit or her tears. "That's

enough," she said, finally. "To bed." It was midnight and Clare's
rooms were nearly dark. She got up from the couch and walked
to her dresser. A thin and delicate shaft of light pierced a hole in
her drapes and entered the room, casting her in silhouette as Jack
watched from the couch. He had been a long time gone, but not
long enough to forget Clare's body, so fit and taught. It looked
geometric, the lines from the outside point of her straight, wide
shoulders to her waist and back out to her hips like two sides of
a scalene triangle. This was a sculpture of stone, not organic
growth, her admirers agreed. How, exactly, could such a woman
walk, built, as she was, like a cut-glass vase? And delicate like a
vase, too, Jack thought, as he sat in the darkness.

———

In the middle of the night Jack awakened suddenly to the
sound of Clare crying. His watch read 2 a.m. In the light from
the streetlight outside, he could see Clare sitting up and holding
her head in her hands. Her shoulders heaved as she sobbed.

"Clare, what's wrong?"

She continued to sob and could not speak. Finally, she calmed
and wiped the tears from her eyes.

"I dreamed, I dreamed, I dreamed . . . ." She sobbed and
wiped her eyes again. "I dreamed we did the photos for the
newspaper and your . . . your . . . your face was in them."

Jack held her head tightly against his chest. Sweat drenched
her face and neck. Her hair was tangled around her head in a
wet ball. He pushed her hair gently back from her red face.

"It's okay, it's okay Clare. It was only a dream, okay? Only
a dream. I won't be in those photos. Look at me." He held her
by her shoulders until their eyes met. "I won't be in the photos."

Clare sighed the longest sigh Jack had ever heard.

"Look at me," he said again. "I refuse to have my picture in
The Collegian. Rocco and Stumpo would never let me forget it."

She smiled through her tears and nestled her head on his

chest. He kissed her softly on her forehead.

"Thank you," she whispered. "I love you so much."

———

Jack and Clare rose early the next morning. Neither said a word about Clare's dream. Jack put his things in his small backpack. When they were ready to go for a walk, Jack asked:

"Do you know where my duffle bag is?"

"No, I thought you brought it in."

Jack looked around the room and in the closet.

"No, now I remember. I left it in the hall."

Jack opened the door and looked down at the bag. There was a red "peace" sign painted on one side of the green bag.

Jack shook his head but said nothing. He brought the bag back inside the room and held it in his hands for Clare to see.

"Downstairs neighbor," Clare said. "She's crazy."

"You know who did this?"

"Pretty sure I do."

"Well, I guess it's back to the war for me this morning. Even when I'm home, when I'm here with you, it kind of follows me around. You'd think there would be some kind of safe harbor here, in your own house. But I guess not." Jack shrugged. "And how about you? Are you safe with these crazies all around? What's the penalty for fraternizing with the enemy? And I don't mean the Viet Cong. I mean me. Let's get out of here," he said, shaking his head. "I'll put my stuff in the car. I wonder what they did to the car. Not that it couldn't use a paint job."

Clare closed the door to her room behind her and they descended the stairs together. No one around, Clare thought. Thank God.

They walked to the pond at the center of campus. The pond was snowman-shaped and fed by a stream. Across the middle of the pond, where it narrowed, was an old stone bridge. Low whitewashed post and beam fences lined the walkway leading to the bridge. The bridge arched over the water to allow rowboats and kayaks to pass. Twenty-five vertical keystones held the horizontal stones of the arch in place. As the stepped onto the bridge Jack noticed a bronze plaque but he did not stop to read it. They stopped in the center of the bridge.

"Sorry about your bag," Clare said.

"You get used to it," Jack said. "Why even talk about it? We're the unwanted guests back here at home. I guess they want us to feel smaller. They want to see shrinkage. They want us to disappear. We're reminders, in flesh and blood, of what they want to forget. Or maybe they're like your dream: when I walk in the room they ask themselves, is he the next man to die?"

"Don't say that."

"Alright, but maybe they think, does he know the next man to die? Or did he know the man who died last week? I don't think they hate me. I'm just a symbol of a war they hate. They want the war to be over, so they don't have to think about it anymore, not one minute more. Anyway, this is mild stuff, the bag, stuff like that. Like you're friend in the cafeteria, the lovely Sarah, knocking over my drink. This is mild stuff. Hear what they do to soldiers getting off planes back in the States, in uniform? They spit on them."

"Why would anyone wear his uniform on the way back home?"

Jack paused for a moment. This was not the response he was expecting, or the response he had hoped for. He knew the answer to Clare's question, but in the seconds before he spoke he felt something become very clear in his mind, as if water had turned instantly to ice. Clare's question gathered all of his worries and frustrations into one simple sentence. There it was, the divide that Tiemo had warned Jack about, "between those who had gone to war and those who hadn't." "There will be a gap, a mile wide . . .," Tiemo, who had seen war, had said to Jack. Amen, Jack thought.

Jack struggled to stay calm and answer Clare patiently. "Why are they wearing uniforms when they arrive?" Jack began.

"They were drafted. Some of them haven't had civilian clothes for a long time. Or they were never in places where they could wear them. They have to fly home in their uniforms. So they fly thousands of miles, finish their trip at a civilian airport, walk into the terminal, and someone spits in their face and screams 'Baby-Killer'!"

Clare said nothing. They stood side by side, leaning against one wall of the bridge. "Well, okay," she said. "Now I get why. And I think that it's wrong to treat them like that. They don't deserve it." She threw up her hands. "We've talked about this a lot, Jack. We write back and forth. I still don't know why you volunteer to do this. And now Rocco tells me you might sign up for another tour."

"I have thought about all this, more than you know," Jack replied. "Your friends, they think we like killing people. We don't. We don't hate the people we're fighting. And you know what? We really don't love all the people we're fighting *for* there, either, at least not their government. Your friends think we do it for some vision of America, for the people back home. But I don't see how the people back home come out better or worse in all of this, except for the sons they lose." He paused for a long while. "I know you think I might be doing this because of the older guys who knew my father. I'm not. It's about me, not them. About my future, not their past."

"And not your father's past?" Clare asked, looking closely at Jack for his reaction.

"No. Those memories of him—those memories are theirs, not mine. This is about my future."

"Well, I'm not so sure," Clare said. "You sure know a lot about him, at least from them. I still don't know as much as I'd like to know about my mother. My father barely mentions her. I think he talks more about your father than my mother. How do you think that feels? To be constantly compared to someone long gone, but still in the dark about her. It's like being robbed of my time together with her—twice." She paused for a moment. "Well, I guess we both miss them in our own ways. Are we trying to live up to an ideal of someone who is gone? I wouldn't deny that if I were you." She took his hand. "So where does that leave you, and where does it leave us?"

Jack looked at her but did not meet her eyes. "I still might re-enlist when my hitch is up in December. I don't know exactly why. It's not like there are a lot of people my age to talk to about this. I thought I could talk to you." He looked away. "Maybe not."

"That's not fair, Jack," she said, raising her voice and pointing a finger at him. "We have talked, a lot. I keep thinking of ways to help you, you know, to help you decide. But you're not the easiest person to talk to. My friends here call you 'The Unknown Soldier'. Sometimes you're like a planet far, far away. That's it—you're planetary. You don't orbit in a circle, you orbit in an ellipse . . . you're elliptical. Sometimes you're close, then you're far. You rotate, so sometimes we can see you, then we can't. Sometimes you reflect light, sometimes you don't. When you do, you light up a room. When you don't, you're as dark as outer space. Sometimes you're hot, sometimes you're cold. You turn on your own axis, but no one knows what your axis is. No one knows what the hell drives you, what makes you go over there, what makes you tick. Is it an idea? Is it duty? Is it memory? You don't tell anyone. Ever. I'm not sure you know yourself."

Clare looked at him, so sternly that Jack cringed. "And that's why you like Rocco—he never calls you on anything, anything at all."

Book V

Chapter 1

Jack's plane touched down in Vietnam in late July, 1970. The ride from the airport seemed longer this time. He spent less time looking out the window than during earlier trips. The sprawling city had become all too familiar, its sights now a reminder of where he was, not a preview of a strange and dangerous new world. He stared straight ahead at the seat in front of him and reflected on his trip home. He silently ticked off the names of those he had visited and others that lingered on his mind. Not one of the people he loved seemed stable. He imagined each in a rocking motion, to and fro, buffeted by events like a buoy bouncing in a wind-blown harbor. Tiemo, Rocco, Clare. Each seemed beset in their own way: Tiemo, by the forces of change; Rocco, by his doubts; and Clare, caught between the loudest protestors, and, Jack admitted, her love for him. Jack thought suddenly of Towny, too, and felt guilty that he and his friends knew an even younger man in greater danger.

In the next few weeks, Jack struggled with his work and his endless reports on conditions in the hundreds of hamlets assigned to his group of analysts. He felt fit, but his focus often wandered. Not even evenings with the irrepressible Stumpo could shake him from his lethargy.

Three weeks after his return, the war snapped him back to attention. The captain had ordered Jack's group to make a new round of visits by helicopter to remote hamlets for closer inspection. The captain's briefing was scheduled for the next morning and their departure early the morning after that.

Jack spent a restless night before the briefing. Clare's face appeared to him as he drifted in and out of sleep in the pungent, humid air. In a dream, she recounted to Jack the same college debate at *The Collegian* over publishing the faces of the war dead. At the end of the dream, she was crying. He awoke suddenly, in a sweat.

When Jack rose the following morning, he felt tired and light-headed. He dressed as if in a trance and opened the door of his room. He nearly ran into Stumpo as he exited into the hall.

"What's new in the war business this morning?" Jack asked.

"Nothing. It's still a very dirty business," Stumpo said. "And getting dirtier by the minute."

"I know. It's going to get a little messier for me soon."

"Why?"

"We're headed back out for some on-sight looks at the hamlets tomorrow."

"Oh," Stump said, serious for a moment, an uncommon state for him. "Well, . . ." He did not finish the sentence.

"Yeah, I know," Jack said. "I will."

Jack gave Stumpo a quick half-smile and turned away and walked out the door at the end of the barracks. He crossed the compound to a concrete building with offices and conference rooms. He slid into his usual seat at the back of the briefing room and closed his eyes for a minute, hoping to grab a moment of rest before the captain entered. Jack was jolted awake by a slamming door and the sound of heavy boots on the wooden floor of the room.

"Good morning, gentlemen. I hope that you are all ready for some fieldwork tomorrow. We leave at 0800." The captain looked around the room for reactions. Some of these guys look more ready for action than others, the captain thought. He frowned. "Here are some things that might help you get the information we need and keep you from getting killed.

"First, when you get to the hamlet, keep your revolver where they can't see it.

In each household, find and talk to one adult. Make it a conversation. It's not supposed to be a cross-examination. You have to try to make them feel relaxed. You are supposed to be their friend, an ally. If they try to challenge you, or your authority, don't respond. Keep talking about what's going on there and what you're trying to find out. Keep your cool, and don't vary the sound of your voice.

"Do not touch any objects. Don't eat or drink anything that they give you. Nothing. Don't touch the women or the girls. Do I make myself clear on this? Do I?" He was shouting now, jolting Jack from his sluggishness. "Treat them like your sisters. If I hear that any of you have fooled around with the women, I'll kick your ass from one end of this sorry country to the other.

"Stay focused. Read the questions off the sheet if you have to. What's been happening in the hamlet? That's what we need to know.

"Don't trust the translators. Some of them are sloppy. Others have divided loyalties. Vietnam is their country, not ours. Keep looking in your subject's eyes. You've heard the phrase 'Lost in translation,' haven't you? Well, I don't want you to lose anything in translation, not the information we need, and not your life.

"Don't trust anyone, even when you can understand them. They will play you. Don't you see the game? They know what we need to know. But they also know what the Americans like to hear. They know we're the big cow—the money comes from us, for buildings, food, everything. They want to keep sucking the cow's milk. So they'll tell you that the hamlet is secure as the White House because that's how they'll get more milk. Why should they tell us that the Viet Cong comes through the hamlet every night if it means they'll get shut off from the cow?"

"You won't feel comfortable there, even when you've done this a few times. If you feel comfortable, it means your guard is down. That's bad. We don't want that. We want you on the balls of your feet."

He looked to the back of the room. "Right, Dunne? You've been out there, right?"

"Yes, sir," Jack said.

"You'll feel like you're not understanding anything they say, even in English," the captain continued. "You'll feel like you can't trust anyone there. I repeat, for you new guys: This is not easy. No one knows who the friendlies are. They all look alike out there, have you noticed?"

He paused. "Questions?" There were sideways glances, but no questions.

There are plenty of questions, especially from the new guys, Jack thought. But no one dares ask.

"Gentleman, I don't like this piecemeal approach anymore than you do," the captain said. "I ask myself all the time: Why are we fighting this war hamlet by hamlet? Won't we all die here of old age even if the Viet Cong or the North Vietnamese don't get us first?"

Here we go, Jack nodded to himself. Wait 'til the new guys hear this rant.

The captain started to pace around the front of the room. "I've been thinking. Let me try this out on you. Maybe we should try to fight the whole goddam country at once. You know, go whole hog. Maybe we are bombing the wrong end of the country, up there in the north. Maybe we should all leave on ships, circle south, and land from the ships on the southern shore of the country. You know, invade. Then march all the way up to the north, all the way to the Chinese border, and take the whole country prisoner. Build a stockade fence around the country. Then pave over the whole thing, south to north. With giant road graders and asphalt trucks from a good old US company like Caterpillar. Lots of jobs for everyone. What do you think?" He stuck out his chin and looked around the room. "Huh? Anyone with me?"

The captain paused to gauge if the new recruits thought he was serious or crazed. He had a reputation for loose talk, and, like most reputations, it was informed by facts. He saw only eyes filled with amazement or staring at the floor.

"That's all, gentlemen, see you at 0800 tomorrow. And gentlemen? Try to come back in one piece."

Chapter 2

The next morning, Jack boarded a UH-1 "Iroquois" helicopter known as a "Huey." Whenever Jack heard the name "Iroquois," he thought of the Native American tribe by the same name, the tribe that had conquered the Abenaki who lived in the river valley near his college. The name was chosen, he guessed, for the tribe's taste for war. The Hueys were made for a helicopter war.

Jack, a lieutenant from his group, and two others climbed into the chopper. It was already filled with its four-man crew: a pilot and co-pilot up front at the controls and two door machine-gunners. Before Jack's first mission in the field, he was told about the chopper pilots by a friend: "They are confident, almost cocky, but competent to a fault. Watch the way they check their instruments, gear, and crew before take off. They check it all. Every time. No exceptions. They learn early that flying is not inherently dangerous, but it is extremely unforgiving of mistakes. In combat, though, you want these guys. They act decisively. They don't stall their decisions. Sometimes they have only a split second to react."

One door gunner was the crew chief. Before the engines started, he had been silently puffing on a small cigar with a plastic tip. As he checked his weapon one of the newcomers asked him "What's with the tip on the cigar?" "In this hell-hole," the gunner replied, "I need to keep both hands free."

Everyone on board wore body armor known as "chicken plates," ceramic held against the body with Velcro. For the first-timers, the guns and the plates flagged the imminent danger. The copters often flew low, as low as the tree tops, exposing them to enemy ground fire and, worse, rocket-propelled grenades.

As the twin engines opened up, Jack heard the familiar whirring sound of the main and tail rotor blades, the chop, chop, chop that also reminded Jack of a beating heart. He heard a second wave of sound coming from a helicopter gunship that would accompany them on their flight.

In minutes they were airborne, headed to the first hamlet. They climbed first over the lush green canopy, then out over large rice paddies, flying about 500 feet from the ground. Jack saw the familiar tree lines dividing the rice paddies, lines that eventually would lead to their first stop.

"Those tree lines, very dangerous," the crew chief and gunner to Jack's right yelled to the newcomer in the back. "Keep your heads down!"

Just as he finished yelling, small arms fire broke out from the trees. "Okay, boys here they come!" the chief yelled. Jack's heart beat hard against his chest, pounding up against his chicken plate. This was not the first time he had taken fire on a mission to the hamlets, but it never felt routine. The gunners began returning fire from the side-door machine guns, cursing as they fired.

There was a loud boom from the back of the chopper. "Tail rotor!" Jack heard the co-pilot yell. Bullets tore into the engine casing above him. He smelled smoke and oil. The chopper dipped and swerved to the left, nose down, toward the ground. A rice paddy loomed but the pilot steered the chopper over the paddy and onto drier land, near a grove of trees. The chopper slammed into the muddy ground at an angle, nose first. Jack and the others lurched forward in the fuselage. He lost his balance and slammed his head against a metal object inside. He lay on the floor, dazed, still smelling the smoke and oil seeping in. He raised his head and looked toward the front. The pilot's head hung forward against the panel, twisted in an unnatural way. The co-pilot was alive and yelling on the radio, "Mayday," calling in their location and casualties for a medevac chopper—the helicopter ambulance.

Jack gripped the floor and tried to move. The side of his head had already swelled badly. He touched it and felt his hair caked with blood. As he looked from the floor, he saw only one gunner: did the other land outside the chopper? He heard no one from his group of four moving in the back. The co-pilot had finished his call and sank back into his seat, holding his ribs and breathing hard.

Their companion gunship hovered over the crash sight but could not land. A soldier from the gunship started to descend down his lift line, but the wind from the propeller of his chopper blew him from side to side over the tops of the trees. The gunship moved forward fifty yards beyond the crash scene and landed.

Within fifteen minutes, the medevac chopper arrived over the site of the crash. It made a tight, high-speed approach onto the small patch of land alongside the downed chopper. A medic jumped out of the chopper and raced toward the wreck. He saw the small flame coming from the twin engines on top. He knew that the flame might engulf the wreck at any moment. He heard small-arms fire coming from the tree line. He knew that he had little time: his crew aimed to spend only thirty to sixty seconds on the ground for the rescue.

The medic examined Jack's head. Jack was barely conscious. The medic quickly moved on to the other casualties. The pilot was dead, that was certain. The co-pilot was breathing. The men in the rear of the chopper had been tossed about like beanbags and slammed against the fuselage. All were alive but not mobile. The four medics moved the dead pilot and the injured soldiers to the medevac, carrying their bodies on stretchers across the open ground. As soon as the chopper rose, the medics began their treatment. They would be landing again soon, but every second counted in their high-stakes jobs. Jack felt the chopper lift and heard the welcome sound of the chop-chop-chop of the rotor blades. He thought of his mother, then Clare. Then he lost consciousness.

———

The compound protecting the evacuation hospital sat on a bluff on a river bend, overlooking a wide ribbon of slow-ly moving water. The hospital was not far from the fighting;

there was no "front" or "rear" in this part of Vietnam. The wounded were lifted directly from the battlefield to the hospital. Most of them arrived within fifteen minutes after pickup by a medevac chopper in the field. Some were near death and could not be moved farther to the rear for care in a safer place.

The compound was ringed by a tall, barbed-wire fence. Outside the fence lived other casualties of war: the Vietnamese from the countryside who had left their own homes to flee the fighting. Men, women, and children squatted in hundreds of wooden huts next to the hospital, desperate for food, safety, and medical care. A mission statement for the hospital was scrawled on a whitewashed wooden board near the entrance to the compound. It read:

SUPPORT THE U.S FORCES, VIETNAM
FREE WORLD ASSISTANCE FORCES,
AND CIVILIAN WAR CASUALTIES.
TREAT ALL CLASSES OF PATIENTS
WITHIN CAPABILITIES.
CONSERVE THE FIGHTING STRENGTH.

A tall guard tower at each corner of the compound kept watch over the chaos outside and in.

Twenty Quonset huts formed the spine of the compound. The huts held rooms for surgery, treatment, and recovery. Each recovery hut held sixty beds. The beds had only one setting for height and were made of heavy steel. Nurses raised a patient's head by lifting one end of the bed and putting something under its feet. Electric generators powered hospital lights and equipment. Water came from wells for bathing, laundry, sterilization, and toilets. Larger latrines were built off the ground outside with steps leading above and with large tanks below. Each evening the tanks were carted away, filled with incendiary liquid, and lit on fire outside the compound. The smell often mixed with the damp night air and wafted back over the huts outside and the barracks within. Extending from the spine of Quonset huts there were a few dozen low slung, makeshift buildings, mostly barracks and offices and utility buildings.

Mortar fire had hit the hospital the previous week. It had flattened a clinic and a medical supply building. Sand bags piled high served as bomb shelters during these raids. When there was no time to prepare for a mortar round, the nurses moved the patients from the bunks to the floor and pulled the mattresses down over them.

At the end of the compound was a paved helicopter pad. Each corner of the pad was painted with a large Red Cross symbol on a white background, the target landing spots. Beside the helicopter pad was a row of olive-drab-colored trucks with the Red Cross symbol on their sides. At the edge of the landing zone there was a building to view the landings and receive the wounded. On the side of the building facing the helicopter pad someone had posted a sign:

DANGER: HELICOPTERS CAN KILL YOU.
NEVER APPROACH ONE FROM THE FRONT OR
REAR. BEND DOWN TO 5 FEET OR LOWER.
ALWAYS APPROACH MIDDLE SECTION DOOR.
DON'T LOSE YOUR HEAD, USE IT INSTEAD.

The medevac carrying Jack and his group hovered then descended slowly onto one of the marked spots. Jack sensed noise and confusion as he was moved on a stretcher into a building. His eyes were closed, but he could hear loud voices and the clang of metal on floors. He moved in and out of consciousness, lights on, lights out, the noise first overpowering, then gone. He drifted off again and heard and saw nothing.

It seemed a long time later that Jack stirred. He blinked his eyes. He believed that someone was looking down on him, but the image was first blurry, then clear, blurry, then clear, like an eye test as different lenses are tried. He tried to focus. Someone was holding his wrist, checking his pulse. Then Jack heard the soft, warm voice of what sounded like an angel.

"Welcome back to the world, soldier."

Jack tried again to focus. His sight slowly cleared. He blinked and looked up. The young woman with the voice of an angel looked like an angel, too.

Chapter 3

One week later Jack was back at his barracks and back to work. Few mentioned the crash or the death of the pilot. He met with his captain and wrote a report but heard nothing further. The glances of the newer men told Jack they knew about the incident. But they said nothing to him. We just do war, Jack thought, we don't talk about it. It did seem to Jack that the new guys were paying closer attention in the briefings. The briefings before field visits were now more intense, with more notes, more questions, less chatter, and no jokes.

With a day off on the weekend, Jack and Stumpo headed for an afternoon at the Café Normandie. Jack still felt rattled from the knock-out punch in the chopper. He walked slowly and carefully along the crowded sidewalks leading to the café. He thought of his friend next to him and smiled. He felt safer with Stumpo as his wingman on any adventure. At any sign of trouble, Stumpo followed the practice of all Viking rugby players: get your retaliation in first.

They entered the café and walked to the back of the patio. Jack chose a round table with a small vase holding a flower. Three chairs circled the table. Stumpo looked at the chairs and said: "One for company? I swear, Jack, all this dark hair is boring me to death. What I wouldn't give to see a blue-eyed blonde in a sundress some time . . . . " Jack smiled but said nothing.

They ordered drinks. Jack said: "So, how are the love letters going?"

"Pouring in like the monsoon rains," Stumpo smirked.

"Heard from Lola?"

"Ah, yes, the lovely Lola, from Saratoga." Stumpo broke into a wide smile. "Known to many as a window of opportunity, open to receive a warm summer breeze, but also prone to slam shut without warning when the thin, delicate straps holding her sash suddenly give way."

"You're crazed," Jack said, shaking his head.

"Actually, I'm thinking of using a whole new method to screen potential mates."

"Oh, is that so?" Jack asked. He could feel his friend warming up. This never gets old, he thought. Thank God for Stumpo.

"I know what you're thinking. But I'm serious this time. It's kind of a checklist. I'm calling it 'Stumpo's Signs.' I'm drawing on my Scottish roots. I read that in the old days in Scotland, the burglars had a system of identifying houses for possible breaks."

"Really?" Jack said, egging Stumpo on. "And . . . ?"

"Well, the system intrigued me. I thought I might use it for my own modest efforts."

"Your efforts at . . . burglary?"

"No, with women."

"With women. And that's like burglary because . . . ?"

"Because, if you think about it, I'm trying to break in."

"To steal . . .?"

"Their hearts, of course."

"Right. Their hearts. You. Stumpo."

"You're too cynical. Hear me out. The Scottish burglars scratched secret symbols on the fronts of the houses that they were casing. They had different symbols for their different assessments of the houses."

"Like we do with the hamlets?"

"Very funny. Actually, I hadn't thought of that. I'll bet their assessments were better than ours, friend."

"You got me there," Jack admitted.

"Here is my list," Stumpo, said, sliding a single white, lined sheet of paper toward Jack. Jack read the list: "Too Risky. Too Wealthy. Nothing Worth Stealing. Good Target. Vulnerable. Alarmed."

"Get it?"

"The symbols aren't on this list."

"I know. I'm still working on them. Viking symbols should do fine, don't you think? So do you think I can apply these to women? To their hearts, of course."

Jack feigned seriousness as he looked back over the list. When he reached the end he looked up and said: "Alarmed? Really? I can just imagine what the sign is for that one."

"You haven't met any women who seems 'alarmed'?"

Jack thought for a minute. Stumpo had lured him in again.

"Well, now that you mention it, I think I have tripped a few hidden wires. Is that where the word 'siren' comes from?" Stumpo laughed. "Too bad Odysseus didn't have my method on board." "So," Jack continued, "how would you judge your friend Lola from Saratoga on this scale? What sign would you write on her house?"

"Alarmed. Definitely alarmed. Even her windows. With a trap door hidden under her front step. If I ever trip that wire again, I will turn and run down Caroline Street and all the way home."

"I think you've been in Paradise too long. It's twisting your brain, partner. But you're not the only one who is losing it. I think Rocco's been in Professsor McUsic's lab too long." He pulled an envelope from his pocket. "I've got his report from the scene of the Spring Festival. It is a few months late, but worth the wait. The guest list makes me think the boys could have used your system that weekend."

"I can't wait," Stumpo said, sitting up in his chair and smiling. He rubbed his hands together. "Read it all."

"Dear Boys," Jack began,

"Hope you are keeping cool in Paradise. Bet you can't wait for my report on the Spring Festival. Sorry to keep you waiting; 'twas an unusually rich cast of characters this year, a volatile mix, as you'll see. It took me a while to sketch the scene for you. I hope that I have done it justice. Any libel is unintended, or at least subtle. Many of the alumni and visiting beauties asked for you two, though the interest of the young ladies in your status ended as soon as I said 'Vietnam.' Oh, well. These are trying times, even at parties. Your old pal Rocco, your faithful correspondent, stays the course for you, though. So here goes:

"From Boston, there were Mr. and Mrs. Crowninshield '36,

Mr. and Mrs. Entwhistle '38, and George Ballantyne '33, and his chauffer, Langdon, who drank a keg himself. We were also graced by the presence of the esteemed Dr. Lancelot Boilet '50, of Boston General Hospital, who was back to his old self, fresh off his acquittal of the charge of murder of his patient last spring.

"From New York came the H.M.S. Hansens, the lawyer ('29) and his wife, and their guest, Robert E. Lee Calhoun of Charleston, who left ten silver flasks of bourbon for the boys, 'reparations for Chancellorsville,' he said.

"There was an old man with long, orange hair who wrapped it around his head like the tail of a squirrel. He cut an odd figure, fondling the banister all night. 'Honduras mahogany,' he kept saying to himself, as he moved his hand up and down the rail. 'Best in the world.'

"Professor and Mrs. Teaneck were chaperones, though by Saturday night Mrs. Teaneck needed her own chaperone and a medical assistant. Professor Fishhead's wife had the reddest lipstick on the planet, some of which later appeared on the collar of Pierre Loch's shirt.

"There were girls everywhere, from the attic to the basement and everywhere in between. There were so many, in fact, that if they were all laid end to end . . ."

"We wouldn't be surprised at all!" Stumpo interjected, roaring with laughter.

"He set you up for that," Jack said. "He knows how your mind works."

"There were triplets from Wellesley named Plank, but only two of them left on Sunday. The third awoke on Monday. Pierre Loch, ever the gentleman, nailed the last Plank into a Greyhound bus bound for Boston with a note pinned to the lapel of her camel-hair coat.

"There were four girls from Wheaton: J.E.B. Nightingale, an equestrian known for her midnight rides; Juniper Jump, an art history major studying male nudes; Betty Bismarck, a political science major whose thesis topic is 'Queen Victoria as Dominatrix,' and a music major named Caterina Slosh, who offers private voice lessons and is known at Brown as 'High C.' 'High C' brought her large lungs and another vocalist, a friend from Regis named Consuela Stutz, a native of Argentina who claims to be descended from the last Kaiser on her father's side. (Pierre was impressed.)

"There was only one fight. A '55 slugged a younger guy who had taken liberties with his wife. Not that the wife objected, mind you. But the '55 hit the younger guy hard, and the young guy flung a cut-glass mug back at the face of the '55. The older guy went down like he was shot.

"Dr. Felix Feuerwasser '55, from Philadelphia, rushed across the living room and, upon examination of the prostate body of his classmate, declared that the gash that had spilled a gallon of blood on the victim's jacket and the floor was a mere 'hockey cut' to the thin skin on the forehead. Pierre commanded the scene, bellowing to the crowd: 'Does anyone have a tourniquet for this guy's neck?' The campus police arrived and removed the blood-stained alum by stretcher. With the victim safely removed, Pierre drew an outline of the body with a stick of chalk around the blood stains on the living room floor. He found some yellow tape and a couple of hockey sticks to rope off the scene of the crime. The next few groups of female visitors, entering the living room, walked quickly past the grisly scene. 'Told you this was the place to be, girls,' one said, glancing briefly to her right on her high-heeled walk to the bar.

"Bronco delivered a score of kegs to the rear parking lot. He sends his best. He said that Joe said that our boycott of the boy-cott worked wonders, and the protests have lost some steam. Joe sends his regards and thanks. Alcoh-diplomacy is the wave of the future, I truly believe, and we are well positioned to take charge.

"We had our usual interlopers from Williams and Amherst. I think their annual trespass is part of an Outward Bound pro-gram, or maybe a weekend study of primitive cultures. You can guess who I mean—the Sutpen twins, drooling all over our guests from Wellesley again, and that bum Kennedy that Stumpo knew at Exeter. Pierre lit the bottom of Kennedy's left pant leg on fire

Friday night, and he wasn't seen again. Aldo, the bookie from downstate, came early and stayed late. Business was brisk, he said."

Jack and Stumpo stared at each other, wide-eyed, and burst into laughter.

"I think he's outdone himself this time!" Holding their sides, gasping for air, they howled: "And the thing is, some of it's true!" They roared again as heads turned at tables nearby. Tears streamed down their faces as they bent their heads down, almost to the table. Finally, rocking and panting, they lifted their heads and shook them in wonderment.

"Leave . . . it . . . to Rocco," Jack managed to say, still laughing. "What would we do without him?"

They had finally stopped laughing when their eyes caught a young woman walking across the patio. She had blonde hair parted at one side and swept across her opposite eye. She had full lips and bright white teeth. She wore a flowered sundress. The dress had white shoulder straps that lay on her wide, tanned shoulders like they had been fitted by a tailor. The straps lay smoothly over two of the starkest clavicles that Stumpo had seen in his young life. The dress stopped well above her knees, featuring legs that looked like they were drawn by da Vinci at the height of his powers. Stumpo looked at Jack with an open mouth and two very arched eyebrows. She seemed to be walking directly toward them. Then Stumpo heard her say:

"Hi, Jack!"

"What the . . . ?" Stump thought, mouth wide open, still processing the vision before his eyes. She walked up to their table.

"Stumpo, this is Kate Freechild," Jack said. "She took care of me at the hospital. Kate, Stumpo Stewart."

Leave it Jack Dunne, Stump thought. My Saigon dream has arrived, but she's looking for Jack. Stumpo stood up quickly to offer Kate the third chair, but tripped and fell back, nervous and embarrassed. Kate smiled. She was used to the reaction.

"I was just going," Stumpo said quickly.

"Please stay," Kate said.

"No, thank you," Stumpo said. "I'll let you two catch up. I was just . . . Nice to meet you."

Stumpo shot Jack a glance as he turned to leave, raising his eyebrows, this time almost to the top of his forehead.

Kate sat down. "Good friend of yours?"

"The best, whether at college or war. Crazy. Fearless. He set a record for fist fights his first year at Exeter. He would hog-tie some of the upperclassmen and leave them out on the football field at night. He told the headmaster he had learned to rope and tie on his uncle's cattle ranch in Montana. He said it was not his problem if they didn't teach kids how to fight in Greenwich."

Kate laughed.

"And he's always the comic relief," Jack said. "Very welcome, over here."

"In other words, a good friend to have."

"You bet. How are you? Beautiful dress, by the way," Jack said.

"Thank you. It's not that I don't like my fatigues . . . ." She laughed. "But, you know, special occasions." She smiled mischievously. She bent her head forward to look down at the front of her dress. "It's different from my fatigues . . . this dress doesn't have my name sewn on my chest. Will you remember it?"

"Your name, or your chest?"

"Hah, hah," she laughed. "So, how are you feeling these days? How's the head?"

"Okay, thanks to you and your crew. My head still hurts, but I am otherwise operational, like a banged-up chopper."

"That's good. Sorry about the pilot. There was nothing we could do."

They were quiet for a while. At that moment Jack noticed around the corners of Kate's eyes and in her face the beginning of lines of worry from months on the front lines.

The waiter brought Kate's drink. "So how did you land here anyway?" Jack asked.

"Good question. I guess the story starts back home, at St. Agatha's in Adams, Iowa. That was my Catholic girls high school.

I got interested in nursing and went to college at St. Mary's in South Bend. You might have heard of the other school, the one for boys, that's there?"

Jack laughed.

"I studied a lot, but I had some dates, too."

"I'll bet," Jack said quickly.

"Those boys liked the nurses from St. Mary's. They were nice boys, hard-working boys, the best boys that the Catholic schools of the Midwest can offer. And they had plans for me, all right. They wanted to marry me and stick me in a big house in Wilmette or Winnetka while they went to Chicago to sell bonds and drink their lunch. No, thank you, gentlemen, I told them, I've got a world to see.

"I'm still in touch with a few of those boys. I don't think any of them are over here. Why? Who knows? Medical issues? High numbers in the draft? I don't know. I know they don't understand what the hell *I'm* doing over here. I write them and tell them that it feels like being back home in South Bend—lots of French Catholic churches and statues of Mary, dear ol' '*Notre Dame*.'"

Jack laughed. "Well, you landed a long way from corn country. I guess you got to see the world after all. But maybe not the part you were expecting to see . . . ."

"No, I was not expecting this." She narrowed her eyes and looked at him closely. "You know," she said slowly, "you remind so much of someone—someone from your college I met in the ER in Chicago," she said. "He played football, like you. My God, you two could be twins. Do all the guys up there in the woods look like you? Put me down for a visit. This guy worked the ER all day and all night. He never slept. The nurses said he could sleep standing up. On bloody Saturday nights in the city, the ambulances would be lined up outside our ER like the planes at O'Hare. Come to think of it, it looked a little bit like the Evac hospitals here. Except that here it's every day of the week. I've wondered what happened to him. I wonder if he is over here—he was someone always looking for the action, like he was going to die any minute."

Jack was nodding as she spoke. "I know exactly who you are talking about," Jack said. "He was a legend on and off the field. A great football player, but much, much more. He graduated *Phi Beta*. He majored in math and biology. He was a math whiz. He could count cards. He was the best poker player on campus—by far—including the faculty. He took on all comers, late into the night in our card room. After graduation, he hopped in his car and headed west for Stanford Medical School. The lore has it that he stopped in Vegas and stayed a week, playing five-card draw until he covered his med school tuition, four years worth plus spending money. The story goes that he got up from the poker table, tipped his hat, smiled, said 'It has been a pleasure to meet you gentlemen,' and walked out of the casino, next stop Palo Alto."

Kate nodded vigorously, as if picturing every scene. "There is not a word in that story that surprises me. Believe me, I've been expecting him to walk into the hospital any day now. And if he weren't a doctor, I would swear that he became a chopper pilot. He is that breed of cat. Brave. Cool. Decisive. The whole package."

"That's the guy," Jack nodded. They both pondered their memories for a moment. "So what was the road from Chicago to here?" he asked.

"I volunteered. I was getting antsy at the hospital. My friends thought I was crazy to go. But I wanted more action and thought I could help. They sent me to San Antonio for the Officer Basic Course. We learned about different weapons and the wounds each can cause. I was a little bit more prepared than the rest, from ER nursing. I had seen some trauma and some intensive care, some real bad stuff in Chicago, but this was different. I had no idea the damage that these weapons can cause.

"We had map-reading and survival training because they said these hospitals aren't in places like we'd ever seen. They were right about that. But I was still only 22 and now a 2d Lieutenant. Things were moving very quickly, but that's what I wanted. We went straight from San Antonio to here. The next thing I knew, I was in an Evac Hospital.

"I'll never, ever forget the day we arrived there. I've never felt heat like that in my life. You could almost smell the heat. Sweat was oozing out of my skin from my head to my toes. I think my teeth were sweating. And the bugs—big bugs everywhere. They seemed as big as the hogs on my Uncle Kevin's farm outside Davenport. Except that the hogs here have wings and they bite.

"We work six days a week, twelve-hour days. We can handle 50 casualties at a time. They are flown in by chopper—the "birds"—real fast, thank God, sometimes right after they've been hit. Some them have tags that say the location of the battle. So you sometimes see the same location on the tags for weeks. We can't help them all right away, so some of the real bad cases are moved to the side. They call these cases the "expectant"—expected to die. It took me a long while to get used to calling them that. I would keep thinking of the expectant while we worked on the ones we could save quickly.

"The concrete floor gets slippery from the blood. At each end of the room there is a faucet and a long black hose. In the middle of the floor between the surgical tables the floor tapers to a drain. At the end of each shift we hose down the floors, pushing the blood toward the drains. The blood mixes with the water as it moves toward the drain. How could a good Catholic girl not see the symbolism in *that*? But you can never escape the smells. The congealed blood. The smell of infected wounds. It's terrible.

"But we help them all, black, brown, or white as white bread. Detroit to Dubuque. Rich or poor. Catholic, Protestant, or Jew, those that lost their faith when they lost their leg. We help the angels—who are few—and the devils—who are many. The saints and the sinners, we help them all. We have a separate room with cribs for the children. We fix them up and send them back to the huts outside the wall. It breaks your heart.

"Some of the wounds are bad, like I've never seen before, not even in Chicago. We get to do things here that a lot of the nurses back home are not allowed to do—mix IV solutions, place central lines, insert chest tubes. Every pair of hands counts, so we do a lot on our own. We teach each other—doctors, nurses, medics, everybody. It's how we survive.

"The guys all need a friend, too. They're young. They are brave, brave in the way they fight, but also in the way they fight to get better, even knowing that if they recover they'll be going back out there. For a blind date with death, my friend says. They still want to be with their buddies. They live—and I guess we live—with the danger every day.

"We are told not to get close to them. But it's hard not to. They're a long way from home. They miss their families and friends. They miss their girlfriends. So they look at us a little differently than the doctors. They need someone to empty their hearts to. And they need someone to empty their pockets if they die. When they say their good-byes, we're there. We're there for their last breaths. They are so, so young. Younger than the doctors and nurses. More like younger brothers.

"How are you handling it all? I mean, yourself?"

Kate sighed. "We all do the same things, I think, to keep going. Music, cigarettes. I cry alone a lot. We drink a lot, too much, in my medical opinion." She laughed. "I pray, but not as much as I used to. I know I will carry all this with me when I get home. The sounds of the choppers. The shouting and crying in surgery and recovery. The people I've met. The boys we've lost. The knowledge that even the guys who survive will never be the same."

"Going back home will be hard for you, too," Jack said.

"Yes, it will. But when I get home, I don't see me marching in any protests. I know that some of the nurses and the vets do. That's their choice. They want to stop the killing. I do, too. But it wouldn't feel right to me. Marching, I mean. I'd feel like I left some guy or nurse behind, you know, unattended. Unsupported. Uncared for. Someone like you. Or the next guy in line. Or the next nurse in line.

"My sisters go to the protests. They think that's the way to get me home. I get it. I write them about what I'm doing and how much I'm needed, but they don't really listen. They're scared. But the louder their letters get, the more I dig in. That's me. I think more about who I'm trying to help here than what happens next for me. As for my family . . . I get it, but they'll have to wait."

In the silence that followed it occurred to Kate how little Jack had said about himself.

"Family?" she asked.

"Mother in Iowa."

"Iowa boy," she nodded and smiled. "I should have known. So polite. 'That's where the tall corn grows . . . ,'" she sang the *Iowa Corn Song* deliberately off-key.

"Whereabouts?"

"Madison."

"Father?" she asked.

"Died when I was two years old."

"I am very sorry to hear that. That's so sad." She reached across the table and took his hand. He drew in a breath.

"What happened?" she asked.

"I still don't know much about that. He worked for the OSS and the CIA in Europe during and after World War II, my mother told me. He disappeared in Prague in 1952. I was two years old. They never found his body. It's all pretty vague. But all the old guys at the College—his college, my college—talk about him constantly. They worshipped him. They keep his memory alive. I guess that's how I know him best—through them. I know more from them than from the stories from my mother."

"And they all want you to follow in his footsteps."

"Tell me about it." Jack's voice drifted off, and he took a drink.

"It's not easy to follow a legend," she offered. "But he would be very proud of you, you know."

"Well, we'll never know," Jack shrugged. "It's a very strange thing, though—to have never met someone, but to live as if he's standing right next to you, whether you're in a chopper, a bar, or on a football field."

"You're an interesting man, Jack Dunne. You seem different from most of the other guys I've met over here. You're more of a listener."

Jack managed a smile.

"Everyone who knew him wants me to be like my father. Or be like the memory they have of him. They see him in me, I guess."

The flirting stopped for a moment. Kate became serious. "But what do *you* want?"

Jack spoke deliberately, as if quietly forming a list of his answers. "To do my job. To not let my buddies down. To get out of here alive. To go home and play football." He smiled. "Not that I mind the company tonight."

She smiled and nodded, as if to say, That's one for you, boy.

"To finish school and get my diploma before I'm old enough to be my friends' father. They're starting to call me 'the Dinosaur'. That's what my friends call me, I mean. The students against the war call me 'Baby-Killer'."

He looked at her closely. "It is strange, talking with you. I don't get to talk this way, especially at school. Why is it that the only time I can really talk about the war is *at* the war, or *in* the war?" He shook his head.

"Things that bad on your campus?"

"Pretty bad, though ours is not the wildest. Let's put it this way: no one is rushing to join Stumpo and me over here in Paradise. Or join you here, either. Though if they saw you, they might change their minds."

She smiled and nodded again, as if to say, That's another one for you, boy.

"All men at that school, right?"

"Right."

"Female visitors?"

"A lot. Stumpo calls it a co-ed school, on weekends."

"Do they have views on the war?

"The women? Definitely. Very anti-war. They're leading a lot of the protests on the campuses. They're out in front, organizing things. There are not many like you, at least that I've met."

"Like me, how? What do you mean by that?"

"Well, I mean . . . supporting the war."

"'Support.' Hmmm. That's not the word I'd use," Kate said. "But I wouldn't say I'm anti-war, either. I'm different from the protesters, because I'm here. That's pretty different. And I did feel like I was different from them in college. Maybe you did, too. Sounds like it. But that doesn't mean I don't think about the war, or why we are here. It doesn't mean I don't question the war. I've got plenty of questions. And I pray for the answers. But those big questions? Go? Stay? I don't have the answers. Those are for someone else to decide. For now, the guys are here. And they are getting shot and killed every day. So I'm here. I wish we all could go home. I pray for peace every day, like the good nuns at St. Agatha taught me.

"I love these guys. What can I say? They are so scared when they come in. They are so far from home. I can't leave them here. At least not yet. I don't like the smell of it all, and I don't like the taste, but I just can't leave now. So I'm signing up for another tour."

Jack raised both eyebrows but said nothing.

"Besides, what would I do? Take vital signs in a hospital in the suburbs? That's not what I was trained to do. I was born to be here, like some of the others I've met here. Soldiers, nurses . . . have you met any of the journalists here yet?"

"No, but I know that my commanders don't like them very much."

"Probably not. But you know what? They're like me. They volunteered. They couldn't wait to get into the action. Writers, photographers, the best of the best. They're here. We're like them, Jack, you and I. We want to be here. You may not want to admit it, but I will. I want to be here. My family thinks I'm crazy. My mother asked the nuns to pray a daily novena for me—as if they don't have better things to do. I keep telling her, 'I'm a big girl. I can make my own choices.'"

She looked up from her drink, which she had been slowly stirring. She looked at him hard in the eyes, as if to be certain that he did not miss her next point.

"I know what I want and I go after it."

She let that shot land and waited for a reaction.

Jack smiled. "I can resist anything but temptation," he joked. Kate laughed. "But no," he said, shaking his head but still smiling. "Sorry. I have a girlfriend."

Kate laughed loudly. "Ha! Girlfriend? Don't all of you guys have them? Downtown? Let me guess. Short? Dark hair? Seventeen?"

"No, no," Jack laughed. "I mean a real girlfriend."

Kate laughed again. "A *real* girlfriend? That's cute."

"Back home."

She nodded as she set up her next shot. "Home's a long way from here, Jack. It's not even the same day there anymore. It's already tomorrow. Soooooooo . . ." She smiled a clever smile and took his hand. "Whatever we do tonight, she's really not involved. She's far away, so far away that she is already living in tomorrow."

"You sound like Stumpo. He thinks he can talk me into anything, because he can talk himself into anything."

She got up as if to lecture him, mock-serious, spreading her long, finely-boned fingers on the table and leaning over him. She locked her stunning blue eyes with his.

"Okay, Jack Dunne. I get it. You are a very loyal man. And your girlfriend, she is one lucky woman."

She bent down and gave him a long kiss on the cheek. She whispered in his ear. "I'm leaving now. But I just might see you again." She stood up straight, arched her back, and brushed her golden hair off her face. She turned slightly away to leave, then looked back over her shoulder and winked. "And if I ever do see you again, you'd better be ready, Jack Dunne."

Book VI

Chapter 1

Professor McUsic arrived early at the president's office for his Wednesday evening ritual with Sam Onion. He had many things on his mind as he reached the top of the marble steps, turned, and greeted Penny at her desk. "He's expecting you," Penny said. "You can go in straightaway."

"Thanks, Penny. Have a good night."

Sam Onion rose from his desk and moved to the mahogany sideboard that held the decanters of bourbon and branch water. He was still in his tweed jacket, bow-tie, and starched blue, button-down shirt, still in uniform despite a day of mud-wrestling with deans, faculty, and alumni.

"Drink?"

"Make it a double."

"You're on." The president poured the drinks and walked over to the conference table.

"We have some company tonight," he said. "The governor and his chief of staff will be on the line from the capital. We'll be hearing from the brooding omnipresence of state government himself. He wants to review our recruiting, get our ducks in a row, take our pulse, he said, and give us a report from his own kindergarten. Duncan, you've heard we're going to have another protest here next week, right?"

"I do know, Sam. And another faculty vote next week, too."

"Oh, yes, the faculty. I hope they have their fun. The Esteemed Faculty. The Conscience of our Campus. The great Revolutionaries. The Jacobins of our time. They're revolutionaries, all right—they are all for the young and oppressed until you try to shrink their office space or change their parking privileges. Then they're all seniority, all tradition, all 'wait your turn.' When their own skin is in the game, they're as conservative as the Catholic Church. No "Teachings of Karl Marx" or "*Egalite, Fraternite*" are allowed in debates over *those* perks. No, those comfy corner offices and nearby parking spaces are a matter of divine right! They're pitiful." He spit out the last few words in disgust.

"The governor may want to know how we are doing on recruiting, where we see this thing headed. He is always asking me 'What are our known unknowns?' That question is giving me a headache, frankly. I have no idea what it means. I keep telling him we are busting our humps looking for the best and the brightest and getting them on board, but lately it's like trying to find the pony in a pile of manure. We keep up our hope—we're like that little boy on Christmas morning in that story—we know that there is a pony somewhere in that pile of dung—so we just keep digging. But it's getting harder and harder. This war is a tough sell, Duncan. Some days I have my doubts . . . ." He looked at his trusted friend. "But onward we go. How goes your project?" Sam asked.

"Going well, mostly thanks to Rocco Marconi. Now there is a guy going places. I'd want him in my foxhole any day. I wish I could buy stock in the guy. He works hard. Day and night, sometimes, when he is not working one of his other jobs. He knows the problems with the project. He solves them. In other words, he does his job. We both know that in any operation, it's all in the draft picks. If you blow your picks, you blow your plans. Oh, and he keeps his mouth shut."

"What a concept," Sam broke in, as he took a pull on his drink, his sarcasm mixing with the bourbon. "All I meet lately are young people who run their mouths."

"Not Rocco. He's our kind of guy. You could have used him in your group back in the day. He would have fit like a glove. Not now, though. Some of the same traits make it hard for him to fit in on campus now. He doesn't mesh too well with his peers. He likes the lab and the library. But it's not that he doesn't like people. He likes the boys at Asgard a lot. And they like him."

"That's interesting," Sam said. "He's not typical of the group, right? When I met him at the house I wondered how he fits in, you know? With the footballers, the ruggers, the ROTC guys—or what's left of them. What's this small, brainy guy doing in there?"

Duncan laughed. "Part co-incidence, part plan. He was Jack Dunne's freshman roommate. That might have been the housing office's idea of a joke on both of them, but they really hit it off. They are very complementary in their personalities. Jack is an Asgard legacy and there was no question he would be joining, so Rocco tagged along. And every guy there has loved him ever since."

"So that was the co-incidence," Sam said, still curious. "What was the plan?"

The professor laughed again. "Typical Rocco. He thinks things through. He knew that people would wonder why he ended up in Asgard. When I asked him about it he said: "It was very much my choice, Professor. You know the old World War II story about the small paratrooper? The colonel is inspecting the paratroops before a big jump. He marches up and down the rows, looking over the troops. When he comes to a small, scrawny guy he stops and barks: 'You like to jump out of airplanes, son?' The small guy answers loudly 'No, sir!' The colonel glares at him and says: 'Then what the hell are you doing in the paratroopers, son?' Without missing a beat, the small guy answers: 'Because I like to be *with* the men who like to jump, sir!' See, Professor? That's why I'm in the Hall. I like to be with the men who like to jump.""

"I laughed and laughed."

"You've got a good man there, Duncan." Sam thought a minute and asked:

"And how is Jack Dunne?"

"Tiemo just got another letter. He's doing well after that bad crash. I guess you know about that. It was a near miss in that chopper. They lost the pilot."

"Is he back on duty?"

"Yes. It would take more than that to knock him out of the line-up, I'd guess. He's been getting great reviews from our friends over there. A born leader. He can be anything he wants to be."

Sam snorted. "Yeah, ironic isn't it? The young person you just described used to be honored on this campus, by the faculty, by the students. And not just for military service. I'm talking about those qualities—the brains, the courage, the athletics, the leadership. That was the kind of student that the others always looked up to. Now? If they serve? Then, in the eyes of the students and faculty, those qualities don't count anymore. They're cancelled out. In fact, their service to our country brings scorn— that they are somehow morally wrong to serve, and worthy of contempt. These same guys, the ones who were once so honored here, get spit on at airports on their way home. They're lucky to be back here alive, yet they get scowled and hissed at in class. It makes me sick to my stomach."

Sam stood up to get another drink. "But Jack's father would be damn proud of him, we know that. He wasn't one to brag, but he would be busting his buttons with pride if he knew what we know about his son."

Duncan nodded. "I've been thinking of Jack's father a lot lately. I guess we all do. I've been wondering what he'd think of this war we have now. He never worked in Asia. I think he would have been cautious about our moves over there. He was a realist. He always wanted to know the facts on the ground, in France or later in Eastern Europe. I guess that's what took him to a bridge too far—that desire to *understand*. I don't know if he would have thought that it was feasible to 'win the hearts and minds' of the Vietnamese, like the head honchos in DC think we can. He'd learn the history of the country cold, he'd look at things clear-eyed. He'd want the info the boys like Jack are looking for. We both know that he was a young man on the rise. He could have gone far, maybe all the way to the Director's chair. There's one for you: it's 1961, and CIA Director John Dunne is briefing Kennedy on Vietnam. What would he have told Kennedy to do?"

"We'll never know, will we?" Sam said, sadly.

They were silent, lost in thought, borne back again to the memory of a special friend and comrade.

Sam changed subjects. It was not his way to wallow. "And how is Clare? I haven't seen her since she was in this room with a couple dozen of her fellow 'visitors.'" He laughed.

The professor laughed uneasily. "Hope they left some bourbon." He looked to see if Sam laughed. "Clare . . . where do I start? With my pride or with my worries? She's still storming the barricades, just like her mother. Her mother was from the Wallace clan, remember?"

"Remember? How could I forget? I watched her decapitate a few snide, male faculty at my own dinner table. She was a real champion of women scholars. God, those dinners were fun. I miss her, Duncan."

"I do, too. Every day. The pain dulls but never leaves. Well, Clare is lot like her. Born to fight. She likes life at the tip of the spear. And with two Scots-Irish parents, well, Clare's like an electrical circuit on overload. It's the warrior gene, and it's in guys like Stumpo and the guys from Appalachia and the South who are over there now. Clare's got some variant of that gene. It's an anti-war strain that she has, but it burns with the same fire. Maybe deep down in that Tartan-red blood she senses a doomed fight, the Scots at Solway Moss, you know, or their legacies at Pickett's Charge. Maybe she knows a Lost Cause when she sees one. But whatever the reason driving her, she's a leader on her campus and beyond. Like many women these days. Maybe she and I are closer than we think on things," Duncan mused. "She objects to a war that is sending poor boys to die, and we're trying to get the college guys into the same fight. Maybe we agree, at least on the unfairness of it all."

Sam said nothing.

"As for Clare and Jack . . .," Duncan continued, "I think they're finding it hard to bridge their differences on the war. Love and respect can take you far, but these days it may not be enough. She doesn't tell me much. But I can tell the war's a strain—that and the distance. They're eight thousand miles apart, geographically and politically, you might say. If they don't make it, I guess you can count it as another casualty of war.

Anyway, I've tried to stay clear of it with her. She knows what I think of Jack. She doesn't need me to beat her up about him. But you and I both know that it will be a cold day in Saigon when she meets someone like Jack Dunne in some smoky tea room in Amherst."

The phone on the president's desk rang. He was expecting the call. "Governor Smith on the line, sir," Penny's brilliant voice sang over the intercom.

"Thank you, Penny. Spike, how the hell are you? How are things on Olympus?"

"Olympus, Sam? I think you've got the wrong number. These days I feel more like I'm broiling in a lower ring of the Inferno."

"Is there a special ring for failed politicians?"

"Right you are. It's hotter than hell and getting hotter by the day. By the way, if it's okay with you, I've got my chief of staff here—Andy Wesson. We are trying to tend our garden here but you need to tend yours. You've gotta save ROTC. You need to get more recruits, and hold the line on those protests. Be ready to go to court again if they go launch another bourbon-and-cigar-hunt in your office. You've got to hold the line, Sam."

Sam and Duncan heard the chief of staff voice his agreement. The governor continued:

"You'd think people would support our effort—you know, trying to get these college guys in the fight. Everybody knows that these colleges aren't sending anyone. The numbers are piti-ful. It's the kids from the trade schools who are going over there and coming home in a box. Why can't they see that we are trying to change that?

"I spoke to the White House last week. He's trying to get some support from the universities. They know it's an uphill climb. But here's what they want. They want a letter from uni-versity and college presidents like you and they want it to say:

    'We pledge unqualifiedly to support the Government
    of the United States and place at your disposal all of

our resources in the present emergency. The University is taking steps to intensify the training which it is already providing to equip its students for more effective national service and wishes to augment its present programs by work in such different branches as may be desirable in the crisis. We respectfully request that you designate appropriate officers in the appropriate services with whom the University may consult.'

"Governor, with all due respect, you must be joking," Sam said bluntly. "You want me to sign that and send it to the White House? What if it gets out? Will they give me a cigarette before my firing squad up here?"

The governor laughed. "You should ask for a Cuban cigar. You'll want to leave that ship of fools in style. I'll tell you what: we'll bury you on the golf course at your favorite tee or green, after we push your pine box down the ski jump once for old time's sake. Sound good?"

"No sympathy from you, as usual, Governor."

The governor laughed again. "Gotta go now, Sam. Affairs of state and all that. Keep the faith."

The governor hung up the phone and turned to his chief of staff.

"We'll, there you have it. I know things are a bit rocky here, but I wouldn't want to trade my job for Sam's job. Our dear ol' College up there is buckling. The trustees are running scared. Sam's a good man, a tough man. He's been under fire before—the real kind. But he knows that the mob is at the door. *Apres moi, Le Deluge*, he says to me privately. But that is not much of a rebuttal these days. *Le Deluge* is what the mob wants."

The governor sighed. "Should we get back to the business here in the Puzzle Palace?" They stared at each other across the long, polished conference table in the governor's office, a table used by his predecessors for a century, sometimes as an altar for sacrifice, sometimes as a confessional, and sometimes as a butcher's block, where legislative careers were gutted, cut, and carved,

the scraps fed to shifting alliances of hungry wolves waiting outside the door in the stately marble lobby.

"This building is full of rumors, most of them false," he said.
"Yes, I support the President of the United States. But I am not
his confidante. I know his flaws. He is a man of very few ideas,
but for the few he does have, he would rather die than forsake
them."

"Amen," said the chief. The chief had two new bills in his
hands, the latest from what he called "The Rabble" in the State's
200-member House. The tide of protests was rising—that was
certain—and the first small waves of revolt were now lapping up
against the governor's office door.

The governor and the chief had been together from the governor's earliest campaigns. The chief saw his job as Lord Pro-
tector—the defensive shield deflecting his boss from the daily
assault of spears and arrows from the legislature, press, and public. He was also the Royal Messenger of Bad News, charged (due
to the craven cowardice of the others on the staff) to bring the
worst news of each day to the governor.

The chief handed the new bills from the House to his boss.
The governor looked over the first. The chief read its title: "A
Resolution for the Withdrawal of All American Combat Troops
from Vietnam." It read:

> "Be it resolved, that we declare our disagreement
> with the present United States policy in Vietnam.
> Be it therefore further resolved that we urge upon
> the President, the Congress, and the people of
> the United States the adoption of a policy of im-
> mediate cessation of all offensive military action
> in Vietnam and a total, unilateral withdrawal of
> American combat and support forces to be com-
> pleted no later than the end of 1970."

"Predictable," the governor said. Then he read aloud the
next bill: "An Act Defining the Rights of the Inhabitants of

the State Inducted or Serving the Military Forces of the United States."

"Pompous, don't you think? Who do they think they are, General Eisenhower?"

The chief continued. "Two parts to this second bill. The first part says, and I quote, the 'inhabitants of the State inducted or serving in the military shall not be required to serve abroad in an armed hostility that has not been declared a war by Congress.'

"It also commands the attorney general of this State to file a lawsuit claiming that the war in Vietnam is illegal because Congress has not declared war, and that the citizens of this State are being denied their rights under the Constitution when they are forced to fight in an undeclared war. It directs him to file the case directly in the United States Supreme Court.

"Are these all going to pass the House?"

"We think yes," said the chief. "Unless we find a way to head things off."

"Chances in the Senate?"

"Dead even."

"Good God."

"Senators Schoolcraft and Prostantino want you to oppose this now," said the chief. "To kill it in the House. Before they have to vote on it."

"Typical," the governor snarled. "They want cover. Their gut tells them to vote no—that this bill is going way too far—but they feel the tide rising. They're gathering the women and children and the family dog. Next thing you know they'll want small boats out there in the park or maybe a helicopter to pluck them off the top of the State House. Maybe they want us to haul them up in one of those medical rescue baskets like they use in helicopters to remove the wounded. We could adapt it to extract the cowards here. Oh, and make sure you find us a soft place to land, they say. We don't want to take the political hit. Those gutless wonders, they think this storm will blow over soon. I'm not so sure. They need to stand up and be counted or go home."

The chief said nothing. There was a long pause as the governor looked out the window to the front lawn of the Capitol grounds.

"Well, let's get to it. But, believe me, they will pay. I don't need to whip people. Squeezing them slowly is more my style. It if they cross me this time, God help them. Sometimes I think the Etruscans had it right."

"The Etruscans, sir?"

"Ancient Italians, pre-Romans. The Etruscan pirates tortured their prisoners by strapping a corpse to them, face-to-face."

The chief of staff formed an "ouch" with his face and turned his head partially away as he contemplated the image. "I think we're still a few steps away from that."

"We'll see," the governor said, making no promise of restraint. "Who is causing the most trouble in the Senate?"

"Senator Harrington."

"Figures he's the ringleader of this mob. But he won't stand and fight. He always runs to ground when the predators take the field."

"He pisses me off!" shouted the chief, spitting out his words. He threw up his hands, quickly making two fists and slamming them down on the table. Fresh smears of sweat formed on the glossy table. "Goddam it, we paid good money for that guy!"

"Damn right we did," agreed the governor.

"Well, we'll deal with him later. We have other points of entry in the Senate, other grommets, other portals."

"Yes," the chief said. As he looked at the governor he thought, *He's working down the list of senators in his mind, one by one, like a thief checking doorknobs.*

"We can take care of the Senate," the governor said, without expression. "Now, who is causing all the trouble in the House?"

The chief answered. "Representative Lawrence Lively."

"Of course," nodded the governor with a thin-lipped smile. "Must be having another fit caused by the absence of mind. That's a common affliction in the House. It must be contagious. What's he saying this time?"

"Oh, the usual. He says you're a war-monger, says you are

still living in World War II."

"Oh, yeah, sure. I knew him when he was chasing ambulances and picking his nose on that city council downstate. He's had a problem with the bottle for a long time. He's anti-war but he's pro-whiskey. He's had a recent arrest that we're looking into. I might just have to give the Speaker an update on what we've found. I've had Lively right in here for drinks a few times, you know. He likes them strong. He doesn't realize I pour a weak one for myself each time. He loses control; I don't."

The governor looked at the chief calmly. "Their tongues are smooth," he said slowly, deliberately. "They have two faces, and that's on an honest day. They make charges without proof. They won't lift a finger for even a good cause unless I stuff their other hand with jobs or cash, or both. He looked out at the statue. We once had statesmen, now we have these . . . ."

The governor returned his gaze to the bills in his hands. "Well, I'll deal with Lively later. The speaker will reign him in if I give him the latest goodies that I have on that guy. When you can get to the organ grinder, why bother with the monkey?"

"Agreed," the chief said.

The governor looked over the papers on the table. "What about this thing about the Attorney General filing suit? Against the President of the United States, for God's sakes. These donkeys can't tell the AG what suits to file—what ever happened to the separation of powers? He looked up from the papers over his reading glasses. What is the AG saying about all this? I appointed him to help me with this crap. Get him in here, will you? He may not like to be in the middle of this, but he should remember, if you are not at the table, you're on the menu."

A few minutes later, the attorney general hurried into the room and took a seat at the conference table. He folded his hands and placed them on the table. He wore large, square black glasses and had black hair. He had large blue eyes and small, light lids, that rarely blinked, leaving him to appear as if he was in a state of perpetual wonderment as he made his way through the important tasks of his day. He had thin gray lips that moved only slightly when he spoke. And he rarely spoke. As a mouth-breather, his mouth would also hang open as well, adding to the effect that he was caught continually off-guard, a naïf in the treacherous cockpit of state politics.

He looked across the table at the governor, his benefactor for many years. The governor had sized him up long ago: a brilliant lawyer with the spine of a jelly doughnut. He could not be elected dogcatcher, the governor had laughed to the chief. But the governor needed him. His appointment as attorney general received applause from the bar and the judges—the target audience. But legislators were circumspect. "Lap dog for the governor," some said, quietly. Others were less kind. "He put his manhood in a blind trust," they charged. Even the lawyers among the legislators knew little or no law. They distrusted this odd, reserved creature with his fancy law degree. He seemed to speak a different language. And, more ominously, he was the chief enforcer of the state's ethics laws. That role worried them a lot. He could make trouble for them. So they eyed him warily, year after year, like long-time residents of a jungle eyeing a threatening newcomer.

The state constitution said that the attorney general, once appointed, could only be removed by the governor for "cause," but the attorney general never assumed that that paper dike would hold. Surely not this time, he thought, if he defied the governor and filed the suit that the bill, if passed, would command him to file. If he filed the suit, his head would surely fall. And he knew that he would not contest the firing—it was not in his nature, and, after all, he had to live in this small State. Conscience is one thing, he thought, but stupidity is another.

The attorney general looked at the chief. "How did I get my ass in this wringer? I thought this war stuff was your department."

"We need a plan," the governor said simply.

The attorney general looked over the bills. "This bill—the part about me— it's beyond their writ," he said. "They can't tell me what suits to file—especially not this one. People will think I work for the Viet Cong, for God's sakes."

The chief watched the governor carefully as he weighed his options. The governor folded his hands with the tips of the left fingers touching the tips of the right fingers to form the shape of a church steeple. But, the chief thought, this was no church service on offer, unless it signaled the imminent funeral of the attorney general. The governor spoke:

"Here's what I want you to do: You announce that you won't file the suit. You say that the act exceeds the power of the legislature and violates the separation of powers under the state constitution. You say that they can't tell the AG which suits to file and which not to file. You say you sympathize with their goals—to bring the boys home—but that your hands are tied by the constitution. You quote Sir Thomas More in his fight with Henry VIII—that will impress the blockheads. You say you can't lay the constitution low even to pursue a worthy goal. We are a government of laws, not of men, and so forth. You refuse to file the suit."

"Oh, and one more thing," the governor added quickly. "You keep me the hell out of it."

The attorney general's mouth hung open, again. "What if the press asks me if we discussed this?"

"You say 'attorney-client privilege.' God, do I have to think of everything around here? You're the lawyer!"

"But the act says 'shall file' the suit," the attorney general said, with a pout that made him look like a little boy.

"I don't care."

"The constitution trumps the act," the chief said. "End of story."

The governor looked at the attorney general closely. He started to speak, then stopped. He made sure that their eyes met, and when they did, he spoke deliberately. "Don't worry," he said, "*they* won't remove you."

The attorney general said nothing as he pondered the governor's threat.

"So do we have a plan?

"Yes," the attorney general said, "we have a plan." He rose from his chair and left the room.

"Trust him?" asked the chief.

"Not entirely," the governor said. "I try to read their eyes. The story is always in their eyes, every one of them. I really don't put much stock in what they say anymore. Sometimes I don't listen to them at all. But I do listen to what they don't say."

"What?"

"What they are leaving out. What they are holding back. Sometimes you can tell. They struggle. They look down. They look around. They change the subject. But I don't let them. I bring them back. I know that if I can just keep them in that room, I can get the thing out of their mouth—the thing they are trying so hard to keep in. Sometimes it resembles the extraction of a tooth."

"What is he trying to keep in?"

"The fact that he fears the mob in the Legislature. The fact that he's ready to go with them."

"And?"

"If that bill passes, he'll file that suit. I know he will."

The governor looked at his watch.

"What time does Lively speak in the House on the bill?"

"Should be soon. He's going to rake you, you know. I saw his press release with a preview. He and the others want to inflict some pain on you. They want you to feel it. They are desperate to show that they are doing something against the war. To strike back at Nixon, strike back at you, at the National Guard. Anything. Who feels the pain doesn't matter to them. A pound of flesh must be taken, preferably yours. He is going to say that you are supporting an immoral war."

"Oh, right, a sermon from the moral pillar of our community, the Honorable Lawrence Lively," the governor scoffed. "The Prince-Bishop of the House, whose powers reach all matters of church and state. Lecturing me on matters of morality. The 'immoral' war. My 'immoral' stance.

"Who's he? Now he's the moral compass of the state? I

thought we dumped rule by divine right. How far does he think his writ runs, anyway? I'm tired of his preening, his playing to the crowd. Camera-hound! And do you know what's next? Probably an award for him from some pointy-heads at some college no one ever heard of, a "Profile in Courage" award or some such. Yeah. Courage. To cut our troops off at their knees. To give aid and comfort to the enemy. Right! Courage! A lecture from a guy who spent World War II shoveling shit in Missouri."

The chief said nothing.

"We should get going. I've set up a meeting with the Speaker in his hide-away office in the basement. That's where he does his drinking and his dealing. Sam Onion tipped me off about his lair. Sam and the Speaker were in France together in '45." He picked up an envelope on his desk.

"What's in that?"

"Some 'Lively' photos, you might say. Taken by the State Police at the scene of the esteemed Representative's most recent adventure downstate. The troopers said that his hotel room looked like an experiment involving gin and a water buffalo. And the young ladies present did not look at all like Mrs. Lively. Not in the least."

The governor and the chief left his office and turned left into the marble hallway, passing the portraits of his predecessors. They had it easy, the governor thought. They turned into a long corridor and walked to the end. They turned again and entered a smaller hall known as the "Hall of Flags." It was empty, a refuge from the storm brewing in the House chamber. The small hall was built entirely of Italian marble. A large, faded mural dominated one wall. It depicted the State's troops from the Civil War returning their regimental flags to the then-governor in 1865. Glass cases were built into the other walls. They held United States military flags from all of the nation's wars. All the wars, that is, except one. They looked around the hall, into every case.

"No flag from Vietnam," the governor said. "Thousands dead already, and no flag."

"No," the chief said. "Not yet."

"Instead, they're burning our flag," the governor said. "Maybe they want me to put a North Vietnamese flag in our hall. Or maybe the Viet Cong's. They're waiving them at the protests. Why not put one in here? I'll tell you where I'd put those two flags. I'd stick them right up their ass, one after the other, until I saw the first one come out their throat."

The chief knew better than to comment. The governor finally cooled and turned away from the flags. "Come on," he said with a dark smile and a curled lip, "we're going to cancel this show right now. I will grind them finer than snuff."

Chapter 2

The old chamber of the House of Representatives filled quickly that day. The chamber held two hundred old wooden desks. Each desk had a hole for an inkwell in its top-right corner.

Three enormous portraits dominated the wall above the dais. Each measured ten by six feet. They were displayed in gold-leaf frames. Left to right, they depicted Washington, Lincoln, and the State's military hero of the Revolution.

The room had a musty smell, a combination of the smoke in the air and the tobacco stains in the ancient carpet. Long benches stood side by side the length of one wall. These were useful resting spots for white-haired, groggy members seeking a late-afternoon nap, eyes closed, contemplating dinner. Sometimes they talked to one another out of the sides of their mouths, whispering, nodding, glancing side-to-side, murmuring a "here, here" from time to time during a debate.

They represented a mixture of professions and trades, a barber, a hairdresser, and a few too many lawyers, according to the dentists, who would extract a few of the lawyers if they could. There were accountants and insurance agents of every description, all of them alert to bills that might harm their competitive position in their professions. Those with tight races for re-election trusted the Speaker of the House to steer them into the safe harbor of another term.

A curved balcony ran from one front corner around the rear and over to the other front corner. The balcony was open to the public and quickly filled for the day's debate on bills related to the war. Chandeliers on long chains hung from the ceiling, but their dim light and the small windows over the balcony lent a sense of late night even to the day. The lights did not reach the areas under the balcony, and no smaller lights lit that space. These dimly lit alcoves, removed from public view, served as fertile soil for many a *quid pro quo* between members. The clerk of the House and his assistant sat a granite dais in front of the Speaker's rostrum, surveying the scene and recording the debates and votes. The proceedings under the balcony were "off the record."

The presiding member of the House called the session to order and motioned toward Representative Lively to speak. Lively stood at the podium in the well of the chamber and began: "Our bill presents the grave question whether and in what circumstances a person may be required to serve in an armed conflict that lacks a formal declaration of war by Congress under the Constitution." As he continued making his argument, his rotund body seemed to burst out of his clothes as he raised his voice and flapped his arms. He had an enormous bald head, with a thin ring of unwashed curls. He had a wide face that registered his every emotion. And he had another feature that added to a sense of at least slight derangement: he had eyes that seemed not to match, one eye far smaller than the other, and both mostly covered by large, drooping multi-layered lids. His mouth was covered by a curly, drooping mustache. It was rarely closed.

He was a lawyer downstate with a busy trial practice and a specialty in the defense of his political colleagues accused of ethical lapses. He bragged that he was the "first responder" to any scene of alleged political corruption. He freely admitted that many of his clients had "the appearance of impropriety."

He once spent a week in jail after a judge had found him in contempt of court. Even his foes in the courtroom admired him as daring and astute, if short on scruples. In criminal cases, he was known for finding flaws in indictments. He once freed a thief with the claim that a stolen key was not personal property, but real estate. When a reporter from a downstate newspaper described him as a "corrupt clown," he barged into the newspaper office and grabbed the reporter by the throat. With the tide of anti-war sentiment rising in the House, he knew that he had found a new and larger stage for his talents.

As the audience in the galleries grew that day, his voice rose to fill the old chamber.

"The State Constitution of 1780, which preceded the Articles of Confederation and the United States Constitution, provides that none of our citizens may be forced to fight a war outside the State unless he gives his consent or consent is specifically given by this body—the state legislature. And when we ratified the federal constitution, we expressly said, at our convention and in our ratifying resolution, that we were reserving this precious right. If Congress declares war, so be it. But it has not."

A member of the House who sat directly in front of the podium rose from his desk. Representative Lively narrowed his eyes as he viewed the interloper. He turned up his nose slightly, as if sniffing for a foul odor that might have wafted into the chamber.

"For what purpose does the gentleman rise?" the presiding member asked.

"I wish to offer an amendment to the bill in the form of a resolution," Representative George Foote said. He was a tall, lean, sandy-haired fuel oil dealer from upstate. He represented a district filled with small business owners and tradesman and dairy farmers. He had served in the House for twenty years and was a loyal supporter of Governor Smith. "My amendment states as follows:

> 'Resolved, that this House affirms its support for the President in his efforts to negotiate a just peace in Vietnam, expresses the earnest hope of the people of this State for such a peace, approves and supports the principles enunciated by the President that the peoples of South Vietnam are entitled to choose their own government by means of free elections, and that the issues in controversy may be peacefully resolved in order that the war may be ended and peace may be restored at last in Southeast Asia.'

"I am advised that the governor supports this resolution," Foote added. With these last words, Lively slammed his fist on

the podium where he still stood. "The governor! The man behind the craven puppets in our midst! Pulling the strings as they
dance! This resolution is nothing less than an attempt to subvert
the will of this House and the people it represents! If you adopt
this resolution, you will be giving the President of the United
States *carte blanche* in Vietnam. When you 'affirm your support'
you are handing him full power to sink us deeper into the bloody
abyss. You will regret this bow to the President, you will regret
even more petting his lapdog, our governor. This resolution is a
political gambit, plain and simple, to deflect us from our main
objective—to stop this undeclared, immoral war!"

Lively glared directly at Representative Foote and continued:

"Once again—at this critical juncture in the country's history—the Governor and his lackeys attempt to bring into disgrace,
ridicule, hatred, contempt and reproach this House and this
State. Never in the history of this State has there been so base,
so gross, so unjustifiable an attempt to steal the apparatus of our
government and use it to seek immoral ends. The governor is
an impersonation—the living, breathing, embodiment of those
in Washington who pursue this immoral war. In fact, I have recently received information that shows that he is conducting a
back-channel campaign with the White House to support the
war."

The crowd roared. The presiding member at the dais pounded his gavel. Then he turned to his right and saw the large, ornate double-doors to the chamber open. The Speaker of the
House entered. He strode to the podium in the well where Lively
was speaking. When he reached him, the Speaker gently put his
hand on Lively's elbow and motioned his head to one side, as if
to say: "May I have a word?" The two took three or four steps
away from the podium. Lively nodded as the Speaker spoke. His
face, florid from speaking, turned ashen. He nodded glumly and
walked downcast to his seat, leaving his notes at podium. The
Speaker was expressionless as he watched Lively take his seat.
The Speaker then turned and climbed the steps to the dais. He
took the gavel from the presiding member.

"Is there a motion to table all matters currently pending before this House?"

"So moved," said Representative Foote, who was still standing.

"Is there a second?"

"Second," came a reply from another loyal supporter of the governor, Representative Elizabeth "Betsy" Westmoreland. "Ayes? Nays? The ayes have it. All bills and proposed amendments and resolutions are hereby tabled. The House is adjourned, *sina die*." The Speaker laid down the gavel and skipped down the stairs and out of the chamber. The House erupted in protest, members and public alike. The howls continued for minutes after the Speaker disappeared.

High in the balcony, standing behind the back row of seats, the governor and the chief watched their carefully orchestrated chaos unfold. The governor nodded his approval. "It's done," the chief said. "That should kill it." The governor shook his head. "Only for now," he said. "Only for now. Today is only one battle in the war within the war."

———

The next morning Duncan McUsic was grading engineering papers at his desk in his library. He sipped from his coffee as he gazed over the pond below him. He heard the telephone ring. He picked up the phone on the small table next to the German jet engine.

"Duncan, it's Sam."

"Hello, Sam."

"A real circus at the State House yesterday, just as the governor predicted," Sam said. "But we'll call it a win, and live to fight another day."

"I know, I heard," Duncan said. "The newspapers in the capital called it 'The Suicide of Lawrence Lively.'"

Sam continued, "Lively told the governor privately that he

knew about the governor's involvement with recruiting for the war up here. But Lively did not get to fire that gun before the Governor took him out. It always pays to shoot first.

"See you here on Wednesday?"

"Same time, same place."

The professor put the phone down on the receiver and walked back to his desk. The phone rang again. He again picked up the phone and said "Hello, McUsic here." He listened and suddenly took a short breath. His chin dropped to his chest. His eyes closed tightly, as if trying to understand the words he was hearing. They seemed spoken in a foreign tongue.

"Yes, I understand," he managed. "My heart is broken." He placed the phone back on the receiver. He stood there, rocking slightly on his feat, unsure whether to sit or stand. He stood for minutes that seemed like hours. He picked up the phone and slowly dialed a number he knew by heart. He heard a familiar voice at the end of the line. He took a deep breath and said:

"Clare, it's Dad. I have some very bad news from Vietnam."

Book VII

Chapter 1

The helicopter raced low over Saigon. Its destination was the large airfield on the outskirts of the city. In the far corner of the field, past the fighter jets and massive cargo planes, the pilot saw his target: a helipad marked by a large white circle. The pad sat outside the gate of a compound filled with small, low-slung, unmarked buildings and three larger buildings that looked like small aircraft hangers. A twenty-foot concrete wall enclosed the compound. A guard tower kept watch over each of the four corners of the wall. An American flag flew from each tower. The pilot radioed ahead to the compound.

"Two minutes out," the pilot said. He approached the pad and landed the helicopter gently, as he had hundreds of times before. A van rolled slowly out of the gate to meet the helicopter. The van parked near the pad. Two uniformed men stepped out of the van. The helicopter rotor blades stopped. The men from the van reached the side of the copter. Two men inside the copter slowly lowered a full, zippered green body bag into the hands of the men on the ground and gave them a quick salute. The men on the ground moved the body to the van. The van carried the body through the gate and pulled up to the wide double-doors on the side one of the larger buildings. Inside the doors, they placed the body on a gurney and wheeled it to a station manned by a mortuary officer.

Lieutenant Joseph Arimatoni would perform the work of identification and preparation of the body for transfer to the United States. He was twenty-five years old, with curly black hair and dark brown eyes and a wide mouth. He had soft hands and long fingers like those of a concert pianist. In fact, as a teenager he had played the piano at his home church. He was working in his family's funeral business in South Philadelphia when he was drafted and sent to Vietnam. His draft induction file read: "Highly qualified for mortuary duty."

In the large hall with other mortuary officers Joseph performed his work. One twenty-foot high wall in front of him displayed ten large American flags in a row. At one end of the hall,
there were stacked row upon row of aluminum "transfer cases,"
the temporary caskets used for the flight home. At the other end,
near the large doors, sat a dozen wooden pallets. The pallets held
the full transfer cases before their trip across the tarmac to the
waiting planes bound for home.

Joseph examined the papers with the new body. Two witnesses had testified to the identification. He carefully examined the
body for telltale scars, birthmarks, and tattoos. He took fingerprints and made a dental chart. The chart recorded teeth that
were missing or cavities filled. On another chart, he recorded
body characteristics and wounds. He matched his notes against
service records for the deceased soldier. It was only after this
slow, painstaking process that the next of kin of the deceased
would be notified.

"*Che giovane* . . . too young," Joseph said quietly to himself as
he stepped back to view the body. He talked to himself a lot these
days. "You have done no unjust violence," he said, looking at the
body, in a slow, formal whisper. "Your mouth held no deceit. You
have done no inequity."

He started to clean and embalm the body, closing the wounds.
When he was finished, he scanned the hall to see if anyone was
watching him. With his left hand, he slipped a small vial out from
the large left pocket of his white coat. He opened the vial and
dabbed its perfumed balm on his right thumb. He rubbed his
thumb and forefinger together. Then he reached over the body
and gently traced the sign of the cross on the forehead.

Joseph carefully taped ID tags to one arm, then a toe. He
wrapped the body in a plastic sheet and bound it with tape. He
had done this hundreds of times. Each time seemed like the first.
He remembered his first body clearly, like a vivid dream or the
memory of a moment of intense fright. His first body was a
nineteen-year-old African-American Marine from Mississippi
named Robert Gould. He knew that name as well as he knew

his own.

Lately, at this last stage, with the identification confirmed and the body wrapped, he would step back from the corpse. His mind would drift as he surveyed the large hall and the stations where his colleagues performed their tasks. His eyes would fix on a corner of the hall. This had happened several times in the last few weeks, at the end of his work on each body. In the corner of the hall, thirty yards from where he stood, there would appear a radiating light, glowing outward from the figure of a woman. The light was undulating, first bright, then dim, then bright again. The woman's hair was dark and long and she wore a simple brilliant white robe. The white robe gleamed with a color that seemed not a color at all but the absence of color, a transparent portal into a world beyond. He was sure beyond doubt that the figure he saw was Mary Magdalene, standing watch as if she were standing at the tomb of her Savior and holding the linen shroud.

Joseph told no one of his daily visions. When the vision first appeared, he had tried averting his eyes from the corner as he completed his work. When his eyes were drawn there, he would blink several times, as if testing his senses to prove, once and for all, whether the vision was real. But each time he looked up from the table, and no matter how many times he blinked, she appeared, and she remained visible until the moment that the body in front of Joseph was wheeled by his assistant away from his station to the waiting wooden pallets. The vision brought Joseph no fear or confusion. In time, the vision brought him a feeling of comfort. It seemed to help to have the vision present, he decided, and nodding toward him with love, though Joseph also sensed, even from that distance, that she was fighting back tears of her own.

This time, as in the others, the vision gradually receded as he completed his work. In time, only the bare corner of the hall remained. Joseph readied himself for the final step. He raised his right hand to signal an orderly that he was ready for assistance. The orderly wheeled another gurney to Joseph's side, this one carrying an open, reusable aluminum case. Joseph and his assistant placed the body in the case. Then Joseph said the same thing he always said before he closed the case. "You're going home, soldier."

They slowly closed the case and attached a final ID tag to its outside. Then they secured the case by two straps and two metal clips. Joseph stood silently as the orderly rolled the case to the far end of the room. The orderly and an assistant—an an older Vietnamese man named Dinh Giuse—called "Giuseppe" by the American staff and known for his quiet, respectful work in the mortuary—placed it on a wooden pallet next to three other aluminum cases. Giuseppe draped each case with the flag as he had been taught: so that the "union," the blue field with fifty white stars—symbolizing the fifty States—the States that were sacrificing the cream of their youth in a war far from home—covered the head and left shoulder of the deceased.

Joseph watched them finish at the pallets then walked over to his desk along the wall of the hall for his final duty: to sort the soldier's personal effects for mailing to his family. As he performed this duty each day, he was aware that he, Joseph, knew of the soldier's death, yet the soldier's loved ones, as they went about their lives half a world away, did not know the same awful news, indeed, had spent much of their day pushing the possibility of this fate from their troubled minds. On this day he screened the clothes, letters, and photos of the deceased, looking for anything that may cause further grief—if that were possible—to the family. There was none. He saw a picture of a parent, a mother only. There was no picture of a father. He sifted the letters from home. These were very hard for Joseph to read. At times, Joseph had to stop in the middle of a letter to control his tears. The letters were filled with love and hope but also an unspoken but palpable fear. It was Joseph's duty to read these letters. The family must be protected if possible. All of it—the whole, gruesome business—was a cup that Joseph wished that he could pass. But he was required to read the letters. And so he did.

On this day he read each letter and found nothing that would

further harm the family. He returned them to the manila envelope with the other personal effects. As he re-filled the envelope,
he noticed in its bottom a single gold-plated tie-clasp, shaped in
the form of a hockey stick. He removed the clasp and inspected
it. The clasp held a small, black-and-white photo of a deserted,
frozen pond.

Chapter 2

The First Congregational Church stood on a small knoll a short distance from the center of town and the campus. Early Yankee settlers founded the congregation in the 1700s. Three fires and two hundred northern winters had not deterred the faithful from re-building and snow-proofing their beloved church.

The church was sided with white clapboards. Large, plain rectangular windows lined the sides. No columns or adornments appeared in the front, only two large wooden doors and six red brick steps. A single white spire reached from the apex of the roof toward the heavens.

On this morning in November a brilliant sun shone in a clear blue sky. The sun cast a long shadow from the spire to the front of the church and its brick walkway to the sidewalk and street. In the shadow on the street sat a hearse and two long black limousines. A long line of people stood on the sidewalk, the walkway, and the steps, waiting to enter the church. The line inched forward. Some wore woolen hats and coats against the November chill. Some smoked a last cigarette before reaching the steps, and blew out streams of smoke and steam with their long sighs.

The crowd filled the pews. Latecomers stood in the rear. At the front lay a plain, unvarnished pine casket draped with an American flag. Sprays of flowers surrounded the casket, some with red, white, and blue carnations. The smell of the flowers mixed with the dusky smell of old floorboards. The morning light poured in from the simple windows lining the high walls of the church.

In the front pew sat the parents of the deceased soldier, Cliff and Mary Townsend. Towny's mother clutched Cliff's arm with both of her hands. In the rows behind them sat their extended family, friends, and co-workers. The mayor of the town was there, wearing his ceremonial bronze medallion. Sam Onion sat motionless next to Duncan McUsic. Next to Duncan sat Clare, sobbing softly, leaning her head against her father's shoulder. Sookie Park sat next to Clare, holding her friend's hand. Kanti Martin, who had eulogized her father at Asgard Hall, sat with her mother a few pews behind, like Sookie, awash in memories of Korea and the lives lost there.

In the left-hand pews sat eight young men in varsity jackets. A few score young people sat behind them, each bearing a different look of sadness, shock, anger, or guilt. Joe Goodale from Joe's Variety sat in the rear of the church, wearing his old uniform. It's too tight, he thought, as he looked in the mirror that morning. But he didn't care.

The limousine driver and other undertakers stood in the back of the church, directing the crowd as it entered. The driver, Bill Spiggot, worked for the funeral home when he wasn't driving a school bus. George Buttrey from the College Garage sat at the end of a pew, stricken. As George sat down he nodded to Rocco, who stood in the side aisle holding the handles of Tiemo's wheelchair. Sam Onion noted the full chest of medals that Tiemo wore that day. Sam had not seen Tiemo's medals for a long time.

The readings were from Isaiah and Ecclesiastes. Then Reverend Whitfield Saltmarsh took the podium. He paused as he looked over the crowd. No one spoke. No one moved.

"We often say," he began, "with solemn respect, that a soldier 'gave his life.' But what, exactly, does this familiar phrase mean? Sometimes, it is used as a short-hand for 'he died' or 'he was killed in action.' But I do not think that those who originated this phrase—gave his life—had these usages in mind. No, I think they intended to convey a greater meaning, a greater metaphor of sacrifice. 'He gave his life' means he forfeited the balance. He left decades unused. Think of the seven decades in the Biblical prayer—the three score and ten years of life given to the fortunate. When a soldier gives his life, he literally cedes to his posterity his five remaining decades. Two decades used, five never seen. The mind trembles at the tragedy of the loss when we view it in this way.

"And what is lost? The chance to love truly, the chance to laugh, to enjoy the simple pleasures of a longer life. And more. The chance to pursue one's dreams, to expend oneself in a worthy, peaceful cause. To win, to lose, to strive again. All these chances are lost when one gives the balance of one's life.

"In these troubled times common ground is hard to find. Yet we are all children of God, each bearing a spark of the divine. In this respect, at least, we are 'created equal.'

"I have prayed for days to find words of consolation and hope on a day when we desperately seek both. We gather to celebrate the life and mourn our loss of a brave young man who, we know, embodied every virtue and held no vice. We praise his valor and commend his deeds to God, to live now as the immortals live. Yet we shudder, together, at the awful knowledge of his mortal death, the frightening violence of death in combat in war. Who can explain such a passage, from earthly hell to heavenly bliss? Who can explain a world where such a young man may be taken in a single, violent instant?

"We live in troubled times, pitting many of us against each other. War and peace. White and black. Rich and poor. Man and woman. Townsend Badger was in these times but not of these times. He seemed a visitor from a by-gone era, bound by a code of honor to serve without fear or complaint. He recalled for some of us an older, simpler time, a time known for noble action, not pointless words. Today, speech abounds. Towny let others speak. He saw things that needed to be done. He thought it was his duty to do them. He chose his course and followed it to its end. In our memories, he will remain frozen in time, eternally young. May he rest in peace."

The piano and soloist began the recessional. "Mine eyes have seen the glory of the coming of the Lord . . . ." Towny's parents slowly walked down the aisle, following the casket carrying their only child. When the line slowed, Cliff turned to Duncan McUsic and said: "I feel like my life has ended."

The crowd spilled out of the church and onto the sidewalk.

They watched the pallbearers carry the pine casket to the hearse. They heard the heavy doors of the hearse and limousines closing, with their harsh sound of finality. Some in the crowd winced at the sound.

No sidewalk of the town was empty as the hearse rolled slowly by. Cliff stared out the window from the limousine. He saw row upon row of faces, some young, some old, some familiar, some strangers. The cortege rolled by Cliff's old elementary school. He saw his friend the new janitor holding his hand over his heart. Then he saw the children. They stood in a long row on the sidewalk, their principal and teachers behind them. Some waved small American flags, others saluted. Tears ran down the faces of the teachers, some of whom remembered Towny as a boy. "I can't believe my eyes," one whispered to herself.

Bill Spiggott maneuvered the hearse through the front gate of the Pine Grove Cemetery, the final resting place for early settlers in the valley, several founders and presidents of the College, and six generations of Townsends. A few yards inside the gate, visitors noticed a large rectangular slab of granite that bore the names of townsmen killed in war, from the Revolution to Korea. Spiggott stopped the hearse at the crest of the hill, next to a small steel-frame canopy and a dozen rows of folding chairs. Bill's friend at the bus company later told him that, when the hearse reached the gate of the cemetery, the last cars in line had not yet left the church parking lot, a mile away. Many minutes passed before the crowd from the church re-assembled on the hill.

Rocco pushed Tiemo over the bumpy ground and scattered burnt-orange leaves to a spot near the side of the tent, close enough to smell the freshly turned earth and hear the graveside prayers. He parked his wheelchair under a large oak tree that towered over the gravesite. Long lines ran up and down the bark of the tree, raised lines that looked like a weathered face. In the middle of the trunk, ten feet up, was a stump where a large branch had been cut many years before. The stump was round with a dark rim, like a medallion. Lines crossed the medallion like a ship's compass or a clock.

Reverend Saltmarsh concluded his graveside prayers. Tiemo caught Rocco's eye and nodded to a spot on the crest of the hill, just as a three-man rifle party there fired a volley of shots. The sounds echoed, one upon the other, cascading back down through the crowd, shaking the quiet old cemetery from its silent grief. Just as the echo of the last shot died away, Rocco heard the first few notes of "Taps" coming from over the hill, the sound of the bugle distant and out of sight. As the last notes lingered, then died, the crowd heard only the November breeze moving the last few leaves on the oak tree and whistling through the branches of the immortal pines.

The six honor guards removed the red, white, and blue flag from the casket and folded it thirteen times. One guard stepped to the front row of chairs in the tent. Cliff stood, unsteady on his feet. The officer presented the tri-corned flag, waist high, to Cliff, straight edge first. The guard said, without expression: "On behalf of the President of the United States, the United States Army, and a grateful nation, please accept this flag as a symbol of our appreciation for your loved one's honorable and faithful service."

Tiemo turned in his chair and motioned Rocco to move closer, down to Tiemo's side. He reached into the pocket of his uniform and gave Rocco a small gold pin with a Viking visage. He then motioned with his hand toward the grave, where mourners were tossing in flowers. "Pin this to a flower and toss it in," Tiemo said. Rocco did what Tiemo asked, turned, and walked back to the wheelchair.

"Our work is done here," Tiemo said. He extended his hand to Rocco. Rocco grasped Tiemo's gnarled hand. Tiemo gripped Rocco's hand like a vise and said: "Thank you, my young friend."

Chapter 3

Jack heard about Towny while still in Vietnam. Rocco's letter to Saigon followed soon after the funeral. The end of December marked the end of Jack's tour of duty, the question of his re-enlistment still unresolved in his mind. Recent letters from President Onion and Professor McUsic had put unsubtle pressure on him to stay and help train their new recruits. Stumpo had signed on for another tour. "I need to teach these people some rugby," he joked. "There's a lot of work to be done." And, Stumpo half-jokingly added, if Jack decided not to re-enlist, Stumpo would feel duty-bound to check in on Kate Freechild, strictly for humanitarian reasons, of course. Jack laughed. For now, he told Stumpo, he needed some time to forget. And some time to decide. "I might be seeing you sooner than you think," he said.

It was dawn when Jack's plane from Saigon landed at an air base in California in early January. He would hitch two more rides in military planes until a final, short leg to the airport nearest the College. From California to a base in the Midwest, he rode a nearly empty cargo plane for troops, vehicles, and supplies. Only a few other passengers sat on the long canvas seats along the sides of the plane.

The next flight east was a medevac flight in an old DC-8 filled with wounded soldiers headed to hospitals. Jack climbed the ladder into the fuselage of the plane. He could see or hear little in the dark, but could make out lines of cots with young men arrayed in rows along both sides of the plane. The men were heavily bandaged, and many had lost limbs. As Jack made his way slowly to his seat in the front, he felt one grab his arm, then heard him rasp:

"Goin' home?"

"Yup," Jack said. "You?"

"Me, too."

The plane lifted into the air and flew through a star-filled, cloudless night sky, across a country that looked strangely peaceful from above. Jack heard murmurs and groans as the medics moved from cot to cot. He dozed off as the plane droned on through the night.

The plane touched down at a military base at dawn. The wounded were slowly wheeled from the plane to the tarmac, then to a line of waiting ambulances. The plane had parked about thirty yards from a steel fence. There was a gate mid-way in the fence for the ambulances to pass through. Jack surveyed the scene from the tarmac as he boarded a bus. That's when he first heard the screaming. He saw a row of about fifty people with signs along the fence. He heard wild, loud screaming:

"Murderers!" "Baby-killers!"

Louder screams followed as the crowd swelled. Four dozen or more waved hand-painted signs. A large woman with flaming red hair yelled through a bullhorn:

"Murderers! Baby-killers!"

The crowd pressed against the fence, then slid sideways toward the opening gate as it opened. Armed military police stepped in against the human tide. The ambulances, now loaded with the wounded, their lights flashing and sirens howling, formed a line to exit the tarmac. They proceeded slowly through the gate. The large woman with the megaphone and two tall men beside her took turns spitting at the ambulances as they passed close to them through the gate. Jack and the others on the bus sat silently as they watched the spectacle from their seats behind the ambulances. The vehicles moved toward the gate.

"Welcome home," Jack said to the soldier next to him on the bus.

"You, too," the soldier said.

———

A cold January wind blew hard from the north as Jack tipped

open a wooden hatch and stepped onto the flat top of the roof of Asgard Hall. His summer visit seemed a world away. He closed the hatch and walked to the chest-high rail. To the west, over the river, he saw familiar snow-capped hills, the boundary of a patch of land and a valley that sometimes felt like home. If you can breathe enough of this cold, clear air, Jack thought, you feel that you can do anything. He hadn't felt that way for a long time.

Jack leaned on the railing. He tried to focus on the view, but his mind drifted back to re-enlistment: Yes, or No?

He left the rail and walked the perimeter of the roof, first looking north, then east over the campus. My father's campus, Jack thought, everywhere I look, his footsteps, his rooms, his fields, his haunts. The dozen places where he had worked to pay his way. His undying love for what he called "my Shangri-La." Jack's mother had shared many of his father's stories, though "shared" was not the apt word. Bequeathed. Imprinted. Branded.

It had been a strange life to this point, living in the world of a man he had never known. His father's friends were eager witnesses to the deeds of a remarkable young man with whom he shared a name, and more. These men, like the stories they told, permeated Jack's world. He seemed to be moving in the same orbit as his father, but at a distance behind, measured in time, not space. Or was his father not ahead of him in the same orbit but actually the star itself, with Jack orbiting around him? If so, this star was unseen, and Jack might as well be a planet without a star, moving in the dark, hidden from the eyes of the world. He had heard so many stories about his father, all so vivid, that Jack wondered if his own memories of the College would ever displace them. Would he ever walk the campus and not think of his father's days here? What would his father have thought of the place now, so changed, so angry, so different? His father's freshman orientation book in the '40s was dedicated to the "genius for unity" shown by previous classes. Where was that unity now? Gone forever.

Jack's reverie ended when he saw the hatch start to lift and a familiar face emerge. Jack smiled and moved in for a bear hug that enveloped Rocco's small frame.

"I thought I'd find you up here. Welcome back," Rocco said. They walked to the rail and looked out over the hills. Neither spoke

"I can't believe Towny's dead," Jack said, finally. "I can't stop thinking about him. He was such a great kid . . . ." He shook his head and rested his chin on his chest. "Dammit."

Rocco wiped a tear from his eye. "The best. He looked up to you, you know."

Jack did not respond. "How are Cliff and his wife?" he asked.

"Not good. Cliff told me at the library that he thinks he might retire."

"That's probably not good for him, but who can blame him? If you were in his shoes, maybe you would want to hang it up, too. I can't imagine what it's like for him. To lose your son."

Rocco nodded.

"I'm going to see Tiemo, then drive down to see Clare."

"Clare was at the funeral."

"I know. She wrote me."

"So if you talk to Tiemo about re-enlistment, maybe you can talk to him about Clare, too. Is everything okay with her?"

"I guess so. We'll see. Anyway, that's not Tiemo's department," Jack smiled. "He's the War Department. For her, I need the State Department, maybe their top diplomat. Someone like you, in fact."

"Me? You gotta be kidding. I don't speak that language. I'm a lab rat, remember? We don't get out much." Rocco thought a moment. "I guess I do have something to tell you, though. Clare's last letter to me was very sharp, very impatient. She was more upset about the war than ever. She didn't say much about you, but she didn't sound too happy about you either. That seemed different."

Jack shrugged. "It's okay. I know that the protests are her world, now. And I don't live there. I just visit from the Dark Side every once in a while, *persona non grata* in the eyes of her friends.

How long is she supposed to go on explaining that her boyfriend is a soldier? Anyway, forget about it, okay? I'll handle it. Or try." Jack looked out at the hills. "So, have you decided anything?"

"No. And I'm tired thinking about what I should do. I figure I'll get shot at no matter what I do, here or there. I'll figure it out," Rocco said.

"You always do," Jack smiled.

"Maybe Tiemo can help you," Rocco said.

"Maybe. I'm not sure. His letters lately . . . it's hard to know what's on his mind these days."

Jack and Rocco descended through the hatch and down two flights of stairs and stepped out on the porch of the house. They gave each other another hug.

"See you sooner or later?"

"One or the other. Home to Iowa first. Maybe back here to play some football some day, if I can remember how to play."

Rocco laughed. "Our rivals are hoping you forget." Jack smiled. Rocco patted Jack on the back. "So long, friend."

Jack walked to the parking lot and climbed into his car. He was headed to see Tiemo but decided to take one more turn around the campus green. As he passed Crouchback Tower, he saw protestors standing next to a mock coffin covered with a shroud that read, "Bury ROTC."

———

Jack arrived at the hospital and took the stairs to Tiemo's floor. He walked to his door, knocked, and opened it slowly.

Tiemo was in his wheelchair and snapped his head up when he heard the knock.

"Sorry to wake you, Colonel."

"Glad you did, Jack. Welcome back."

Jack grabbed a chair and pulled it close, as close as a penitent to a priest.

"How are you, sir?"

"Not bad for an old man, son. How are you?"

"Good, Colonel. My hitch is up, I think I wrote and told you."

"I know that. You've done fine work over there, Jack. So say all of my friends. What's next?"

"I'm not sure, Colonel." Jack paused. "What would you do?"

"Your call, Jack. Only you know what's best for you. They're starting to withdraw some troops now. That's not a great sign about their future plans. But that doesn't mean the guys there now don't need your help. You could do some good. But at some point the balance tips toward greater danger. You don't want to get swept away in a down draft, the last man in an American uniform, circling the drain pipe.

"The current picture is getting cloudy in my old, tired mind. What's the end-game here, Jack? Where do we see this headed? We could stay another while, slog it out, but I know that however long we stay, there is one thing we can't change: It's their country, not ours. When I say theirs, I mean all of theirs—the Republic's, the Viet Cong's, the North's. They are all fighting for *their own* country, at least their own vision of it. And they have been fighting a long time: fighting the Chinese, the Japs, the French, fighting forever. The French made mistakes. But remember, the French were good, tough soldiers. Don't be fooled by the way the Germans rolled them in '40. The French lost Vietnam because the Viet Minh had the will to win. I had a colleague in France who went to French Indochina after World War II. He said that when he traveled through Vietnam every village flew the flag of the Viet Minh, the native resistance to the French. The villagers fully supported the Viet Minh, my friend said. He said the Viet Minh were everywhere and nowhere at the same time. All of them were prepared to fight long and hard. To the death. No one in the rural areas, he said, was for the French.

"We are just the latest uninvited and unwanted guests. Like those guests, we came late, knew no one, drank all the wine, and stayed too late. And you know what else the Vietnamese know? They know that we'll leave some day, too. Like all the others.

"The Vietnamese see us stuck in the mud, like jeeps in those dirt roads I saw in France in '44. It's ironic, isn't it? Fifty years ago—in World War I—then twenty-five years ago, in World War II—off we went to save the French. 'Lafayette, we are here,' we said, and all that. Now we're following the French in again, but this time they've left for good. It's not their country we're fighting to save. They got kicked out, for conduct unbecoming a colonialist, I guess. And we're there to pick up the pieces. Maybe they were the smart ones—they got out. '*Adieu, bonne chance,* would you like our seat at the roulette table? *Pardon,* we are out of chips. You must stake yourself, *mon ami.* This next round will be no *pas de deux.* We'll leave you some wine and don't miss our basilicas. We've left our churches and priests to the faithful, free of charge. Let us know how things go, *s'il vous plait.*'"

Tiemo pursed his lips and leaned forward to drive home his point. "You see, Jack, the people we are fighting, they know their history. They have lived it. They're like the Europeans in my family—they know about horror, and they know about stamina. They've been bullied by history. They should not be underestimated. Theirs is a long distance run. Kennedy said 'We shall bear any burden, we shall pay any price.' But will we? We know our adversaries will pay it. A million dead? Two million? There is no limit to their endurance. And time? Time is meaningless when you are chasing a dream. Time for them means 'In God's time.' Ask any of the priests that the French left behind.

"It's not that it's hopeless. I don't believe that. But the South needs new leadership. Both Saigon and the people in the countryside are starved for new leaders. They want men who understand their needs, and their hopes for the future. Someone said that Vietnam right now 'is a country with an army and no government.' There is a reservoir of spirit there that I think we can still tap. But the spirits of the ordinary people can't be rallied by men in white linen suits who wave at the people as they ride by in an air-conditioned Mercedes."

"But despite it all, we go on, Jack. We keep in mind the old Viking proverb: 'When you are the hammer, strike; when you are the anvil, bear.' Whatever you choose, Jack you must know that you have added luster to the proud history of the Vikings and your family name. You have fulfilled all of your obligations. Your father would be very proud of you."

Jack did not reply. He nodded, stood up and reached over to shake Tiemo's hand. "So long, Colonel. I'll write soon."

———

Jack walked to the parking lot of the hospital and opened his car door. He sat down behind the wheel but did not turn the key to the ignition. He sat for a while, turning the conversation with Tiemo over in his mind. Snow had started to fall when he finally started the car and rolled it down the hill. He turned out of the hospital and onto the two-lane, headed south. The interstate would have been faster, but Jack liked the views on the winding road and the extra time to think.

He drove for an hour in silence. A light snow continued to fall, covering the road. In one winding stretch, the black pavement began to disappear. Suddenly, he felt the rear wheels of the car drift left, then right, and he skidded sideways off the shoulder and down the bank, rear of the car down first. He had spun out just short of a bridge over a steep ravine and some railroad tracks, the tracks on the line hugging the river north to Canada. The car continued its backward slide down the bank and toward the ravine. He turned the wheel and pounded the brakes. He fumbled with the door handle, but his hand slipped off. Then he heard a loud slam and felt the car shudder, as if it had been hit from behind. He peered through the snow-filled back window and saw two saplings pressed up against the back of his car. The twin trees had saved him from a very bad fall.

Dusk was quickly filling the valley. Jack could not move the car from the bank. He grabbed his fatigue jacket and climbed through the snow back up the bank and to the road. He stood shivering in the cold, rubbing his hands, some of the same old doubts creeping into his mind.

He walked back up the road to a gas station. A blue-and-orange "Gulf" sign shone through the snowflakes. It was the station where Jack had stopped on his last trip south, the station owned by a Vietnam veteran. Jack opened the glass door and stepped inside the station. The young owner Jack had seen from his car was seated at the desk.

"I spun out near the trestle," Jack said. "I'm twenty feet down the bank."

"We can tow you back up to the road," the man said.

"I don't have any money."

The man smiled. "Of course you don't."

He looked him up and down.

"Where did you get the jacket?"

"Service."

"'Nam?"

"Yes."

"Unit?"

Jack told him. "Going back soon, I think."

The man looked at him, unsure of Jack's meaning. "I got back two years ago. Got the same welcome-home parade that everyone gets . . . ." He looked down and shrugged. He looked back up at Jack and said:

"Let's go get your car."

———

Jack reached South Tapley at five o'clock and parked the Buick. He was tired from the long drive and still shaken from his near miss over the railroad tracks. He was surprised when Clare met him at the door of her house wearing her parka and a wool hat. She had a button with a peace sign pinned to the front of her jacket. She gave Jack a long embrace and kiss. Jack started to move toward the door, but Clare took his hand and said "No, let's go for a walk, first. Then we'll come back here."

They walked in silence along the sidewalk on the main street.

"It's been a tough fall and winter here, Jack," Clare began. "I keep dreaming of Towny. Sometimes I give his eulogy. Sometimes I see him alive. Then I see his casket, that plain, knotty pine. Sometimes I'm walking alone and all I see is black. Dark, no light. Sometimes smoke. I keep walking but I can't find my way to the light. I hold out my hand but can't feel anything. Nothing.

"The future feels like that to me, too. It's so hard to see. Towny's now part of the past, not the future. How can that be, Jack? And the country keep burying its future—guys like him—every day. How long can this go on?

"There's another thing about Towny that's bothering me," Clare continued. "I could see it coming from a mile away—I mean his enlistment—but there was not a damn thing I could do to stop it." She looked directly at Jack. "You knew him. He looked up to you and Rocco. Why didn't you or Rocco talk him out of it? And I thought you'd be more upset about Towny's death, too."

Jack looked surprised. "I am upset. Very much. He was a great kid. What more am I supposed to say about it? And Rocco did talk to him at the garage. A lot. But he wanted to enlist. Is that really so hard to understand? People do what they want to do. I thought you knew that by now."

Clare frowned as they walked in silence. They turned off the main street and walked down a brick path into the campus center toward the small, frozen pond and the old stone bridge where Jack and Clare often stopped to talk. Six globe lamps lit the bridge. They matched the gold-leaf dome on the top of the nearby library. Stray flakes of snow fell on the globes, sparkling then dying as they melted on impact.

They stopped on the center of the bridge. Clare spoke first.

"I've tried to stay true to what we've had together since we met, Jack, you know, true to the special things. I never took them for granted, not for a moment. But I've grown a lot since I met you. I'm a different person now. Some things are the same, but some are not. You weren't a soldier then. You were not in the middle of this goddam war. And I've done so many things without you. I have missed you. There are things that I still want . . . for the two of us, together. But you're putting them at risk, I think. Our future . . . it must not mean as much to you as it does to me. You're thinking about re-enlisting, I know. How am I supposed to take that, Jack? We all have choices. We can't go backwards. Our lives are what they are, or what they've become. We have to choose in the now, not in the past." She paused and, without looking at him, asked quietly, "So, are you re-enlisting?"

"I'm not sure."

"Why would you?"

"The pay is good."

"Stop kidding me. It's not a joke. Why would you re-enlist?"

"Well," Jack started slowly, looking out over the pond. "This may sound strange, but I've learned a lot over there. About life. About death. About myself. About people. It's kind of become a second college for me, as crazy as that sounds."

"It does sound crazy. What do you mean, 'a second college'?"

"It's a place where I learn."

She shook her head in disbelief. "Great. A war college. For someone who says he's learning, you sound pretty confused."

"That's the mark of a first-rate education, isn't that what they say?"

"I'm serious."

"So am I. If I had all the answers, maybe I wouldn't go back."

"So you're telling me your going back to the goddam war to learn something? Christ, Jack." She cocked her head and squinted at him like he was speaking a foreign language. "Really? What about us? How long are you going to play this Russian roulette with your life? With our life together? My friends ask me if everything is all right between us. I tell them 'yes' but they don't believe me. They say they don't know how I can love a soldier.

"I keep looking for signs that we are still a pair. But it's hard when you are so far away. You're not at my side, you're not even on the same continent. Sometimes you're living a different day on the calendar, if you haven't noticed."

"I've heard that," Jack said. "But I'm here now."

"That makes me happy."

"Is there really that much distance between us, Clare? And what we think? Are we really as unalike as your friends think? I admire all you do, for the protests, your writing . . . all of it. You're a leader. I don't see us at odds the way they do."

"I know you do. You're my biggest fan. You are. That's what makes this all so hard. I think we've done all we can to bridge the gap. It's not your fault."

"It's not yours, either, is what I'm trying to say."

"It seemed so much like love, Jack. We always seemed so close to it. I felt like I was just waiting to fall all the way. Waiting for a word, waiting for something . . . waiting for you to hit me with your heart. But it never seemed to happen. Not all the way. You always seem to drift away.

"I don't mean you ran away. I just mean that I felt I couldn't reach you, even when you were lying right next to me. I could touch you, but something was missing. It wasn't just the distance—when you were too far north at school, or a long, long way west—it was something else. It felt like you were right next to me, but then you were gone. Some times were great. I felt I was so close. I thought I was there, right there with you in something so right . . . God, I could barely breathe at first. But then it was gone. I know I tried. I did. And I think you did, too, in your way."

Jack said nothing. He felt like a spent force. He looked away, up at the cars on the main street. The traffic light turned green, then yellow, then red, then green again. The cars stopped and idled. Jack saw exhaust fumes mixing with the cold, damp air.

He turned again toward Clare. "I am sorry for the words I never said. I do love you," he said. "But I don't know if that's enough."

"And I don't know if that's enough now, either," Clare said. She took his hand. She looked in his eyes and brushed the hair on the side of his head. She moved closer against him. "But I do know this: I can't go to your funeral." She rested her head on his chest, still talking. "I hate what this war has done to us, to Towny, to everyone. I hope that some day we can look back at these days and think of happier times."

"I hope those days come, too," Jack said.

"I won't be going back home after I graduate," Clare said. "Maybe Towny would have gone back . . . well, maybe not."

They stood side-by-side again, backs resting on one wall of the bridge.

"Should we go back to the house?" Clare asked.

"Sure," Jack said. Clare stepped away from the wall, but Jack remained. "I think I'll just stay here for a few minutes. You know, clear my head. I'll be there in a while."

Clare looked surprised, but shrugged and said, "Sure." She stepped closer to him and kissed him on his cold cheek.

Jack watched Clare walk up the hill from the pond to the sidewalk. The wind from the north came over the hill and hit him hard in his face as he watched her walk away. He leaned his back against the wall of the bridge. He noticed a small bronze plaque on the wall opposite. He walked over and bent down to read it.

IN MEMORY OF KAY CORCORAN
NURSING SCHOOL CLASS OF '50
KILLED IN ACTION
M.A.S.H. UNIT 999
REPUBLIC OF SOUTH KOREA
JUNE 15, 1952

As he finished reading the plaque he heard a sound from the far end of the pond. He straightened up and turned, still hearing a familiar, rhythmic, "tock, tock, tock" sound from the ice. He looked closer and saw a single skater with a stick and puck. A boy from the town or maybe a boyfriend of a student, Jack thought.

The skater stopped and stood motionless, as a hockey player

stands at attention on his blue line for the anthem played before the start of a game. Jack could see steam form as the skater's breath hit the cold air above the ice. This was not a boy, Jack noticed, but an older man, probably in his late forties.

The skater resumed his rounds, drawing wide circles with long graceful strides, one leg crossing over the other, then pushing off, inside out. He first cradled the puck delicately, then began dribbling, "tock, tock, tock," the puck and stick moving side to side, the two in tandem, as if held together by magnetic force.

He made circle after circle, faster and faster, then, with the grace of a dancer, he spun to skate backward, carving his skates in a heart-like pattern, out in a curve and then back in line, one side and then the other. He switched again to forward motion for a long, looping turn, then suddenly came to a violent halt in the middle of the pond, throwing a cloud of ice shavings six feet high into the cold air. The shavings fluttered to the ground, mixing with the snowflakes of the gathering storm.

The snow fell harder as the skater stood. The fluffy flakes covered the round globe lamps on the bridge, casting Jack into darkness. The skater rested his stick in front of his skates with his left hand. He looked up at the bridge and lifted his right arm and waved, inside out, as if making a wide salute.

Jack hesitated. When he lifted his arm to wave back, the skater had turned away. Jack watched the white shadow glide toward the end of the pond and disappear into the thickening snow. Jack lingered for another moment. Then he zipped his jacket up to his neck and turned back into the wind.

Made in the USA
Las Vegas, NV
11 February 2022